unprepared

Gavin Shoebridge

D1528441

For Samantha

Civilization begins with order, grows with liberty and
dies with chaos.

Will Durant

Prologue

There are three kinds of disaster. The first is confusingly insignificant, like an earthquake so mild that you aren't really sure if you felt it. You might check Twitter to make sure you weren't just imagining it. It's not even worth mentioning on Facebook.

The second kind of disaster is intense, but unlikely to result in death or destruction, such as a blizzard or a Category One hurricane. In a perverse way, some find these events a source of enjoyment. It's a chance to hunker down, go head to head with nature and, as a bonus for narcissists, it offers some great fodder for 'cyclone selfies' on Instagram.

The third kind of disaster is destructive in its intensity. It's frightening. Take Hurricane Katrina, Isabel, or Andrew, for example, or the wildfires of California. The arrogance of man soon evaporates when road signs become projectiles and suburbs are engulfed in walls of flame. There's no time for updating Twitter.

You flee or you die.

8

Chapter one

Flee

"Hi, welcome to Chick-fil-A, how may I serve you?" asked the voice trapped in the drive-thru speaker.

"Hi. Can I have a number one with extra crispy fries and a number four with waffle fries, please," asked Kelly as rain dotted the windshield.

"And to drink?" asked the speaker.

"One Coke Zero, one Doctor Pepper," said Kelly.

"OK, that's twelve-forty, please drive on to the next window."

Kelly edged the car forward about five feet, unable to move further due to the vehicle waiting in front.

"Is that more expensive than normal?" asked David, sitting in the passenger seat.

"Not sure. I hardly ever come here," she responded. He turned the music on the car stereo up a little and checked his phone for the latest weather update.

"It's a category four now, but it's still 80 miles away, according to weatherwatch.com. Though you can't really trust anything they say; they sensationalize everything to cause panic. It's good for clicks," David lamented.

The two sat in their warm Toyota station wagon as Hurricane Henriette raged somewhere in the distance. It was the eighth time meteorologists had used the name Henriette for a hurricane but, other than sprinkles of rain on their windshield and trees moving about more enthusiastically than normal, there was no sign that anything bad was at their doorstep. Regardless, they were prepared. They'd done this before. Living near the east coast of the USA meant that hurricanes were a part of life, especially now, in September.

The car edged up to the drive-thru window and Kelly paid by card. Hot food was passed through the driver's window over to the passenger side with David placing it on his lap. Kelly then relayed him the drinks; David holding one in each hand. She thanked the fast food employee and moved the car around to the parking lot, picking a spot facing the main road.

Lynchburg was normally a pretty unadventurous small city in central Virginia, but this afternoon it was as chaotic as Christmas Eve. Cars were bumper-to-bumper on Wards Road, all en route to evacuate or get last minute supplies. It was free entertainment.

"Dinner and a show," chuckled David. Kelly hummed in agreement as they ate their meals, watching a line of shiny metal boxes crawl painfully into the Walmart parking lot down the road. Between bites, Kelly responded.

"It baffles me. Why don't those idiots plan ahead? I mean, they *know* this happens every year. It's hurricane season. It's not rocket science. You put a box of emergency crap in the car and you just go."

"Yeah, but then we wouldn't have this free entertainment."

The two chuckled as spots of rain continued to land and thick, gray clouds swelled in the sky above.

David and Kelly wouldn't dare admit it to strangers, not wanting to look like nut-jobs, but they were 'preppers'; meaning people who enjoy being prepared for disasters. It was a satisfying hobby for them. Now, to be clear, they weren't the kind of larger-than-life preppers you might see on TV, featuring bearded rednecks with stockpiles of guns, showing off their underground shelters while decked out in camouflage gear.

No, David and Kelly had pretty normal preparation supplies, like most people who choose to live in the regular, yearly paths of hurricanes.

At home they had a few months' worth of canned and dried foods, a few gallons of water, batteries, a radio, and other miscellaneous items. They almost certainly had more disaster preparation gear than their neighbors, but nothing out of the ordinary for anyone who might need to hunker down for a few days while the idiotic masses raid the supermarkets at the last minute.

Shouting interrupted their meal.

"Kel, look... Are they fighting?" David asked. They both had their heads turned, looking out the raindrop-dotted passenger window.

"Shit. Looks like it," Kelly responded, both of them now watching the commotion surrounding a couple of cars parked a few yards away. David turned to Kelly, sauce on the edge of his mouth.

"Should... We do something?"

Kelly was a step ahead. She had her phone in her hand, dialing 911 with her right thumb. She was a policeman's daughter, after all.

"Yeah, hi. We need the police, please."

David watched two men grabbing at each others' shirts in the rain.

"We're at Chick-fil-A, just outside River Ridge Mall. There's two guys fighting."

The dispatcher said something inaudible.

"Two guys. They're behind a car. One black guy and a white guy. Both about forty or fifty. Oh my God. It looks like their girlfriends are fighting too. Shit, what a mess," Kelly responded, food still in her mouth, but unable to turn away from the freak show taking place outside the car window. David took the handgun out of the glove box just in case things turned south.

The dispatcher asked for more information about the description of the now four people brawling like gorillas in a rainy fast food parking lot.

"Dave! Look look look. He's got a gun," said Kelly, no longer chewing. The white man had retrieved a handgun from his truck and was now aiming it at the other man, shouting, clearly audible above the sound of rain and car tires on wet tarmac.

"Get on the ground! Get on the fucking ground, nigger!" screamed the man with the gun, in-between heaving breaths, blood dripping from his lip.

A white man shouting that word at a black man would normally be cause to fight, but they were already well passed that, so the six-letter insult did seem to have lost some of its impact.

The other man, knowing when the odds were stacked against him, stared at the white guy for a few seconds. He slowly hunched down, putting his knees on the wet asphalt, his chest rising and falling visibly from three minutes of fighting. Although he now had a gun aimed at him, the defeated man almost seemed relieved that it was over. Their ladies, however, were not done yet. While no longer physically fighting, they stood a few feet apart, screaming at and taunting each other, throwing every clichéd racial insult you could imagine.

Cracker, gator bait, white bread, nigger, honky, etc, all while their partners poised motionless like mannequins; one with a gun, one without, but both still gasping for air, both overweight, soaked and exhausted.

Police sirens erupted from what was a distant wail to an ear-piercing scream with the arrival of a police cruiser which turned off the road and into the lot. The suspension of the vehicle absorbed the impact of driving up the ramp at a brisk speed, creating a thumping noise audible above the sound of the sirens.

Both Chik-Fil-A staff and customers were now craning their necks at the restaurant window as two officers got out with sidearms drawn, screaming at the man with the gun to drop it. He complied, seeming relieved that the mess he'd created was taken care of for him. He was immediately handcuffed and the two groups were separated to try and get to the bottom of whatever caused 'Exhibit A' of our shared ancestral connection to apes. In the Toyota, Kelly and David had enjoyed the show, but were glad it was over.

"You can put us in cars and suits, but we're still just primal animals underneath… It just takes one thing and our lizard genes kick in," said David with a mouthful of waffle fries. Kelly wiped her fingers on a napkin and got out of the car, still on the phone to the 911 dispatcher. She went over to one of the officers to explain what she'd witnessed. David waited in the car, aware that another person's presence wouldn't help the situation in any way. The wind and rain had increased slightly in the time since they'd ordered their food, meaning that when Kelly returned to the interior of their warm and dry Toyota Venza wagon, her hair and shirt were damp.

"You won't fucking believe it," said Kelly, slumping behind the wheel.

"What?"

"The fight. It was all about water."

"Water?" David responded.

"Yeah. The cop said that the black guy has about a dozen water containers in the back of his truck. He bought the last ones at Walmart down the road. The white guy got pissed 'cause he couldn't get any and wanted to buy a couple off the black guy in the Walmart parking lot, offering the other guy some money. The cop said the black guy didn't want to sell any to the white dude, and an argument began. The white guy followed the black guy here and then they started fighting."

"Far out," David said, staring out the window.

"All that for water? But... It's fucking *raining*!"

"Yep. The cop said it's pandemonium over at Walmart. People have cleaned out the aisles. Everything except soap and vegan food is gone."

David chuckled at the thought.

"Well, given the choice, I'd rather eat soap, too."

"It's like this every fucking year," sighed Kelly. "Every damn year we get Hurricane Titface flying off the sea, and every year people panic."

Resuming what was left of their meals, their faces flashed shades of red and blue in the overcast, late afternoon light.

"Well, we'd better hit the road ourselves. Henriette is heading straight for the coast of North Carolina and if it's anything like Isabel back in 2003, it's gonna wipe this town out for a few days," David responded, crushing his empty box and fries container into a ball.

Kelly eased their Toyota, full of food, water and general supplies, into the traffic on Wards Road and headed north towards I-81. They had no set destination; only heading southwest for as long as it took until the hurricane either changed direction, ran out of puff or wiped out Lynchburg. Whichever it was, they'd done this before. It was not only routine, it was a chance to have a little adventure together, camping in the back of the car for a few days.

I-81 was gridlocked but moving. It wasn't only Lynchburg that was taking part in today's exodus, but the cities of Norfolk and Richmond and dozens of smaller towns, too. Cars and trucks with their trays and back seats filled with supplies, bedding, children and pets rode alongside each other at two miles per hour as the sun, already rendered useless by the storm clouds, disappeared behind the horizon. Occasionally the passengers and drivers made eye contact across the lanes, as headlights and taillights illuminated a thousand faces, all heading in the same direction.

"Look at that, Kel," David said, pointing to a gas station off the highway with three lines of cars waiting to get to its forecourt. Right at that moment, the gas station must have run out of gas itself, because just as their car was crawling past, the building's lights turned off. People waiting in line began to get out of their cars and walk towards a frustrated looking man standing by the pumps, gesturing motorists to keep going. As the gas station slowly crawled past, arms were waving about and pointing, belonging to obviously frustrated motorists who had to try their luck elsewhere.

"Idiots," lamented Kelly. "They *knew* this hurricane was coming. It's all over the news. Everyone has the Internet. You fill your car up just in case, not when the storm's in your rear view mirror."

"I can promise you they didn't bring reserve gas tanks either," chimed in David. "They'll probably be whipping up a delicious casserole of soap and vegan food on the side of the road tonight!"
David checked weatherwatch.com once more. The storm was around 80 miles from the shore. Nothing to worry about.
It was just after midnight when their gray Toyota crossed the Tennessee state line. The small township of Colonial Heights was to be their destination for this particular escape. Kelly turned off the highway and into a side road which soon led to a parkland area, surrounded by trees. Parking under a tree, the two climbed into the back of

their station wagon which had a foam mattress and several blankets, all warm from six hours on the road.

"I do declare, my good lady," grinned David in an appalling attempt at a southern accent, "We're in cahtton an' hwhiskey cauntry now!"

Kelly groaned, shaking her head.

"Canna offa y'all a dree-ink? Or maybeh some cahtton?" he joked.

"Oh, Jesus," Kelly sighed.

"David Shepherd. Just pour the drink, you yokal."

David grabbed a couple of crystal tumblers, wrapped up in a towel. They may be squashed in the back of a car parked amongst the trees, but at least they could drink in style. From the small cooler, he fished out some ice cubes and a bottle of Crown Royal Canadian.

"Ohhh, that's blasphemy, *eh*. Bringing Canadian whiskey down here, *eh*," joked Kelly, having better luck with a Canadian accent than David had imitating a *good ol' boy*.

After a couple of glasses of whiskey and some free adult fun (which caused the windows to fog) the two went to sleep. This was turning out to be one of their best hurricane exoduses so far.

David awoke first, with the sound of birdsong permeating the cold, thin walls of Chateau Toyota. The lack of a decent cell phone signal meant that he was quickly bored and started reading the back of a Campbell's soup can.

"Twelve grams of sugar per serving. That seems like a lot for soup. Why the hell would you put sugar in soup, anyway? It's soup, for God's sake," he thought.

He then studied the front of the can.

"How the hell did Andy Warhol make a soup can famous. Why didn't I think of painting a picture of a soup can? Maybe there's still a chance for me. Maybe I could paint something else that's completely boring and be rich. I'll paint… uh…"

Fortunately, for the safety of Andy Warhol's legacy, Kelly stirred and awakened. She rubbed her eyes and turned to David, his face coming into view.

"Hey babe" she said with morning breath.

"Morning," he responded, putting down the soup can and leaning in for a kiss.

"What happened with the hurricane?" she asked.

"Not sure. Cell phone signal is seriously weak here."

Kelly stretched her arms back as much as the Toyota Venza would allow, before slumping back into the foam mattress.

"Sooo, what's for breakfast?" she asked.

"I was thinking we should hit a cafe or something," he responded. "There's got to be something around here. I can't be bothered firing up the cooker to boil water for a coffee."

David opened the rear hatch and pushed it with his foot. It raised up, revealing dew-covered trees and grass. The morning air was cool but not freezing as it swelled inside the now-open vehicle. They snuggled together under the blanket. It really was one of their best escapes yet.

"I hope the house is OK," Kelly said, breaking the calm atmosphere with a cloud of reality.

"Yeah. We won't know what the damage is until we get online. The storm surge will probably be in full swing right now. Let's follow the road into town, get a coffee and figure out the damage, hey?"

Kelly agreed, getting out from beneath the covers and folding up the blankets, while David put on shoes and climbed behind the wheel.

Both now clothed and needing coffee, David turned the key and started the engine, while Kelly brushed her hair using the fold-down mirror on the passenger sun visor. The disaster back home could wait a few more hours.

"Starbucks? Dunkin Donuts?" David asked.

"Hmm. I want something more… real," Kelly responded. "No more fast food."

"Alright. What about that place? It looks alright." Kelly nodded. Their 2011 Toyota wagon pulled in to the parking lot of a small, locally owned cafe and stopped next to a Ford F-150, where the Japanese-designed wagon was dwarfed by the American giant.
Kelly picked a seat by the window and ordered coffee and scrambled eggs. David chose jam on toast.

"Ah, you won't believe it," she said, finally looking at her phone, reconnected with the modern world.

"The hurricane turned north and weakened to a Category 2."

"Oh for fuck's sake," laughed David. "You mean we spent seven hours in the car to come to the fucking boondocks for nothing?"

"Umm, if you'll remember... It wasn't for *nothing*," Kelly said, winking.
David laughed and shook his head.

"Oh well, it was still a fun adventure. I'll call my boss and ask if the office is open today. Though, if it is, we're not gonna be there till after lunchtime."

"Oh this is cool," Kelly said, staring at her phone. "I've got a second interview for that management job with Goodyear. They say I can expect a call next week."

"That' damn good news," David replied.

"We can't be Double Income No Kids with only one of us having an income. What is that… SINKS?"

Kelly looked up from her phone and met David's gaze.

"Oh. No, I didn't mean it like that," he said, worried he'd implied she had been unemployed too long.

"I know you're joking, Dave. I'm just giving you 'the stare'. You know I'm desperate to get back to work again. My last job sucked and I was glad to leave, but shit. I'm sick of being out of work. It's been like four months now."

The server brought over their food and coffee, while the TV in the corner of the cafe was playing CNN. It was admittedly a nice start to their day, even if the whole thing was ultimately a waste of time.

"Uh oh, what's he up to now?" David said, while pointing at the television with a corner of toast.

Footage of President Trump was showing on the screen. It was old footage, taken during his historical meeting with the 'Supreme Leader' of North Korea, Kim Jong Un. The text on the base of the screen read NORTH KOREA THREATENS WAR.

"What do they want *now?*" Kelly asked. "I thought things were all smoothed things out with North Korea after the summit?"

"Kel, it's CNN. If I spilled my coffee they'd report it as a major environmental disaster. They're nothing but clickbait journalism in televised form," David stated. "It'll be nothing as usual."

"True. And even if North Korea declared war on us, what are they gonna do? Throw spitballs?" Kelly joked.

"Well, they could throw food… oh, wait, no they can't," laughed David.

"Yep. That country's poorer than a gender studies graduate," Kelly joked.

Technically, David was right. North Korea had nothing. No food, no freedom and no economy. However they did have *something*: they had an intercontinental ballistic missile. That, and endless threats.

In mid-2018, President Trump met with Kim in Singapore, with the media eating it all up. There were promises of peace, North Korea took down their anti-US propaganda and they began to disassemble their intercontinental ballistic missile launch sites - or at least they said.

It looked genuinely hopeful. But, new intelligence was revealing that it was all just a show.

In North Korea's typical style, they commenced issuing threats of war until they received what they wanted, then they backed down, before threatening again for something new. It'd been this way for years. It was normal. The only difference is that now they had a dangerous weapon which they kept a closely guarded secret. The ultimate weapon, in fact.

But they wouldn't dare use it. The missile was just a bargaining tool. It remained unlikely that they even had the technology to get it off the ground.

Finishing their breakfast and using the bathroom, it was time to hit the road. The news, although sensationalized, gave the impression that Lynchburg had escaped without any serious damage, other than a few signs blowing over and the local rivers and creeks being a little higher than normal. Sitting back in the car, David called the office. There was no answer, so he found his boss's cell phone number and called that instead.

"Hi Paul, it's Dave. How's things there?"
Kelly listened, while the voice on the other end of the phone spoke, inaudibly.

"Oh that's good to hear. Yeah, Kel and I left

yesterday after work. We're in Colonial Heights. It's in Tennessee, about two hundred miles away."

David's boss continued to speak. She couldn't hear what he was saying, but David seemed calm and upbeat, so it must be all OK back home.

"That's a relief. I was worried it would have blown away," said David. "We're about to head back up now. Are we opening today?"

Kelly could hear from the tone in Paul's answer that he was calm.

"OK, no problem," David continued. "In that case I'll see you tomorrow.... Alright... See ya."

David pressed the *end call* button on his phone's display and turned to Kelly, smiling. "Well, guess who's got the day off?" he asked.

"Oh, that's good, babe. No stress for us today then. Let's head home."

Chapter two

Unprepared

Driving from Colonial Heights, Tennessee, to Lynchburg, Virginia takes around three and half hours, providing you're not facing unusually heavy traffic flow. Unfortunately, heavy traffic is exactly what all motorists on the I-81 faced, as what seemed like half the state was attempting to return home. David and Kelly were among those early returners, of course.

Most evacuees had no doubt planned to stay with friends or relatives inland for up to a week, so many were still at their inland places of refuge. But in the age of the Internet, information about the sudden weakness of Hurricane Henriette spread quickly, and some attempted to beat the rush home. The result was traffic not unlike what they saw the day before, when they attempted to flee, but heading in the other direction.

After two boring hours of driving, the conversation had withered away. Both driver and passenger stared blankly through the windshield as the cars edged forward. Kelly readjusted in her seat.

"Maybe we should try taking the regular roads," she suggested.

She picked up her phone and opened the Waze application, looking for alternative routes.

"If we take exit 81, we can get off the interstate and take the I-77 inland. We'd be able to get off the interstate all together and make our own way home via the back roads. In this traffic it says it'll take the same amount of time, maybe a bit longer, but at least we'll be moving."

"How far away is that exit?" David asked.

"Uhm. Hang on." Kelly scrolled and pinched at her phone.

"Not far. About six miles from here."

The idea sounded excellent. After now almost three hours behind the wheel, David was eager to feel the sensation of actual movement, even if there was no real time saving advantage. The wait for exit 81 was eternal when traveling at twenty miles per hour, but eventually it appeared. Turning off that highway was a voyage into the unknown, but the change alone was beautiful.

The journey inland was worth the stress relief, but it came at a cost. The trusty Toyota might be reliable enough to survive a movie-style zombie apocalypse, but without gas, it wasn't going anywhere. With its gas needle falling closer and closer to the white 'E' at the bottom of its dashboard display, David was on the lookout for a gas station, aware of how heavy his foot had been on the journey so far. Meanwhile, Kelly was trying to look for the nearest gas station online, though her cell phone signal was weak on the hilly side roads.

"Oh thank God," David said, some miles later, causing Kelly to look up from her phone.

"Oh good," she said, with the view of the Copper Hill gas station and hardware store appearing in front of them.

Laughing, David admitted, "I was, uh, actually getting a bit worried there. Got some range anxiety seeping through. I can unclench my butt now!"

Kelly gave a laugh as the Toyota pulled into the gas station, stopping in front of pump number four. While the pumps were all available, the place looked like one of those gas stations that also sell a few cars out the front. There were about fifteen late model cars all parked off to the side.

David flipped the gas cap and got out of the vehicle, looking forward to stretching his legs. The attendant came out of the building and walked over to him.

"Sorry bud. We're outta gas," were the first words out of the attendant's mouth.

"Oh shit. Seriously?" said Kelly, overhearing.

"'Fraid so. That hurricane caused a run on us, draining our tanks last night and we're still waiting for the tanker truck. They reckon it should be here in about an hour."

"I guess that explains all those cars," David said, pointing to the fifteen vehicles parked to the side of the gas station.

"Yep. Most people took the risk and carried on. There's another gas station fifteen miles down the road, but they're empty too. Some of the car owners realized the situation is pointless so they're sitting inside, buying drinks and sandwiches. Tell you what, it's been good for business, if nothing else," the attendant joked.

"If you two want, you can park up next to those cars and wait too. Just leave enough space for the tanker truck to get in here."

David looked at Kelly. They both knew what each other was thinking.

"Nah, it's OK. We'll carry on. We still have a bit of gas left in the tank. Just wanted to be extra safe and fill it right up, even though we can make it home. Thanks anyway, though," David said to the attendant.

The attendant smiled, not worried about losing business when he had a captive audience waiting in his store.

"Alright then. You two drive safe," he said.

The gas light was glowing orange on the dashboard.

"We need to find a discreet place to fill up," David said, getting nervous. They didn't want to mention on the gas station forecourt that they actually had a four gallon container full of gas in the back of the car. The last thing they wanted was to be the target of some frenzied bidding war, as people with much more money attempt to buy the gas off them for ten times its value.

And, considering what they saw back in Lynchburg, when four adults devolved to brawling for water - in the rain, no less - they both knew it was prudent to keep such information undisclosed.

Telling people you have what they need in a time of crisis can only lead to escalated consequences. Not only that, the number one rule of being a "prepper" is never to tell anyone you're a prepper.

"There. That gravel driveway. Behind those trees," Kelly said, pointing.

David braked and pulled the car off the road. The gas needle was pointing lower than he'd seen it before.

"It must be running on fumes," he said, as he turned the car around, so that the gas filler cap was facing away from the road, then he stopped the engine.

Kelly lifted the trunk hatch and, carefully looking around, removed the four gallon gas container from the back, placing it around the side of the car.

The average observer would never have known there was a gas shortage sweeping the state, as there still seemed to be cars passing by every ten or twenty seconds on this winding country road. Perhaps they were all in the same situation?

"You know, that explains why we've seen so many breakdowns," Kelly said, fishing out the funnel from inside the back of the car.

"I reckon most of them are just out of gas," she added.

"Makes sense," David responded.

"Remember last night at the gas station by the highway? Some of those folks are probably still there now. They're lucky the hurricane was a flop."

David screwed the spout onto the top of the gas container's mouth and waited.

Another car went by.

They stood there in silence; the rear of their car partly concealed by a tree on this empty driveway leading somewhere around a corner.

Silence.

"Go. Do it now," Kelly said quickly, looking towards the road, listening intently.

"OK."

He lifted the four gallon container up and quickly aimed the spout into the gas tank's gaping esophagus. Tilting it, the distinct sound of gasoline sloshing down the spout began. The container weighed about eight pounds, but was getting lighter with each second.

"Stop! Car!" Kelly said.

David yanked the spout out of the car's gas filler and it fumbled in his hands. A stream of gasoline flowed out as it slipped from his fingers and landed on its side, pouring precious fuel all over the dusty driveway.

"Fuck!" he said, grabbing it and standing it upright as a car went past; its occupants looking through the car window in their direction, craning their necks before disappearing around the next bend in the road.

The two stood motionless next to the car.

"Do you think they saw anything?" he asked.
Kelly didn't immediately answer as she was busy listening to hear if the car would turn around.

"I don't think so," she said.

"Besides. Maybe they didn't need gas. Maybe they live locally."
David picked up the container and continued pouring its contents into the car's tank.

"I might have lost us a few miles by spilling that gas."

"Shit babe, don't worry about it. The gas stations on the highways are probably refueled by now anyway," said Kelly, reassuringly.

"Besides," she added, "Worst case scenario: even if the gas stations are all still empty, we have more gas at home. We just have to make it back."
It was ridiculous that they had to refill their car in such a clandestine manner. It was just a few gallons of gas. The world hadn't fallen apart. They were in a first world country.

"I actually think we're overreacting. No one's gonna stop us and try to buy our gas from us... Or worse. I mean, yesterday was different, with those guys and the water. The hurricane was coming and everyone was on edge. But it's all good now. I reckon we're being paranoid," said David.
While waiting for the last few ounces to slide down the spout and into the car's filler hole he did some basic math.

"I think we'll be OK. It's what... about seventy miles to get home? The car gets around twenty-one miles per gallon. I put in four gallons-"

"Well, almost," Kelly interrupted with a smile.

"Hehe, almost," chuckled David.

The last few drops left the container. David gave it a shake. Every droplet was another foot of vehicular movement and there was no guarantee all the gas stations back in Lynchburg had been replenished yet.

David put the now-empty container on the ground, just as a red SUV drove past. The occupants looked over at them, standing behind their vehicle, with its back positioned behind a tree. The SUV continued onwards, going out of sight as it followed the curve in the road.

"What the hell is everyone looking at. We're just two people standing behind a car," David said, mildly annoyed at the inquisitive passers-by.

"They probably just think we pulled off the road for a quickie," Kelly said.

David paused for a moment and silently contemplated sex in the car once more.

Kelly laughed.

"I know what you're thinking!"

"What?" he responded, smiling.

"I know you," she laughed. "This is Bible Belt territory. Sex is basically illegal here unless it's for making a quiver-full of babies. Let's just get home and have a shower."

Kelly picked up the empty gas container and put it back in the car, closing the rear hatch.

"Here," she said, pulling out a packet of wet wipes and handing them to David. He opened the packet, took out a moist towelette and wiped the smelly spilled gas residue off his hands. He then tucked the scrunched-up wet wipe in the back of the car and got behind the wheel. Kelly resumed her position as navigator in the passenger seat. Turning the key, the Toyota sprung into life and the gas needle began to rise up like Icarus flying toward the sun. Unlike Icarus, however, the needle only went up a fifth of the way.

"I'm pretty sure that should be enough to get back. I reckon we'll be home in a couple of hours," he said as he slipped the shifter into "D" and released the parking brake.

◆

Hypermiling, meaning driving as economically as possible by feathering the accelerator and adjusting a vehicle's speed well in advance of corners and other motorists' actions, is only really fun when it's optional. Ask any early adopter of city electric cars, with their small batteries and short driving ranges, and they'll tell you that driving economically is a bore, especially if there are cars close behind you, desperate to go faster. When seriously hypermiling, your butt hole is constantly clenched, concerned about getting a gentle run-up before every hill, while trying not to piss off everyone behind you. It's a fine line between driving so slowly that you become a dangerous hazard on the road, and driving fast enough in order to not annoy your fellow motorists, but doing so at the risk of possibly running out of fuel or electricity before you reach your destination.

◆

David was treading a fine line between economy and speed. On the single-lane, twisty back roads heading to Lynchburg, there really weren't a lot of opportunities for the seven cars behind them to pass, either. This meant David and Kelly weren't really making a lot of friends on their slow and methodical journey back.
They were too far from the interstate to make it worth changing course and getting back on it, and besides, the closer they got to home, the heavier the traffic would be. It was now getting close to 2 PM and the journey had taken much longer than anticipated. The traffic, the back roads and the stops all took their toll and the fun was quickly draining from the journey home.

The town of Bedford was about five miles ahead and Kelly tried to lighten the mood by changing what was being played on the car stereo. They had been listening to a recent album by Sting featuring the artist known as Shaggy, but neither of them thought it was Sting's best work. Kelly connected the stereo to her phone via Bluetooth, ending the "Mr. Boombastic" singer mid-sentence.

"Oh thank God. I was starting to get sick of that," David said. "I mean, I get Shaggy. He has some good songs. But partnering with Sting? It's like oil and water. Sting is… Sting. But Shaggy? Shit. The guy has all the vocal range of a car horn."

Kelly let out a chuckle, phone in hand. She decided on a comedy podcast and clicked the *play* button on her phone. After a second, the stereo replaced the voice of Shaggy with the voice of comedian Bill Burr. The podcast launched in the middle of an episode, straight to the point where Kelly was last listening two days ago. The comedian was giving relationship advice to those who dared to write in to his show. His last listener had asked him for advice on a cheating spouse. In his usual comic style, Bill Burr went on a rambling tale of sports references and anecdotes, before coming to the obvious conclusion that the relationship had to end.

"Dude. It's over. But there's plenty more fish in the wahhteer!" the comedian said in a Boston accent, almost shouting the word *water* in falsetto. Bill Burr then moved onto reading an advertisement. He'd only just begun singing an improvised ditty about one of his podcast sponsors, a underwear manufacturer, when the familiar vibration of the car engine stopped.

"Whoah-whoah-whoah. What… What the hell…" David said, as the vehicle lost momentum.

"What's happening?" asked Kelly, flatly.

"I don't know. The engine's dead."

"Was it the gas?" she asked.

"It can't be. The car wouldn't just die if the gas was bad."

The Toyota coasted. Forty miles per hour. thirty-eight miles per hour. Thirty-five miles per hour.

"Fuck... FUCK!" David said. He'd had enough. What had started out as a routine hurricane evacuation had quickly become a pain in the ass. He sighed a heavy, angry sigh.

"I'd better pull over."

He flipped the blinker stalk, pulling over to the right but the blinker didn't blink. The car continued to coast. Twenty miles per hour. Fifteen. Ten. David put the car out of its misery, turning the wheel slightly onto the edge of the road, applying the brake.

"It must be an electrical fault," he said as the car came to a stop.

"That's weird," he said, looking in the side mirror. "No one's passing us. They're all stopping too." Indeed, the seven or so vehicles that were stuck behind them had pulled over as well, all at different distances. David pulled the parking brake up, pressed the hazard light button in the middle of the dash and undid his seat belt. Kelly did the same. He popped the hood release lever at the bottom corner of the dashboard and opened the car door. Kelly opened her own door, holding her mobile phone in her hand.

As the two got out of the car, they turned, looking back at the seven cars behind them. The convoy, created by David's hypermiling was spaced out. The Volkswagen Passat wagon that had been tailgating them had stopped right behind their Toyota, with the vehicle's occupants undoing their seat belts and clearly arguing about something. The passenger in the Volkswagen was a woman, mid thirties. She was gesticulating to the driver who sat there like an idiot. It was obvious he was tired of her shit.

Some vehicles in the convoy had also pulled over on the side of the road but a couple of cars had stopped right in the middle of the road. One of them a big Chevrolet Silverado. It was a strange spectacle. Kelly turned to David, the roof of the car separating them.

"What is going *on?*" Kelly asked.

His expression blank, he said nothing, not being sure himself. They both turned, facing the vehicles behind them.

The doors began opening on the convoy of seven vehicles stopped behind them, spaced out awkwardly over 200 yards or so. The occupants of the vehicles climbed out of their cars. With the sudden lack of road noise and car sounds, Kelly felt like she was having a mild out of body experience, akin to giving a presentation in front of a group of people and you find yourself suddenly hyper-aware of your surroundings and the sound of your voice. People were milling around their cars. One motorist a couple of cars back had lifted the hood on his late model Toyota Camry and was peering at the engine bay, full of plastics and metal, possibly hoping for something obvious to fix, like a big red On/Off switch on top of the motor that had tripped. Of course, modern cars weren't so simple; everything runs through computers now. David was planning to do the same, but the large, bizarre scene playing out behind them distracted them. They stood motionless for a few seconds, watching people exiting their vehicles and wandering around like lost puppies. The driver of the Volkswagen, which had stopped directly behind them, got out and walked over. He was in his late 30s; about the same age as David and Kelly, thin, but already balding. His passenger, a dark haired woman of a similar age also got out, clearly pregnant. She obviously hadn't finished whatever she started in the car, because before the man was within ten feet of David, she continued her discussion.

"Nathaniel, we need to talk about this. Come back here, please," she said, clearly not happy.

The balding man turned back to the woman in the car, looking a combination of annoyed and exhausted.

"Victoria... Please. Not now," he said flatly.

The woman scrunched her face up and sat back in the car, closing the passenger door. She picked up her cell phone, turning it over and squeezed it, a pouting expression on her somewhat unattractive face.

"Trouble in paradise?" Kelly joked to the man. It was possibly not the appropriate thing to say to a squabbling couple, but Kelly didn't have much of a filter. That was one of the things David loved about her.

"Our car just died," said the thin, balding man. "I don't know why. I had it serviced last week."

"Ours is dead too," David said.

"I reckon it's an electrical fault. It's weird," he added.

Just at that moment, David noticed that his hazard lights were not flashing. He must have forgotten to press the button. He opened the driver's door and reached in to press it.

"That's weird. I did already press it."

"What's that?" asked Kelly.

"The hazard lights. They should be working. They're not part of the car's computer," he answered.

"No one's hazard lights are working," she said, scanning the cars on this section of road.

The pregnant passenger in the Volkswagen stopped behind them then got out of the car and called to the balding man. He was standing at the front of their car, rubbing his head, confused by the situation.

"Nathaniel, I want to go home," she said in earshot to David and Kelly.

"Oh, please, Victoria. Stop whining. We're not going anywhere. The car isn't working," he said, aware that the sound of a nagging voice wasn't going to help the situation in any way.

"Well, can't you fix it? I'm tired. I wanna go home. And my phone's stopped working. It's brand new. And I'm getting hungry. Why is the car not-"

"Shut up! Just... please," he snapped.
The pregnant woman slumped back into her seat, folded her arms and began sulking. Kelly turned to David and said quietly.

"They're not gonna last when that baby comes."

"I'll bet they won't even last the journey home. Free show, though." he joked.
Only a few minutes had passed since the impromptu convoy had collectively stopped. As David lifted the hood on their Toyota, another motorist approached him.

"You got the same problem?" he asked.

"Yeah," David replied. "It's electrical, that's for sure. But why it's affected all of us, I don't know. Maybe we passed through some sort of..." He was going to say the word 'forcefield' but stopped himself, aware that it sounded ridiculous. This was not a science fiction movie.

"Passed through what?" the motorist asked.

"I'm not sure, to be honest," David answered.
Kelly approached her husband and the stranger.

"Dave. Is your phone working?"
He pulled his phone out of his pocket.

"That's odd. I think it turned itself off."

David held the Power button down on the side. Normally the phone would give a little vibration once it had began to power on, but it was unresponsive.

"Nah, my phone's not turning on."

David and Kelly stood by the side of the road and pressed at their phones repeatedly. David looked up to see five or six others down the road doing the same.

He felt a sudden chill wash down his spine.

"Kel…"

His breathing increased. He could feel a hit of adrenaline flushing his chest. He felt a tingling as the hair on his arms stood on end.

"Kelly. Come here."

Her expression changed from that of confusion at the scenario in front of them, to worry, evident from the serious tone of his voice. David took her hand and led her out of earshot of the other motorists, toward the front of the car's open hood. He looked genuinely frightened.

"What?" she said, getting scared herself.

"Look at them," he said, pointing to the dozen or so motorists all tapping at their phones, cars and watches, the air suspiciously absent of sound.

"David, you're scaring me," Kelly said quietly.

David was breathing shallow breaths. His eyes were wide open and stared at Kelly intently. He took her hand and led her further away. Once they had walked a few more yards away from their car and the other motorists, he stopped again and turned to Kelly.

"I think... I think I know what's going on," he said hurriedly, gesturing to the convoy with his head.

"The phones. The cars. Nothing electronic works."

Kelly cocked her head to the side, not sure what he was getting at.

"Kel. It's an EMP attack. It's gotta be."

Kelly didn't say anything, nor did her expression change. She did nothing for a couple of seconds. Then she turned her head to the convoy, silently observing the dozen or so people milling about their cars. It dawned on her that he was right.

"Jesus," she whispered, her mouth slipping open ever-so-slightly as a hundred thoughts fought for space in her mind. Her eyes darted aimlessly as her brain processed dozens of scenarios. She quickly pulled her sleeve on her sweater back and tapped at her smart watch. It was dead. She tried turning it on. No response.

"Check your watch," she said.

David looked at his own watch. It was an old style quartz watch. He hadn't yet jumped aboard the smart watch train. Sure, he'd thought of getting one, and sometimes played with them in electronics shops, but was always put off by the idea of having to recharge a watch two or three times a week.

"I think it's dead, too," he said, lifting his wrist up to his ear.

Normally it would be impossible to hear the quiet ticking of the second hand during the day, especially outside. It was something you could only do in bed, when the world was asleep. But the silence of this afternoon was so pronounced that you could hear a pin drop. And yet, there was no ticking sound. He stared at his analog watch. It was frozen at 2:20 PM. They both looked up at each other, making eye contact.

David wanted to say something, but what? He took a breath and began to speak, but stopped before a word could leave his mouth.

"Shit," Kelly whispered, shaking her head. Were they the only ones who knew? Other than the chatter of motorists milling about, completely unaware of the seriousness of the situation, the silence of that moment was almost deafening. But that silence was immediately interrupted.

A sound that could only be described as a plane crashing occurred on a concealed hillside about a mile away from them. Someone in the convoy screamed in fright. An enormous ball of flame and a plume of dark gray smoke rose above the source of the sound, which echoed into the distance.

"The fuck was that!?" David asked, now in a state of heightened alert.

"I don't know," Kelly answered.

He joined the dots.

"It was a fucking plane. A passenger plane. Like, a fucking passenger jet!"

"My God," Kelly said. "Should... We go there? Should we try to help?"

"But what could we do?" he answered.

"Shit, if it really *was* an airliner, it would have hit the ground at five hundred miles an hour! There'll be nothing left!"

"We should go anyway. Maybe there's a survivor. It might be worth photographing. The pictures would be worth something to a newspaper," Kelly said, her passion for photography becoming evident, before it hit her: her phone was dead, which means no one was going to be photographing anything. Her old Nikon F2 film camera would probably still work, but it was back at home.

"Anyway, whatever happens, we *do* need to get the fuck out of here." She pointed quickly towards the convoy of cars and people, all frozen in confusion, looking in the direction of the explosion.

"They clearly don't know what's going. They don't know what's happening. They haven't figured it out yet. They're not preppers. If they knew..." she trailed off.

They were both breathing shallow breaths. David was sweating.

"OK. If this is an EMP attack, it's bad. But we don't know how bad. Maybe it's just this area? Maybe just this part of the state is affected," said Kelly, trying to be optimistic.

"Maybe. Or maybe the whole country is wiped out," continued David. "It must have been North Korea. Remember the news this morning?"

"Or it could have been Russia. Or China," Kelly responded.

"Shit. We're not ready for this," David said, worried. "I mean, seriously, we're not prepared for this kind of shit."

The atmosphere in the convoy was quickly becoming a mixture of fear and confusion. Kelly and David quickly returned to their car, pretending to be equally confused, but they knew they needed to get away from this group before anyone else figured out what was going on. Someone - some country – must have attacked the USA. At that moment the damage wasn't yet known. Who knows how those people behind them would handle it if they knew that their friends and families could be dead, or about to enter a world of starvation.

"What on Earth is going on?" the balding man asked Kelly as they returned to their Toyota and lifted the trunk hatch.

"Not sure. We're going to go and get help," Kelly said, lying.

In reality, she and David were simply going to get the fuck out of there. There were too many unpredictable people in that convoy and, as the realization of the situation's seriousness became evident, those motorists were more and more likely to do something stupid. It's Virginia, after all. Half the people in the stalled convoy behind them probably had guns in their cars.

A couple of guys from one of the cars near the end of the convoy walked up and approached David. They explained that they were going to see what that explosion was behind the hill, and if anyone needed help.

"We reckon it was a plane that crashed. Do you guys have a first aid kit we can take?" asked the older of the two men.

"Unfortunately not," lied David. Trying to act as calmly as possible, he wished them well and told them to be careful. He added that they were going to get help at Bedford, the next town, about four miles away.

While the two men, carrying whatever first aid items they could scrounge up, started walking across the hilly field, Kelly and David filled up their backpack with essentials: a portable gas cooker, their metal water bottle, eight cans of food, some chlorine tablets for purifying water, a shortwave radio, a map of Virginia, a compass, rope, their pistol and their first aid kit. They stood shoulder to shoulder, blocking the view of the people in the convoy behind them as they placed the last item in the backpack, before zipping it up.

"We're going to Bedford to get help. It's about four miles from here," Kelly said to the miserable looking driver of the Volkswagen Passat behind them, who stood, leaning against his car. His pregnant passenger was clutching her cell phone in the passenger seat, audibly complaining. Again.

"They're not going to survive," Kelly whispered to David.

"You mean their marriage or their lives?" David asked, even though this wasn't really the time for comedy.

"Probably both," joked Kelly.

Chapter three

Going home

An electromagnetic pulse, known as an EMP is a very quick burst of electromagnetic energy. Like the hundreds of tiny earthquakes that happen around the world each day, EMPs happen often on our planet, but typically go unnoticed; coming in the form of naturally occurring phenomena such as lightning, or sometimes as coronal mass ejections from the Sun. Normally, other than a lightning strike setting a tree on fire, such electrical pulses are harmless. But sometimes that is not the case. In 1859, for example, a coronal mass ejection originating from the Sun hit our planet. Once the ejection collided with our planet's magnetosphere, it created a substantial geomagnetic storm, the largest in recorded history, affecting what limited electronic technology we had at the time.

The world's early telegraph systems were overloaded with electricity and put out of service. Some telegraph operators were shocked by their machines and the pylons themselves sparked in the streets. Fortunately, this event happened when humankind was not yet reliant on technology and circuit boards in order to survive. If such an impulse happened today, it would be catastrophic, causing cities or entire countries to grind to a halt.

Another, potentially more dangerous form of EMP can be caused by a nuclear explosion.

During the cold war, the Soviet Union carried out test attacks using bombs which generated nuclear electromagnetic pulses. They learned that detonating a nuclear missile 30 miles above the United States would be enough to send the country into chaos, knocking out important electrical equipment, nationwide.

Depending on the intensity of the explosion and its altitude, such blasts could, in theory, be powerful enough to do more than just destroy electricity grids, but even render cars and wristwatches permanently useless. Anything with a microchip or enough wiring could be overwhelmed by an instant, silent blast of pure energy.

Such a situation is real, and it's entirely possible. So what would happen to society if such an event occurred today? How would we react and, given our slave-like reliance on technology, how would we survive?

Once they had walked a safe distance away from the cluster of cars which had ground to a halt behind their own, David reached around and slid off the backpack, placing it on the roadside. Undoing the zip on top of the bag, he reached in and pulled out their portable shortwave radio. He flicked the *On* switch on the side. It did nothing.

"It's dead?" Kelly asked.

"Yeah"

Of course it was dead. Almost everything electronic, except perhaps for utterly basic devices without microchips, such as an old-style flashlight, had been turned into junk.

David tried removing the batteries from the radio and replaced them but it made no difference. He looked at the radio, turning the dials on the side, but realized he was now holding a plastic paperweight. He sighed and threw it in the ditch on the roadside. Kelly said nothing, aware that the radio was useless as it wasn't protected against such a strong electromagnetic pulse.

They continued walking, the sound of footsteps surprisingly loud on a road with no cars or human activity. If it wasn't so frightening, it might even have been enjoyable.

Walking around a gentle curve on the road, they were then faced with a straight stretch of tarmac, about 300 yards long which dipped downwards. On the left side of the road was an unusual sight: a three-phase distribution transformer atop a power pole was on fire, not unlike a giant Olympic torch on the side of the empty road. It's flammable mineral insulating oil was alight, dripping down and creating firey splatters on the ground.

"Make a wish and blow it out," David joked, finding humor in the absurd. Kelly didn't respond, finding the entire scene surreal.

They walked past the transformer with it's yellow flames and thick black smoke billowing upwards. Against the silence of the countryside, the licking of hungry flames made for a haunting sound in the afternoon air. They pressed on, both pondering the seriousness of the attack. David broke the silence first.

"So, if even my wristwatch is dead, it's got to be a serious attack. A real intense pulse."

Kelly was quiet for a moment.

"The people on that plane," she eventually responded.

David nodded in sympathy.

"Try not to think about it."

"There were families on that plane, Dave. People like us."

"I know. But what can we do? It just fell out of the sky, hitting the ground like a ton of bricks. No one could have survived that."

The sound of their footsteps replaced the sound of conversation for a few hundred yards.

"Once we get to this next town, whatever it's called, we need to figure out how to get home," Kelly said. "But, it's going to be chaos. It's going to be like a real world disaster movie."

She paused for a moment, stopping in her tracks. David continued for a few steps before turning around to face her. After a few awkward few seconds, she voiced what was on her mind.

"We can't possibly go home. It's what, thirty miles from here? And it'll be completely lawless."

David knew there was truth to what Kelly was saying, but it wasn't exactly a matter of choice.

"But where else will we go, Kel? Our supplies in this bag will keep us going for maybe three days, tops. After that, we need to be somewhere safe until either everyone kills each other or the military steps in."

"If there even *is* still a military," Kelly responded.

"Kel, we *need* to get home. Maybe we can stay the night in a hotel or something when we get to the next town. What's it called, Bedford?"

Kelly nodded.

"So, maybe we can stay there for the night, but ultimately we need to get home. And fast. I reckon we have about one full day before it descends into total, lawless chaos," David said.

He stared into the distance for a moment, before continuing.

"Right now, everyone's in the 'what the fuck' stage. I doubt many even know what an EMP attack is. I mean, maybe it's just this area. Maybe help is already on its way. Shit, maybe it was all just an accident."

"Yeah, maybe, maybe, maybe. We don't know anything," Kelly responded.
David found himself getting angry.

"Are we going to start fighting? Now, of all times?"

"We are not fighting. We both just scared. Calm down," Kelly responded.

"Never in the history of being un-calm has saying 'calm down' ever caused someone to calm down," he responded, realizing he was starting to sound whiny. David exhaled.

"Look. I'm sorry, Kel. I'm being a dick. I'm just... freaked out."

"Babe," said Kelly, grasping David's hand. "We are gonna survive. Look, let's just get to this town before it gets dark, then we'll figure out what to do next."
David turned to face Kelly, reaching to hold her other hand.

"I love you," he said.
"And I love you too. We'll be alright, babe."

The town of Bedford, like any town in the USA, is car-centric. People don't walk or ride bicycles; they take their cars. Even if it's just a mile down the road. This made the following scene playing out in front of David and Kelly somewhat surreal. As they entered the outskirts of the town, the streets were devoid of traffic. There were cars, sure, but none were moving. People walked in the middle of the road. One resident was on a bicycle. Neighbors talked over their fences. If it wasn't the eve of the end of the world as they knew it, it could almost be a beautiful scene.

"It looks like Amsterdam," said Kelly.

"But without all the drugs," David joked.

"Uhmm," Kelly responded, unconvinced. "This place probably has more meth than an entire season of *Justified*. I can't imagine there's much else to do. Procreate and do drugs."

They walked past a couple of middle aged neighbors, standing on the curbside, talking. The two neighbors, both women, looked up at the weary travelers, one with a backpack.

"Where y'all come from?" asked the neighbor wearing an oversized brown sweater.

"Our car broke down about four miles back that way," Kelly responded, gesturing down the road with her thumb.

"Did you see what that explosion was?" The neighbor asked. "We reckon it was a plane."

"Really? We didn't see it," Kelly lied.

Like someone standing outside The Matrix, she was acutely aware of the seriousness of the situation. The less information she gave away, the better. It would just take one spark to ignite panic. If only they knew, she thought.

"My husband went off with a group of others, heading towards the plane crash - if it was really a plane crash - to look for survivors," the neighbor continued.

"No one's phone is working though, so I don't know what's going on. I reckon it's a government conspiracy. Probably one of them chemtrails planes, trying to control the population."

Kelly and David exchanged a split-second glance towards each other. They didn't need to say anything. Just that quarter of a second of eye contact, before quickly looking away, meant that they were on the same page. They both thought the neighbor was bat-shit insane.

"Is there a motel or something nearby?" Kelly asked.

"Yeah, in the center of town. End of this street," the neighbor responded, "But the town's got no power at the moment."

The other neighbor finally spoke.

"There's a fire at the big power box-thing in town and the fire brigade say their truck has broken down. It's all hit the fan here so good luck getting a room."

"OK. We'll give it a shot. Thanks for your help," Kelly answered.

They turned and continued walking into town. The neighbors watching silently as they walked away, pretending to act casual.

"This place gives me the creeps," David said when they were finally out of earshot.

"I'm telling you, this is a jaunt down *Methame Street*," Kelly joked.

"Hah. You've been watching too much TV."

They walked past a man working on his car on the side of the road.

"You two know anything about cars?" he asked the two strangers to Bedford.

"Nah, unfortunately not," David lied. "What happened to it?"

"I just filled up the car at the gas station and it died. The gas station ran out of gas last night when all those folks from Washington and Richmond flooded through here trying to get away from that storm. The storm never happened but they came through and bought up all our gas anyway. The tanker truck showed up after lunch, so I went to fill up my car, but after filling up I only got this far before it died. I walked home to get my tools and came back here, but I'll be damned if I can figure out the problem."

"It just died?" asked David, pretending to be naïve.

"Yep. All the cars in town are dead. And the power's out. I reckon it's all connected. Must be something to do with the gas. Or the government's trying to fuck with us. It's the Illuminati, I guarantee it."
Oh great, thought David. This whole town is full of nut-jobs. Kelly was already looking at David and he knew it. He could feel her eyes on his face. He slowly moved his head upwards and allowed his eyes to quickly flick in her direction.
Eye contact.
The two smirked.

"What's so funny?" asked the stranded motorist, now annoyed.

"Nothing," David answered. "I'll bet you're right."

"Damn right I am," the motorist said, matter-of-factly.

"Hey," Kelly interjected. "Is there a motel nearby?"
She already knew the answer, but was desperate to change the subject.

"End of this road," he said.

"Thanks. Good luck."
They continued walking, this time walking in the middle of the road to reduce the likelihood of having to interact with more conspiracy theorists.

"Surely, they can't all be nuts?" David asked.

"Too much Internet and too much spare time," I guess, Kelly responded.
With the sun getting close to the hills in the horizon, they arrived at the town center. It was picturesque, given that

there were no cars moving about. There were people talking in small groups everywhere. There was a general store, which was open. That seemed to be a hub of activity, even though there was a hastily written sign out the front saying 'Cash only! No cards.'

Kelly saw the sign and realized they had a new problem. She let out a pained sigh.

"If the motel is even *taking* guests, how will we pay? The phone system's probably dead. We can't pay by card. How much cash do you have?"

That was a very good point. David stopped and pulled out his wallet, flicking through what banknotes he had.

"Ten... Twenty... Twenty five. Twenty five bucks. How much do you have?"

Kelly did the same, opening her wallet and counting her cash.

"Ten bucks. And some coins."

David inhaled through his teeth.

"This could be a problem," he said.

The motel had a sign out the front reading *Vacancy*, but who knew if that was accurate. It'd now been around three hours since the EMP attack. The normally quiet town of Bedford was still blissfully unaware of the dangers it - and perhaps the whole nation - were facing. David opened the door of the motel's reception and allowed Kelly in first. The two walked up to the counter and pressed the doorbell button on the top of the chest-height front desk, though the button didn't seem to do anything. Kelly gave it a few more presses. It surprised her how even the most innocuous little things all had sensitive electronic circuits which were now fried.

"Hello?" she said in a raised voice. "Anyone here?"

"Coming!" replied a muffled voice from another room. A door opened and an older man appeared.

"Afternoon. What can I do for you two?"

"Do you have a room?" Kelly inquired.

The man seemed unsure.

"Uh, I *think* so. We've had a lot of bookings this afternoon, but the power's out so we're all writing everything down on paper. Also, we got no hot water, so if you want a shower it'll be cold."

He searched through a disorganized sea of paper notes behind the counter.

"It's like working back in the 80s," he said. "No cell phones, no computers. Got to do everything with a pen and paper. You young'uns probably wouldn't remember that time. It was simpler."

Kelly and David made eye contact and smiled. Although both in their mid to late 30s, they admittedly looked fairly young for their age, perhaps that being a result of not having kids.

"Here we go. This key doesn't have a home, so I guess we still have a room left. Room 36."

The motel owner placed the key on the counter.

"Alright, if I could get some ID please, the room will be all yours. It's fifty dollars for the night. Sorry, but cash only. Our credit card system's dead."

"Ah," said Kelly.

"Yeah, about that," said David. "We thought this might be a problem, so we counted our cash outside. We've got about thirty five bucks."

"Hmm. That's not gonna work," responded the manager, his demeanor changing.

"The thing is, we've got money on our card, but we can't get at it," David replied. "What if I give you my watch? It's a Citizen watch. It's worth a couple hundred bucks."

David took off his watch and placed it on the counter. The manager picked it up, suspiciously. He studied the face of the watch, aware that fakes are getting almost indistinguishable from the real thing. He placed it to his ear.

"I think it's broken."

"It just needs a new battery," lied David. "It's a two hundred dollar watch, though."

The manager placed it back down on the counter.

"Sorry, friend. No deal."

This situation was more serious than it appeared. They couldn't go back to the car. It was too dangerous, and it was only a matter of time before society descended into chaos. They just needed one night to sleep and think, then they could figure out how to ride the coming wave of mass hysteria. Kelly acted on instinct. She wiggled off her wedding ring.

"Babe?" David asked, not enjoying what he was seeing.

"Dave, just do it," she responded.

He complied, realizing the gravity of the situation. He placed his ring next to hers on the counter.

"These are eighteen karat gold," Kelly stated, sliding both rings along the counter towards the motel owner.

"You guys really want that room."

He picked up the rings and put them in his shirt pocket.

"Don't worry about the ID. Just don't make a mess."

"Alright. Thank you," Kelly said, collecting the key off the counter.

Slumping down on that bed was like falling on a heavenly cloud. Sure, that mattress has probably endured all kinds of steamy jungle sex by people with questionable hygiene, but for one night it was theirs.

They didn't care, they were just glad to be in a room together in each other's embrace.

After resting for a while, they cracked open a can of salmon and a can of kidney beans from the backpack, with both being good sources of protein and calories. Kelly opened the cans using her Swiss Army pocket knife. They had one spoon in their minimalist survival pack in order to save weight, so they took turns eating. It was the first thing they'd eaten since breakfast all those hours ago at that little cafe in Tennessee. Back when the world had order.

As the room was getting cold, after dinner they finally had the opportunity to brush their teeth - a luxury often taken for granted – before sliding back into bed to stay warm. Simply holding each other was a beautiful form of therapy.

Kelly broke the silence first, allowing the problems of the world outside to make their way into the room.

"What are we going to do tomorrow?"

David took a breath and pondered their options. They knew they had to get home. But they didn't know how.

"We both know we have to get back to Lynchburg. We have our supplies there. We were caught off guard in the car. Back home we have the spare shortwave radio, Geiger counter and spare phone sitting in the Faraday cage. Depending on the strength of the EMP blast, it could all be fine. We have food, water, chlorine tablets, gasoline, you name it."

"Yeah," Kelly responded, "But the question is, how do we get there?"

Kelly pulled back the covers and got out of bed, reaching over to the opened backpack. She fumbled around in the dark and pulled out the map of Virginia. She also grabbed the flashlight and turned it on. A beam of light filled the room.

"Babe, don't use the flashlight. We've gotta save the batteries. We might need them," David said.

"Alright," said Kelly. She switched off the flashlight and put it back in the bag, reaching inside for the zip-lock bag which stored a candle and a box of waterproof matches. Going purely by touch, she straightened the wick and placed the candle between her knees. Opening the box of matches, she took out one match and struck it against the side of the box. It took a couple of attempts to get the potassium chlorate ignited, but soon the room was brightened by the characteristic fizz of a lit match. She placed the flame against the candle and a soft amber glow illuminated her face.

"I am the illuminati," she said in a flat tone. She couldn't see David's eyes clearly, but he rolled them. Sitting in the bed, she brought her knees closer to her chest and placed the map on her thighs. It took her a moment to locate Bedford, then Lynchburg. She had a gentle frown on her face, biting her bottom lip slightly as she looked at their location and the map's key.

"I reckon we've got about 18 to 20 miles to get back home," she said. "But we can't take the roads, so it's going to take an entire day to get back."
David gave a single nod. Kelly was a good navigator and better with figures than he was, so he took her word as fact. She'd always enjoyed orienteering as a kid and was good with maps. Being a prepper, she was one of the few women in the modern world who was as good with the latest Android phone as she was with finding her position with a compass and a sextant.

"We're going to have to cross a lot of private property," she added.

"With armed and probably freaked-out rednecks," David lamented.

"Well, I'm confident I can get us home," she said. "But I don't know what happens afterwards." Kelly blew out the candle and held it for a few minutes until she was certain the wax was cool enough to place it on the nightstand. She moved over to David's side of the bed and they held each other tightly. Perhaps two of a small handful of people in the state who knew what kind of hell was unfolding before them.

Normally, on a Friday morning, David would be awakened by the alarm on his phone. He's a light sleeper, so he used the recording of a babbling stream and birdsong to wake him up. It worked every time. Kelly, on the other hand, could sleep through a nuclear holocaust, so David always tended to get up first. Today, however, their phones provided no other purpose than dust collectors or paperweights. Why they brought them with them from the car was unknown. Habit, perhaps. Regardless, they would be leaving their cell phones in the motel's trash when they left to start their journey home. Birdsong was the only sound in the morning air and it wasn't loud enough to wake either of them. What did shake David and Kelly from their slumber was the sound of a gunshot somewhere nearby. They both thrust themselves upright in bed. A man was shouting something outside.

"Get down!" David ordered.
Kelly slid straight onto the floor, while David grabbed their handgun off the floor next to the bed. He aimed the Glock 19 at a 45 degree angle downwards, arms extended, as he walked quickly to the window. The yelling continued. With his left hand he prized up one slat on the white, plastic venetian blinds and peered outside. A man was crouched on the ground outside the general store, yelling. Wailing. On the ground next to him was a

person. It looked like a woman, but from David's angle it was too hard to see.

"Someone's been shot," he said to Kelly.

"Are they alive?" she asked.

There was a pause. The man outside the store was holding the person but their arms were lifeless. He was crying, shouting for help. Blood was visible on his shirt but it didn't look like it was his.

"There's a guy outside by the store. Looks like his friend or something has been shot dead," David said to Kelly.

"Shit," she replied.

The situation was already falling apart and it had only been seventeen hours since the pulse.

"Kel. Get yourself ready. We've gotta get out of here ASAP."

David continued staring out the window, one finger prying open a slit in the blinds. Kelly threw their essentials back into the bag and ran into the bathroom to fill up their water bottle. There was no time for a shower or breakfast this morning. She unscrewed the cap and turned on the tap, with a gurgling sound emanating from the faucet. She turned the tap counterclockwise a few times and the gurgling became stronger. Eventually, splatterings of water came out of the spout and Kelly placed the bottle underneath it as meager pulses of water fell out.

"Ohhh fuck," David sighed.

"What is it?"

"You won't believe it. That pregnant woman. The one from the car yesterday. It's her."

"She's been shot?"

"Yeah... Oh fuck me. Shit... She's dead..."

David stared in disbelief out the window. That woman was alive just minutes ago. Yesterday she was at the side of the road in the car behind them, complaining about not being able to get on Instagram. Now she was dead.

"Come on, Kel, we've gotta go!"

"I'm trying! There's no water pressure."

It took a full minute to fill the metal water bottle beyond halfway before she took the bottle away and screwed on the cap. The water continued to splatter out in pulses, full of air, turning a gentle brown color. Kelly shut off the faucet and threw the bottle in the backpack.

The morning sun was beginning to rise above the surrounding hills and a small crowd had gathered outside the general store. A policeman had arrived on foot and the owner, a man in his 60s, sat in handcuffs to the side. Someone had gone to fetch a doctor but it was pointless. The thin, balding guy from the Volkswagen sat cradling his dead wife, their unborn child either dead or dying inside her. She wasn't the first victim of the disaster and she wouldn't be the last.

David placed an arm through each of the straps on the backpack and hoisted it onto his back. He placed the gun in the backpack's rear elastic pocket, allowing for easy access for Kelly to grab it if need be. With their shoelaces tied, it was with an air of trepidation that they opened the front door and slipped into their first day in hell.

Paramedics had been summoned by a local resident and they soon arrived on foot, carrying an old military-style stretcher. They looked exhausted, both splattered with dried blood. There was now a crowd of around thirty people surrounding the event. The husband of the dead woman sat motionless, staring at the ground, while the paramedics prepared to take her body to the local hospital, not that it would do any good.

Kelly sidled up to an onlooker.

"What happened?" she asked.

"I heard that woman tried to steal something

from the store and the owner caught her. She tried to run," said the onlooker.

"Shot dead for stealing?"

"Yeah. I heard the owner talking to the police just a few minutes ago. He said he's been guarding his shop all night. People have been trying to loot it."

"Shit. What did she try to steal?"

Another onlooker who had been listening in turned to Kelly and spoke.

"Magazines."

"Magazines? Like nine millimeter?"

"No. Entertainment Weekly or some shit."

Kelly, with her mouth agape, turned slowly to David. He replicated the exact same slow head turn and they locked eyes, staring at each other for a good two or three seconds. If it wasn't such a horrific situation, the comedic effect of their synchronized head turns would have been worthy of a Jim Carrey film.

"Something fucking weird is going on," the onlooker continued. "Did you hear the plane crash yesterday?"

Kelly played dumb.

"Plane crash?"

"Yesterday afternoon. A passenger plane crashed about five miles from here. My brother went out there on horseback 'cause all the cars won't start. It's a mess. No one survived. It was a big plane too, like a 747 or something. It's just a pile of smoldering metal."

"Seriously? Everyone died?" asked Kelly.

"It's like September 11 all over again. It must be a terrorist attack. Some rag-heads must have crashed the plane. They took out the power grid too."

"And the phones," added the other onlooker. "None of our cell phones work"

The two onlookers began to talk between themselves.

"It's gotta be terrorists. I don't know how they did it, but they turned off our cars, too."

"Yeah. Even the police don't know what's going on. Those two medics over there have been all night at the plane crash collecting body parts from the site and bringing them back here to the morgue."

"Yeah, and the county sheriff's riding a horse to get around. It's like we're back in the 19th century. He said he's riding to Lynchburg this morning to get answers. He's spooked. When the sheriff gets spooked, you know something bad's going on."

The two paramedics, both in blood-stained civilian clothes, carried away the woman's body on the military-style stretcher while the husband walked alongside, sobbing. It was a waste of potential. Two lives cut short, one adult, one unborn, because of the stupid actions of the former. All that for a pointless tabloid magazine full of celebrity gossip. It was a terrible thing to think, but David couldn't help wondering if the world was better off without another shallow, narcissistic mother raising another shallow, narcissistic child.

The policeman, meanwhile, crouched down near the ground scribbling in his notepad while the handcuffed store owner stared at the faces looking on. The situation was emotionally charged, with the bloodstain on the pavement outside the store serving as a reminder for Kelly and David that the worst was yet to come. They had to get out of there.

"This way," Kelly instructed, heading northeast through the town on Forest Road. The streets and sections were strangely busy, full of people interacting with each other who normally would be keeping to themselves. Because of the chaos of the shooting, they were able to walk through the town without having to talk to anyone. This suited them fine, as during a crisis, everyone is a potential enemy. Besides, today was all about getting home, where they'd be able to hunker down and wait for help, however and whenever it may come.

"Any society is only three square meals away from revolution," David said after a long stretch of silence.

"Who wrote that?" Kelly asked.

"I thought it was Trotsky... Or Arnold Rimmer."

"Jesus, Dave. You know, if I *do* die on this trip, it won't be from laughing."

"Jawohl, mein Führer. I vill vork on mein jokes." Kelly allowed herself a small chuckle. At least no matter what the world threw at them, through thick and thin, they both had equally terrible senses of humor.
Empty, immobile cars dotted the road as they approached the edge of Bedford. There was something unsettling about walking past a shiny, late model car which had stopped in the middle the road with no one inside. It was a bit like being in a real life zombie movie. Kelly unfolded the map and the two stopped in the middle of the road, just like the car they'd walked past. David's sunglasses masked the direction of his gaze, but his eyes were focused intently on two 20-somethings sitting outside a house on the front step. He faced his body slightly off-center and glanced down at the map often, to give the onlookers the impression that he wasn't watching them. The onlookers, however, were staring intently at David and Kelly.

"Kel, don't look up, but I'm getting a bad vibe from those guys in front of that house over there. On your left. About 9 o'clock."
Kelly reached into her pocket and put on her sunglasses. This allowed her to raise her head ever so slightly so she could observe their observers.

"I think they're just as worried about us," she said. "Well, I hope, anyway. Let's get out of here, hey?" They continued walking along the main road out of town, past a used car lot which had a salesman walking the lot, wiping the morning dew off the cars. He noticed David and Kelly and stopped in his tracks. As the two moved closer to the car dealer, he took off his baseball cap and rubbed his scalp. They still had a safe distance between this new onlooker, but everyone's a potential enemy in a disaster. The only question was, did anyone actually realize yet that this was a disaster?

"How you guys doing this fine morning?" shouted the car salesman.

"Fine," David shouted back. Neither of them wanted any interaction with strangers, but until they could get out of town, off the road and into the fields, this sort of unwanted chit-chat was inevitable.

"You guys walking somewhere? I mean, I don't want to state the obvious, but people walking on the road tells me you're both potential customers from a car salesman's perspective," the dealer said, jokingly. Kelly and David both thought the same thing: how could anyone not be aware of the crisis on the horizon?

"Your uh… Your cars work?" Kelly asked. The dealer looked a little confused. These sure were odd customers.

"Of course they work. Why wouldn't they?" David looked at Kelly. Was the guy joking? Had he not tried to start any of the cars? Cautiously, they changed direction and began walking into the car lot. If they could get a working car they'd be home in half an hour, well before anyone figured out that there's no more air conditioning or gas or running water or insulin. Well before the mass looting and rioting began. They didn't have any cash, but they could always pretend to be customers and take the car home. Besides, the car dealer's going to have bigger problems to deal with once the town wakes up to reality.

"You've got some good looking machines here. What about this one?" David said, pointing to a 2013 Ford Fusion.

"Oh, you've got a good eye," the salesman beamed. "This is a great car. Reliable, good on gas, powerful engine too. It's got low miles for its age. Perfect car for a family. You guys got kids?"

"Yeah," Kelly lied.

In Bible country, people liked to hear that everyone was happily procreating. Fucking for Jesus, if you will. The idea of two people enjoying sex without the 'miracle of childbirth' didn't sit well with some folks, so with strangers that you'll never meet again it was often just easier to lie.

"Yeah, got a boy and a girl," she continued. "The boy's five, the girl's seven. So, about this car. Can you start it for us?"

"Sure can, honey. Let me go get the key."

"Oh, and can you grab the key for this one too? I like the look of it," she said as the salesman walked to the office.

David turned to Kelly.

"These cars can't possibly work. Do you think he knows about the EMP? Has he protected them somehow?" he asked, wondering if they were wasting their time and getting themselves into an unpredictable situation.

The salesman came back from the office with two sets of keys, pointing the key fob at the Ford to unlock its doors while pressing the button. He came to a standstill when the blinkers didn't flash and the doors remained locked.

The salesman hoped the customers didn't notice, pressing it a few more times.

"I, uh, I seriously doubt any of your cars will work," said Kelly.

The salesman briefly looked up at her, bemusement on his face.

"Ma'am, this one's a Ford. It works fine. The key fob just needs a new battery. Don't worry, I have a spare in the office."

He walked to the driver's door of the Ford and inserted the key, turning it. The door locking mechanism unlocked the door easily, and he removed the key.

"There we go."

He opened the door and the interior light came on.

"Hey, look. The light works," David said to Kelly, finding himself optimistic for the first time in 18 hours.

"Of course the light works," said the salesman, as he slid into the car's cold, black interior and inserted the key into the ignition.

He turned the key clockwise into the *On* position, then turned it further to try and start the vehicle's engine.

"The hell..."

"What is it?" David asked.

The salesman turned the key counterclockwise, back to the *Off* position, then repeated the performance. The mid-sized sedan was unresponsive.

"Uh, nothing," the salesman responded. "Um. Gimme a sec."

The salesman worked the key in and out, turning it left and right but to no avail. Kelly turned to David and they exchanged glances. They didn't need to say anything. That glance meant they were on the same page. They both realized they were wasting their time. None of these cars would work. With time slipping by, they just needed to get out of there and hurry home, without upsetting the car dealer.

"Hey, don't worry about it. We'll come back another day. We'll continue our morning stroll," Kelly said, trying to stop the salesman from freaking out. The last thing you want in an unfolding disaster is someone freaking out. Everyone has a gun in these parts and a great deal of those who do, shouldn't. It just takes one spark to ignite a fire of irrational stupidity. Especially when the local police force is overwhelmed and hours away from losing control.

"It's just a dead battery. I'll jump start it," the salesman said.

"Try the other car," David responded. Kelly shot him a dirty look. She just wanted to get the hell out of there. The salesman closed the door of the Ford, embarrassed and somewhat frustrated. These could be his only customers today, for all he knew. He walked around to the passenger door of a beige Nissan parked alongside. The electronic key fob did nothing, so once again the salesman used the physical key to open the door. The interior light came on when the door was opened, but it was a false flag. Car batteries clearly weren't affected by the silent electromagnetic pulse that struck the local county, or perhaps entire country, yesterday afternoon. The circuit for the interior light on these cars seemed to bypass the car's computer. A light bulb circuit is simple, after all, comprising just a few feet of wire and the bulb itself, which is nothing more than a resistor.

It surprised David that something as meager as the amber glow from a 9 watt light bulb was enough to give him false hope. The salesman, now frustrated, worked the key left and right in the Nissan with no result. The salesman got out of the car and stood up, turning to face David.

Kelly was standing near the front of the dead Nissan.

"What have you guys done to my cars?"

"What?" they responded in unison.

"It's all a bit convenient," the salesman responded, folding his arms. "You guys walk in, off the street and say something about my cars not working... You fucked with my cars to get a discount, didn't you?"

"Whoah, whoah, whoah," David said, raising his palms. "We were just walking past and you invited us here to look at the cars. We *are* in the market for a car. We're customers."

"Bullshit. You must have done something." Kelly walked around the front of the Nissan, moving closer to the salesman and David. She had a way of calming situations.

"Stay right there, ma'am," the salesman ordered, pointing to Kelly.

The situation was escalating unnecessarily.

"I'm calling the police," said the salesman.

"I promise you, we have nothing to gain by doing anything to your cars," David said. "All the cars in the town don't work. They're all broken and won't start. All their electronics are fried."

Kelly shot him a frowning glance. Telling a car salesman that he now has around fifteen, shiny, irreparable vehicles on his lot was not wise. Unsurprisingly, the salesman's reaction changed for the worse. He seemed to simultaneously experience a combination of worry and anger, and he wanted to shoot the messengers.

"What... the fuck are you talking about?" he stuttered.

"Look. We don't want any trouble," Kelly continued. "Something happened to the cars in this town. I'm sure they're fine. Maybe all their batteries went dead by, uh…"

"The lunar eclipse," interjected David.

"Yeah," Kelly responded. She could work with that.

"There was a lunar eclipse last night and it caused… a fluctuation in… the batteries… mimetic poly-alloy," David said, almost triumphantly.
The salesman paused, looking at David, before turning to Kelly, while Kelly shot a glance at David, a pained expression on her face. David responded with a quick raise of his eyebrows and a shoulder shrug.

"It's temporary, though," Kelly said. "Trust me, I'm a scientist in… battery technology. At the University of… Phoenix."
Now it was David's turn to shoot a surprised look at Kelly, with a expression that could only be translated as, "What the fuck are you doing?"

"Give it a couple of hours for the moon to pass behind us and all the battery alloys will settle down. I heard scientists on TV this morning talking about it. It's just temporary," David said.
Kelly nodded. The dealer looked back and forward between the two, the two key fobs in his hands.

"Couple of hours, huh? Well… If you say so," the salesman said, not entirely convinced. "So… you guys wanna wait for the moon to go away and test drive these cars?"

"We'd love to, but we're on a tight schedule, unfortunately," Kelly continued. "You've been very helpful, but it's my grandmother's birthday and we're heading to her place. We'll be back this afternoon though, if that's OK?"
The salesman, still wearing a frown of mild confusion and distrust, gave a weak nod. Kelly put on a fake soothing smile and turned to David, taking his hand. The silence of the air was broken by the sound of horse

hooves on tarmac, as they began walking out of the car lot.

"A battery scientist?" scoffed David, smiling. "The University of Phoenix?"

"Hey. It worked. I just gave him the AT&T approach: confuse them with bullshit and hope they won't smell it."

It was just after eight in the morning as the two made it back to the roadside in time to meet with the county sheriff who was on horseback. He had a police radio on his chest, non functioning of course, and a rifle over his back. It was a sight to behold. A combination of modern man and western gunslinger. His horse walked in the middle of the road, meeting with David and Kelly on the edge of town, all three heading in the same direction. For a brief moment, they formed a trio.

"Morning," said the sheriff. "Where are you two heading?"

"Lynchburg," Kelly replied.

"I'm heading there too," said the sheriff. "Our radios and phones are down and I have to get answers."

"Was it true a plane crashed yesterday?" David asked.

"Yep. It's a hell of a mess. A Delta Airlines plane. Looks like a 757. A couple of witnesses said it just fell out of the sky and flew into a hill on the other side of town with no survivors. I can't get hold of the FAA or anyone in Washington and things are falling apart here in town. There's only me and a couple of deputies and someone was already shot dead for looting this morning. I've gotta get some answers. I've got to figure out what caused the crash and what's causing the power cut."

Kelly and David nodded. They had answers to those questions, but they wouldn't put the sheriff at ease, so they kept their mouths shut.

"You guys be careful. A few people wandered into town last night, saying their cars broke down. I expect a great many more spent the night in their cars outside town on the roadside. I can't be everywhere, and it looks like thieves and criminals are starting to realize it."

"Alright. Thank you, sheriff. We'll be careful," David replied.

The horse naturally walked faster than David and Kelly could on foot, and it was only a matter of minutes before the sheriff had got a couple of hundred yards ahead of them.

"Hang on a sec, Dave. Let me get out the map." David stopped and Kelly unzipped the backpack strapped to his back. She reached in and pulled out the map, the morning sun illuminating it brightly. She also fished around in the backpack, feeling for the little compass which had slipped to the bottom of the bag. Reaching around inside the bag was causing David's torso to shift about. She grabbed it and pulled it out, flipping its little stainless steel lid open, taking her a moment to figure out which way was north, then east. Kelly looked at the road ahead, empty except for a late model car parked awkwardly a hundred yards in front of them. She looked at the map. Then the road again. Then the compass. Then back to the map.

"OK. So, we're here," she said, pointing to Bedford on the map of Virginia. "We wasted half an hour with the car salesman, but I reckon we should still get home before nightfall, as long as we don't have any problems."

She studied the map closely. It's a shame it was a map of the entire state, rather than a localized map of their area. With local roads and streams being so minute and often omitted, they were going to have to use it more as a general guide than a trusted pathfinder. Kelly lifted the map and placed her finger on a location just northeast of Bedford.

"If we get off the road somewhere around here, we'll be able to go inland, through the trees. We can continue for perhaps a mile, but then we're going to get to a creek. I can't see how wide it is on this map, so we might get our feet wet. I'm not sure. All I know is that we're best to get off the road."

"Well, we've gotta start somewhere so let's get moving," David replied.

It was going to be a long day.

The sound of birdsong is normally an ignored symphony. You hear it so often you drown it out, not unlike the sound of your windshield wipers in the rain, or "Hotel California". It's everywhere and so common that it becomes forgotten background noise. But on this morning it was louder than normal; emphasized by the lack of human-made sounds, from tire noise to tractors to aircraft. The sounds of nature were loud enough that David lowered his mental defenses and allowed this background sound to the fore.

"I never really noticed how loud the birds were," he said, stating the obvious.

The birds chirped, only being interrupted by their sneakers trudging on the forest floor.

"Well, there is a season, turn, turn, turn," Kelly responded.

David let out an exasperated sigh.

"Music jokes, now of all times? You know exactly what I mean."

"I'm just lightening the mood, but you're right. It really is beautiful out here. Though I'd be lying if I said my thoughts weren't about what waits for us back home."

"Yeah, I know. I reckon the center of town is probably already under military control to stop looting. Our place should be fine though. We're a good distance from the city center."

The sound of water babbling gradually became audible over their footsteps and the sounds of birdsong.

"Can you hear the water?" David asked.

"Yeah. It sounds like it's fairly close. Speaking of water, this morning, in the motel room, I could only fill up the water bottle halfway. The taps had no pressure and it started blowing out brownish water."

"That's interesting," David replied. "Bedford's town supply must rely on pumps. I guess you never think about water until it stops."

The two walked in single file with Kelly in front, being the navigator with the map and compass. She was the first to see a flickering of light bouncing off the ripples on a stream.

"There's the stream."

They got closer. With each step it became apparent that it was more like a small river than a stream. Kelly raised the map as she approached the water's edge. It was a good fifteen to twenty feet across.

"Little Otter River," she commented, looking closely at the map. "It's just a thin blue line on the map so I was kinda hoping we could just hop over it."

"Well, the word 'river' written on the map could have been a clue as to its size," David responded.

The two of them stood at the river's edge in the gradually warming morning air, looking at the body of water in front of them.

"If we wade through it we'll be walking the next 18 miles in wet clothes and soaked shoes," David said, stating the obvious.

"Well, let's see those paper-white legs of yours. We'll strip from the waist down and carry our clothes over."

"Oh," David said. "Yeah, that makes sense."
Kelly began taking off her left shoe and sock, standing on her right foot. David undid his jeans. It took a minute before they were both standing naked from the waist down, clutching their underwear, pants and footwear.

"Ladies first," David said with a smile, nodding towards the water.

"Oh, so *now* you're a gentleman?"
Kelly waded into the water first.

"Shit, it's not exactly tropical!"
David followed her in.

"Fuck me. It's fucking freezing!"
They waded forwards, carefully. Slipping or tripping on a submerged stone could result in wet clothes and shoes, a sprained ankle or perhaps worse. Both felt the ground with their feet, slowly and methodically. The cold water swirled around their waists and their breathing increased. The discomfort was temporary though, as they soon exited the other side, standing on the mud of the other bank, dripping wet. Kelly placed her things on the ground first, grabbing her underwear and wiping water off her legs with her spare hand. She glanced over at David's penis.

"Looks like it was colder for you than it was for me," she joked.
David looked down, wondering what the hell she was on about.

"Oh, ha-ha," he said, sarcastically. "You know, if you wanna perform CPR on it, I think we can save it."

"Tonight," she promised, sliding her underwear up her legs.

With their pants now on, they sat on the leafy dirt, a few feet away from the river and folded their legs slightly, drying their wet feet as best as possible on their pant legs, before slipping their socks back on and doing up their shoe laces. Kelly stood up, map and compass in hand.

"I reckon it's been half and hour since we left the road. It looks like there's a trail less than a mile from here. It doesn't look like a main road, so there shouldn't be any traffic. There are a couple of houses there, though."
David nodded.

"Alright, babe. Let's go."

◆

In a way, being a prepper is a bit like having car insurance. It's a necessity, and it offers a feeling of security, but you hope you never have to use it. Of course, there are those in the prepping community who yearn for the day when some kind of apocalypse transpires, but the reality is that most preppers are living in a fantasy world. They're like commenters under YouTube videos: nothing but talk and ego. When the shit does actually hit the fan, their $40 Amazon.com prepping kits, including some string, a Chinese pocket knife and a box of matches, turn out to be about as useless as a chocolate teapot.
Hobby preppers tend to romanticize a major disaster, imagining themselves venturing into the forest and catching wild animals in peace, but in reality, two or three days after their beer has run out, they would turn tail and head home, only to be shot by some looter in their own living room.
To be truly prepared for a real doomsday scenario, you need to plan professionally, and most importantly, not to tell anyone. Take away a man's food, and friends soon

become enemies. In order to survive, you need to hide, and if seen, paint yourself as being just as helpless as the general populace.

Besides, if you tell anyone you're a prepper *before* any disaster happens, you'll open yourself up to ridicule. Your colleagues will label you as a nut-job or a conspiracy theorist and jokes will be had in the lunchroom at your expense. Until, of course, the shit hits the fan (or SHTF, as preppers write), and those colleagues find themselves knocking on your door for help, or worse.

It's better to save yourself the hassle, both before and after a disaster, by keeping your dry-stored food cupboards stocked full and your mouth firmly shut.

It was about 10 AM by the time they'd exited the forested area and reached a trail. It was a gravel road, which meant walking on it made a fair amount of noise. There was no sign of human activity, which suited them fine. Besides, anyone isolated out here, a couple of miles from town, with no cell phone or TV, probably thought it was a minor event and wasn't yet a threat to their safety. It's only when large groups of people get together does rumor and tension spread.

As they walked around a gentle bend in the gravel road, a house appeared on the left hand side with a confederate flag hanging on the front. Kelly took this not as a sign of the homeowner's sense of pride, but rather as a warning sign to stay away. They moved off the gravel part of the road and walked on the grass alongside, adding a few more feet of distance between them and the house. They were soon spotted, however. The screen door on the front of the house opened, and a woman with dark hair and a shotgun walked onto the porch.

"What're you doing here?!" she shouted.

Their heart rates increased. They kept walking, eyes front.

"Y'all deaf?" the woman shouted. "I said what're you doing here?! This is private property!"

Kelly slowed her walk and turned to the woman, shouting back, "We're sorry. We were just enjoying your beautiful nature. We're leaving your property. We're sorry for bothering you."

The woman didn't respond, standing on her porch with her rifle in her hands, aimed downward. They picked up their walking pace. Kelly was in front, and their Glock was in the backpack, behind them both. It would risk escalating the situation if she were to fall behind and visibly reach into the backpack. They said nothing, now almost race walking.

After what felt like five minutes, but was probably only ten seconds, the woman with the shotgun shouted at them once again.

"Get outta here, you hear me?!"

"Yes, ma'am!" Kelly shouted back, her heart pounding.

They walked quickly onwards, becoming more confident with every yard traveled that they were getting out of range of the shotgun's buckshot. It was a good five minutes before either of them spoke, with David breaking the ice.

"This place is fucking nuts! We were just fucking *walking*."

"I know. But this is why we need to stay off the road. It's only going to get worse as people get crazier."

"I think that bitch was crazy well before the EMP attack," David said, angrily.

Kelly reached into her pocket and pulled out the compass, stopping for a moment. Her hands had now stopped shaking.

"We're heading north. We need to be heading east."

She looked eastward.

Let's cut straight through these trees. Besides, I don't want to deal with any more crazies like Florence Methingale back there."

David exhaled, nodding.

"Fucking fine by me."

"But according to the map, we have to cross a main road in a few minutes. There might be houses there too."

David gave a single nod, both of them still uneasy from their interaction with the mentally unstable woman. They pressed on through the trees and into a clearing.

Kelly led them both along the treeline until they reached the highway, which had a few houses and a small business down the road to their left. They stopped, scanning the area with every sense evolution had bestowed upon them. David raised his hand up.

"Listen."

The two listened intently.

"I hear it," Kelly replied. "It sounds like a lawn mower."

Kelly perked up.

"So maybe… Maybe this was the perimeter of the EMP attack? Maybe some things from here on are working fine? Lynchburg might have escaped unscathed."

David shook his head. Kelly was the navigator and the brains in their relationship, but David was the gadgeteer.

"Nah babe, it'll be a really basic engine. Sounds like a two-stroke."

"So some engines *can* still run? How? How's that engine creating a spark?"

"It must be an older mower which generates its spark by a magnetized disk on top. It's just spinning magnets. No microchips."
Kelly looked disheartened.

"Babe, don't worry," David responded. "This could be good news. It means that the gas we have at home could be useful for someone out there as bargaining currency."
Kelly turned to David, a look that warned him sarcasm was coming.

"Oh yes. Perfect for someone who wants to cut their grass as the world burns."
She was joking, but she knew David was right. Everything useful or desirable has value in a crisis. Gasoline, coffee, cigarettes, alcohol - it all has its price when there's none available. This meant that their little stash of all the aforementioned items, safely hidden back at home, could help them bargain their way out of a future problem, if need be.

Once they were sure the coast was clear, they walked across the road and behind a line of trees on the opposite side. If people were still blissfully cutting their grass, 20 hours after the beginning of the end of the world as they knew it, then perhaps they didn't have to worry too much about muggers shooting them for whatever tiny things they had in their backpack. Not yet, at least.

Kelly studied the map and suggested a course adjustment.
"So, we can't take the roads, and walking through these fields is really slow-going, especially when we come to the next river. So I reckon we should head southeast for a couple of miles. There we should meet with the train tracks, just as they cross over the next river.

Then we can just walk the tracks until we get to the outskirts of Lynchburg."

"Aye-aye, captain," David responded.

Podcasts and music were always great ways for David and Kelly to pass the time when bored, but those things were luxuries of the past. All they had now, as they walked from forest to clearing to forest to clearing, were pop culture references, which they quickly turned into a game. David repeated a line from a movie or TV show and it was Kelly's job to name the title.

"I love the smell of napalm in the morning."

"Easy. Apocalypse Now."

"Nice. Bonus points if you can guess the year." Kelly thought out loud.

"It was just after Star Wars, so I'm guessing late '70s... 1978 or 1979?"

"1979 is correct. Alright. How about a challenge... Alright, what about 'There's no crying in baseball'."

"Oh shit. I know this one," Kelly said. "It was Tom Hanks... And Madonna. Oh... I know it."

"You have ten seconds."

"Oh... It's on the tip of my tongue. There's no crying in baseball. Argh! I know this!"

"Ehhhhhhhh! Time's up," David responded, making a buzzer sound. "It was 'A League of Their Own'."

Kelly turned the tables on David.

"Alright smart-ass. When was it?"

David laughed. "I don't actually know. I was just going to say yes to whatever year you suggested!"

Kelly hit David's arm, playfully. This was a great distraction to the problems of the day.

"Hey, babe," she said, noticing a structure up ahead. "There's the rail bridge."

The two walked up to the tracks and onto the concrete railway sleepers. It was going to be a long journey home, but at least they knew they were, literally and figuratively, on the right track.

     "Can you get the water out? I'm getting thirsty," said David.
They stopped walking, the sun overhead. Kelly reached into the backpack and fished around for the water bottle, before handing it to David.
     "You said that when you filled it up, there was brown water coming out the faucet?" he asked.
     "Yeah. I, uh, don't know if you want to drink it."
     "Hm. We should have filled it up at the river. Can you see if there's a river or something nearby?"
Kelly checked the map while David looked around, scanning for anything which could be a threat or for anything that could be useful. The railway was lined with trees and bushes on both sides. Even if there was a house on the other side, they were safe from prying eyes.
     "The closest stream... is... Hmm... two miles back."
Kelly continued searching.
     "There's nothing in our immediate path, but the tracks will be going through a town called Forest."
David was too thirsty to attempt a Forrest Gump reference.
     "How far away is it?"
     "Looks close. Less than a mile."
     "Alright, let's do it. If it's not safe there, or if we can't get any water, I'll chlorinate whatever's in the bottle and drink that."

The town of Forest is technically part of Lynchburg, but it might as well be part of Auckland, New Zealand, because their home was still several miles on foot through areas that could be potentially dangerous, having been without modern amenities for 22 hours. So far, all the interactions David and Kelly had experienced with strangers, while sometimes frightening, had ultimately resulted in no harm. Their best defense wasn't the pistol in their backpack. Their best defense was staying the hell away from people. People were the problem. A problem which grew with each passing minute.

A gunshot rang through the air.

Kelly stopped abruptly, causing David to walk into the back of her.

Another gunshot.

And another.

Two people were firing guns at each other, somewhere up ahead. Or was it three. It was hard to tell, but the firing continued. Faint yelling could be heard. Several more shots followed in quick succession.

"Let's keep going," Kelly instructed.

They walked under a road underpass, heading in the direction of the gunshots, the train tracks being in their own, man-made gully. This soon leveled out and the trees became shrubs, which became grass as they approached a clearing. A horse with an unmanned saddle walked in their direction, about 300 yards away, but when it saw the two, it changed direction and walked down a side street, heading away from them.

"Shit, that looks like a body," Kelly said, pointing ahead.

They got closer. There was indeed a body lying outside a gas station. Being out in the open in a built-up area didn't feel right after hours of isolation and relative safety.

"No way. Dave, it's a policeman," Kelly added.

David studied the body in the distance, his eyes straining.

"It looks like that sheriff from this morning."
They got about two hundred yards from the gas station
and stopped.

"Kel, look by the door of the gas station. There's
another body."
They looked around, searching for potential threats. The
scene was empty. If there were people nearby, they were
either scared and hiding or they'd not been able to return
home after fleeing from Wednesday's non-existent
hurricane.

"What should we do?" Kelly asked. "We're going
right past that gas station."

"Well, we can't do anything to help. They're
both dead and there's no one to call," said David.
"I know. I'm just not feeling very comfortable here. We
need to get around this scene and carry on."

"But we do need water, babe. Or anything to
drink, really."
A few seconds went by before Kelly came up with a
solution.

"Let's walk past the gas station, eyes ahead,
acting uninterested. But if the coast looks clear, we'll go
in and grab water or whatever drinks they have then
leave."

"OK," David responded, his heart in his mouth.
"Get the gun."
They walked slowly, closing in on the gas station, trying
not to make a noise with their footsteps. Such noise
would make it harder to hear anyone approaching. Kelly
had the gun in her hand, hidden under the sweater
wrapped around her waist.
They changed their course slightly, now moving fairly
directly toward the gas station pump area. The air was
silent yet the atmosphere was electric. Just a little water
or soda, whatever was available, that's all they needed,

then they could get the fuck out of there. Kelly's eyes darted around from behind her sunglasses.

"I think it's clear," she whispered, the pistol grip becoming sweaty in her hand.

David scanned the area, focusing on houses, hopefully empty, grass blowing in the breeze and two dead men. They moved towards the open front door of the gas station, the bloodied corpse of a young man now visible, propping the door open. The image burned into both their minds. The guy looked about twenty. His mouth was open, full of blood, still wet and stuck to his cheek, his eyes open, staring eternally towards a shelf holding bottles of windshield washer fluid outside the shop. A handgun lay just out of his frozen, claw-like reach.

Kelly took their Glock out from under her sweater and extended her arms outward. She went in first, impulsively kicking the young man's gun away and carefully stepping over his body. David followed, his head craning in each direction as he scanned for threats.

The store was a mess. There were papers on the floor and one shelf had been knocked over, but ultimately the building was devoid of food, drinks and people.

"Hello?" Kelly called inside the empty store.

No answer.

David scanned the empty shelves.

"There's nothing here," he said.

"Find something. Anything, and let's go."

He looked around. There was a squashed chocolate bar on the ground, half sticking out of its wrapper, but they didn't need food. They needed water. He noticed a bottle on the ground, rolled under a shelf.

"Tomato juice."

"Take it," Kelly instructed.

David reached under the shelf and fished it out.

"Kel, let's go, let's go."

She turned, gun extended, and walked slowly to the exit. In the silence, the sound of footsteps outside were easily detected. Kelly made eye contact with David. They needed to get out of there. Who knows who was outside. The police? The owner? A looter? It didn't matter, as the rule of law had been eroding quickly, ever since the electromagnetic pulse.

Kelly crouched down behind a shelf, David alongside her.

The footsteps came closer. Whoever it was had changed their style of walking and was now trying to be quiet. The footsteps stopped and a metallic scrape was heard outside the gas station store. Then the unmistakable sound of a pistol magazine being removed, inspected and replaced. Their pulses racing, David and Kelly looked at each other.

"I think he's got the dead guy's gun," David whispered.

Maybe the unknown person outside wasn't a threat? Maybe he or she was just as scared as those two cowering behind the barren shelf? Did the person outside know that they were inside? Kelly's mind raced. The footsteps stopped at the door, replaced by the sound of rummaging around in fabric. It definitely sounded like the now-armed mystery person outside was checking the pockets of the dead guy in the doorway.

The footsteps became slower; more intimate. One was sticky on the floor. The person was in there with them, breathing the same air. By now David and Kelly assumed that the person couldn't have known they were all sharing this room. A moment of tense silence was broken with the sound of rustling plastic directly on the other side of the shelf. There were three people in that room, two of them with weapons, and all of them about three feet apart. They were facing a thief, just like themselves, but one who searches dead bodies for money and takes their guns. In the moral hierarchy, Kelly and David had to believe that they were the ones with justification to act in self defense preemptively. Kelly turned to David. She had an idea. A distraction. With her left hand she quickly waved at David to get his attention. He looked. She mimicked that he should throw something towards the corner of the store, away from them and she would go the other way with the gun. He nodded.

The plastic rustling noise stopped and the footsteps began pacing slowly towards the left end of the shelf, closest to where David was crawling on his hands and knees. Kelly was also crawling, but to the other end of the shelf. David picked up a pair of broken sunglasses from the floor. He turned to Kelly, who gave him a nod. The next events happened unplanned, unexpected and in less than four seconds.

David tightened his chest and threw the sunglasses against the far wall, immediately distracting the armed man who spun around in the direction of the store's corner. Kelly jumped up at the other end with her gun aimed and screamed.

"Drop the gun!"

The man spun back around, and it was the first time she'd seen his face. He was about the same age. He was black. Why was he here? Seeing his eyes and face made the stranger less like a threat, and more like another person, capable or love and laughter, just like herself. Kelly didn't want to pull the trigger, but the man began to turn his torso and raised the gun up in her direction. Both David and Kelly saw this happening, as if in slow motion, with Kelly ducking down. Before he could fire David tried to buy her a crucial second by distracting the man. David shouted and threw a can of engine lubricant up at him.

"Hey!" David screamed; a hidden voice on the man's right-hand side, somewhere behind the shelf.

This caused the man to turn towards David, overwhelmed by the distractions all around him taking place before he could fire.

Kelly popped up to see the man spinning back to face her, his gun racing to aim at her. He fired a shot but he was too soon; it missed in the confusion. Kelly knew that this was now life and death, squeezing the trigger, once, twice, three times in the man's direction. The controlled explosions of bullets immediately gave way to a dry, empty silence.

"You OK?!" She shouted to David.

"I'm OK!" he replied.

The look on the man's face was one of disbelief. His mouth was agape and he was swaying on his feet. Blood had begun to erupt from his chest and neck as his eyes looked around, trying to comprehend what had happened and how to save himself. Kelly fired her gun again. The impact of the bullet pushed him against a wall-mounted shelf. He appeared to immediately lose energy, collapsing and sliding down to the floor. He was dead.

A stunned silence filled the walls of that room. The silence of life being extinguished, followed by a moment of sharp lucidity.

"Let's go! Now!" David shouted, picking up the bottle of tomato juice.

They both met at the exit at the same time, Kelly with her gun still extended, her hands now shaking. They walked away quickly and headed straight for the nearest bushes to get out of sight. Once behind the treeline, they ran. They ran as fast as their legs would allow until they couldn't breathe.

After almost five minutes of running, they eventually collapsed on the leafy dirt amongst the trees. Kelly still had the gun in her hand. David reached over and took it off her as she was still visibly distraught. He threw it a couple of feet away.

"I... I... killed... him..." panted Kelly, between breaths.

"You did... the right thing.... He.... would have killed us... It was self defense."
They sat on the ground, breathing heavily.

"His face," she said. "He was frightened."

"Yeah... I know... so were we."

"I can't get his face out of my mind."
David put the gun on the ground and held Kelly tightly. He leaned in far enough to kiss her on her cheek.

"You did the right thing. Honestly. You mustn't feel bad. You can't."
A tear rolled down her face.

"David, I'm a murderer."

"No, you're a fucking survivor."
He held her tightly for another few minutes. Kelly eventually calmed down and her breathing eased. She wiped her eyes and let go of David, who reciprocated, before giving her some space.

"I just can't believe it," she said. Then her demeanor changed and she became angry. "That bastard. That fucking bastard! Why did he do it?! Why didn't he drop the gun?!"
David sat in silence. She was a tough woman. She just needed space and a moment to get these emotions out of her system.

"He could have walked away! Why didn't he walk away?"
David nodded, looking at the ground.
The sound of the wind in the trees and birdsong continued arrogantly, as if nothing had happened. As if nature didn't give a fuck about human life or death.

"I wish we never... I don't know what I wish... I wish this none of this ever happened," Kelly continued. "Today has been nothing but fear and death. God, I hope the army comes in and fixes everything. We can't go on like this."

David was silent for a moment, but he was also realistic.

"The army might not even exist anymore. Who knows how far this EMP has gone. Maybe army trucks are on their way from Chicago or Los Angeles as we speak. Or maybe the whole country's up shit creek. We don't know, but we have to continue. What you did was necessary. It meant that you and I are here now, alive. I... I'm proud of you."

Kelly was silent. David was right. But she now knew that killing another human being isn't like it's portrayed in the movies. It affects you, even if the other person wanted you dead.

"I love you," she said to David.

"And you know I love you too."

David handed over the tomato juice.

"Here. Drink this."

Kelly raised the bottle to her lips and began drinking. Given its blood-like color and consistency, the tomato juice was possibly the least suitable drink imaginable after enduring a fatal shooting, but the two were thirsty and they downed it quickly.

It was now 24 hours since the electromagnetic pulse had changed their lives. After a full day of exhausting movement, they now found themselves on the outskirts of Lynchburg, continuing on the railway tracks. They resumed their roles, with Kelly acting as navigator and David carrying the supplies. Kelly came to a stop, noticing that they were approaching a bridge over a river, and she began studying the crinkled map.

"I think we're about a mile or two from home now. This river here… I think it's Dreaming Creek. If we want to avoid the roads then we're going to have to walk down it. This creek should take us behind the subdivisions, minimizing the chance of human contact." Right now, all David wanted to do was get home and hide from the world.

"Sounds good, babe," he said, attempting to be upbeat. His efforts were rendered useless by frantic gunshots somewhere in the distance. He looked at her, a serious expression on his face.

"Let's go."

Kelly crossed the short railway bridge first and walked down the embankment with David close behind. They were less than an hour from home, but now they were entering a scenario they'd been trying to avoid all day: they were returning to civilization. Or what remained of it.

They walked quickly along the edge of the creek, going past a small lake, until they had no choice but to head inland.

"I know where we are now," Kelly said. "We're about half a mile away. We need to go east now. But there's no way around it. We have to walk on the streets. We can't cross people's yards while they're starting to panic."

"Ok, let's do it. I've got the gun. Let's go fast."

Kelly walked quickly for about a hundred yards until they entered a clearing and the backs of two houses.

"We've got to get between these houses and onto the street."

"Let's go. The houses look all locked up. I'm guessing they haven't make it back yet."

Fortunately, David was right. The owners of the houses were either hiding inside or hadn't come back yet,

probably trapped on the highways somewhere miles out
of town. If there was a mass influx of residents, it wasn't
going to happen for a day or two. If they even survived,
wherever they were. Perhaps they were all stranded on
the roadside? Many had almost certainly begun fighting
for water and food.

With half a mile to go, David felt the keys in his pocket.
Never had pieces of machined metal felt so good to have
in his hand.

The two of them walked quickly through the back of
another section and approached Leesville Road, normally
busy with traffic at this time in the late afternoon, but
today it was completely motionless. There were dozens
of cars, of course, but they were all stopped in awkward
positions. It's was a strange sight to behold. Dozens of
colorful vehicles, of all shapes and sizes, all clean and
shiny, parked in the middle of their lanes. At this moment
it struck David that an EMP attack was the ultimate
social leveler. Rich or poor, SUV or hatchback, they were
all rendered equally useless. This rare moment of
pondering was broken by another barrage of gunshots
from a nearby street. It might have been a looter. Perhaps
it was the police. Did the police still exist?

It was evening by the time the roof of their modest house
came into view through the trees. It wasn't fancy, but it
backed onto a beautiful reserve, full of trees and
birdsong, in which they were walking. They approached
the rear of the building, desperate to get inside, with
David fumbling with the keys. The rear door unlocked
and David entered first, with the familiar smell of their
home filling their nostrils. God, what a beautiful smell,
he thought.

Kelly turned and grabbed her husband in the doorway, as if they'd just taken ownership of their home all those years ago.

"We're home... We made it... Thank God," Kelly said.

"Babe. Thank *you*," David replied.

Chapter four

Home

One of the reasons they chose to live on the southwest corner of Lynchburg was its greenery. It was a lush, hilly place with clean air. The crime rate was fairly low and the people were friendly, or at least they used to be. It was also close to Richmond and Washington, and close enough to spend a day by the sea. Most importantly, it was far enough from their prying parents' eyes that they could live the way they wanted: purely for each other.

"When are you having kids," was a question repeatedly asked by their families living back in Sacramento, where they initially met and used to live. Surely, by moving two thousand miles away, they could escape this incessant push for them to procreate.

"God said that you should go forth and multiply," David's mother would say.

"Yeah, but at what point do we say mission accomplished, mom?" was always his answer, as the human population sped past seven and a half billion. He thought his answer was witty, but it made no difference. It was an emotional argument, after all, not a logical one. Kelly had tried logic with her mother as well.

"Mom, if people actually wrote down all the pros and cons, no one would have kids. You'd run out of paper on the cons before you could even consider any pros!"

Similarly, that argument didn't hold water.

The truth is, David and Kelly were just happily childfree. In our modern era of child worship, being childfree wasn't something they broadcast publicly, being acutely aware that their lifestyle choice offended some people, but it was who they were and they couldn't help that. They had both long known, since they themselves were kids, that they didn't want to be parents themselves. It wasn't, like some parents imagine, a denial of a natural urge to procreate. Rather, they felt that they were born without the urge to be a mother or father. Of course they liked sex as much as the next couple, but only as long as it came without the unwanted byproduct of children. This meant that Kelly was one of the millions of women on long-term birth control by method of a intrauterine implant, while David opted for a vasectomy in his early thirties.

They traveled the world, ate out regularly, bought themselves gadgets, saved for their retirement, and lived purely for each other. They loved their life, they loved each other, and Lynchburg was home.

Life was good.

David was a light sleeper, which made the single click coming from the other room all the more pervasive in the dark, early morning stillness. His eyes opened fully in the blackened room, a shot of adrenaline flushing his chest. He lay deathly still, waiting to see if he was imagining it. Was one of the window frames simply contracting in the cool outside air? Old houses did that sometimes. Maybe it was nothing?

Clunk.

He took a short breath as a chill went down his spine. His right arm reached to the bedside table, feeling around for

the familiar cold, jagged shape of the Glock 19. His hand slipped around the grip and he slowly lifted the blanket off his chest as not to make a sound. His legs slipped out of the side of the bed, touching the floor. With shallow breathing he carefully stood up and in the darkness of the room, moved slowly forward, his left hand extended out in front of him, waiting to make contact with the door frame. His foot hit his jeans, sitting in a pile on the floor. He stepped carefully over them, gun extended in his right arm, edging closer to the door frame hidden in the darkness. Contact. He could feel the door frame. The kitchen was at the end of the short hallway.
Clunk-clunk.
That sounded like a person putting down a plate. His back stiffened and his breathing increased audibly.

"Babe?" an unsettled voice asked from the kitchen.

"Kel, is that you?" David responded.

"Yeah. Sorry, I couldn't sleep."

"Jesus, Kel. You scared the shit out of me."
David relaxed, dropping his arm down, and walked carefully into the kitchen, using his left hand to follow the wall, with the gun in his right, completely invisible in the darkened room.

"I was trying to make some cereal, but I can't see a damn thing."

"Shit, babe. Honestly, I thought there was an intruder in the house or something. We need to create a kind of secret signal or something."
The dry echo of a gunshot rang out in the distance. It wasn't even 5 AM yet.

"I was going to make some coffee, when I can actually see the damn gas burner," said Kelly.

"That sounds good. Just don't make any light as I don't want anyone seeing we're home. The fewer crazies, the better. I can only imagine the center of town is in lock down. We have a lot of work to do today, inventorying, planning and covering the windows."

"Have you checked the radio?" Kelly asked, hopeful.

"I will, as soon as the sun comes up a little. All yesterday, I was planning to do it as soon as we got home but I just zonked out the minute we got back."

"It was a hell of a day yesterday. One I really don't want to remember."

David felt around in the dark and put the gun on the kitchen counter, before moving closer and holding Kelly, both hands around her waist. She relaxed with a heavy breath and tucked her arms under his, holding his waist. Their warm breath washing over each other's faces and necks, quickly turning into soft kisses, their tongues pressed against each other. Kelly could feel David becoming aroused, his waist pressed against her belly, his underwear unable to hide human nature. That was the thing about David. He might be concentrating in the middle of an important task, or ready to fire a gun in the kitchen in the dark, but the minute Kelly placed her hand inside his pants, his male brain would suspend all operations and hand over control to his smaller, less logical brain.

They made their way back to the bed, going by touch, in more ways than one. At first, they almost tripped over the bed, landing in a sitting position. Kelly climbed in first, sliding under the covers. David followed, grasping her tightly and kissing her mouth, before releasing her and changing focus to sucking on Kelly's curvaceous and sensitive breasts. This went on for a minute, before his right hand maneuvered down, pulling at her underwear. Like most women, she was capable of multitasking. She lifted her midsection off the mattress just long enough to allow David to pull her underwear down to her thighs, all while kissing him and simultaneously reaching inside his boxer briefs. With her underwear gone, David now had access downstairs and fought with the urge to jump on top and insert himself inside her, choosing to stimulate her first with his hand instead. Kelly was breathing rhythmically, whimpering occasionally, wriggling and twitching.

"There. Right there," she panted.
David tried to pinpoint and focus his energy on that exact location, just inside her that seemed to hit the spot, but it felt like the goalposts kept moving. He could never find the same magic spot twice, but he enjoyed the challenge. Kelly gave him the green light to enter her, which was exactly what he was waiting for. Like an entrée, foreplay was fun, but it wasn't the main course. Climbing on top of her, he used one hand to hold up his torso, while the other helped guide his blind and clumsy dick to its ultimate goal; entering her warm and inviting body. Maybe it was the adrenaline of the day before, or the secure feeling of being back home, but David and Kelly released a lot of energy that morning. They had long forgotten about coffee, breakfast or the day before. Funny how sex does that.

"Hey," Kelly said, propped up on her side, supporting her head with her hand.

"Hey," David replied, looking up at his beautiful wife.
His gaze changed direction, looking at the dead alarm clock by the bed; a force of habit.

"What time do you think it is?"

"I honestly have no idea. It looks like about 7 AM. Maybe 8?"
David's face became more serious.

"The shortwave radio. I've got to figure out what's happening."

He swung his legs out of bed and reached over to pick up his pants, putting a leg through each hole, then pulling them up to his waist as he arose.

"I've got to check the spare cell phone too. It's all in the cage."

Kelly remained in bed as he walked out of the bedroom and straight into the spare room next door. They used this room as both a computer & games room and storage of prepper essentials. Under a bunch of boxes sat an old microwave, unplugged. It stopped working a couple of years ago, and rather than throw it out, David decided to use it as a Faraday cage.

A Faraday cage is a simple device. It's essentially a metal box which blocks electric fields from entering or leaving. Microwaves are essentially consumer Faraday cages, protecting you as you watch your oatmeal spin around inside. Without the protective Faraday cage, your face and eyes would be cooked from the high energy electromagnetic waves emitted from the device's magnetron. The concept of a Faraday cage also works in reverse; stopping an electromagnetic pulse (to a certain extent) from affecting the contents inside.

David took three boxes off the top of the microwave and cleared some room in front, so its door would open. This was the moment he'd waited more than a day for. Was it North Korea? Was it an accident? Was the whole country affected? Was the military on its way? Answers were just seconds away.

He opened the microwave's door and took out its precious contents, their value skyrocketing in just over a day, placing them on the floor. He tore the packaging off the unused portable shortwave radio and grabbed two AA batteries from inside the microwave. He didn't need to store the batteries in the microwave as they weren't affected by electromagnetic pulses, but it was just easier to have everything in one place. The radio was on the floor, its battery cover removed, as David opened the packet of four batteries, pulling out two. The batteries went straight from package to radio. Battery number one went into the back of the radio and slid horizontally inside. Battery two had to be pressed in, pushing battery one up against something hidden inside the radio, turning two 1.5 volt batteries into a single 3 volt power supply. Done.

Without bothering to replace the little plastic battery cover on the rear of radio, he flipped it over. This was it. News and information was literally at his fingertips. For no reason, he held his breath as he flipped the on switch. Click.

Did he hear something? He wasn't sure. His face was emotionless. He turned up the volume dial on the side. Nothing yet. His right index finger scrolled at the tuner dial. Was it even turned on? He spun it on its side to check. Yes, the switch was in the *On* position. No light on the front, however. His instinct was the check the batteries. Maybe they were dead. They'd been in storage for a couple of years. He rolled them a few times inside the radio. A pervasive thought was on the horizon of his mind, but he willfully ignored it. He had to ignore it. Doing three things at once, David wiggled the batteries, adjusted the tuner dial and flipped the On/Off switch back and forth.

That unpleasant thought began to claw its way closer to the forefront of his conscious, however. He forced it away. Perhaps it was the batteries. It *had* to be the batteries. With his tired knees making a clicking noise, David got up from the floor and jogged into the living room. There on the sofa was the TV remote with its precious cargo of AA batteries inside. Those were only replaced about a month ago, so he knew they worked.

"What are you doing?" asked an inquisitive Kelly from the bed.

David didn't answer. This was more serious than exchanging pleasant conversation. That can wait for just a few more seconds, when he had some good news. Falling back on his ass in the spare room, he pulled the batteries out of the TV remote and dropped them on his lap. They were still good, he knew this. With his fingers, he tugged on the little piece of fabric sticking out of the radio, which aided the removal of stubborn AA cells. One battery popped out onto the floor. David shook the radio sideways, so the other battery slid into view and fell out by itself.

The new, or at least fairly new batteries went in. One... two... He put the battery cover on the back of the radio. His hands turned the device to face him and he took a breath.

Click.

He held the radio up to his ear and turned the volume knob but there was no sound. His breathing tightened and he clamped his jaw, pressing his molars together, hard. He'd invested everything into this moment.

"...Fuck!" he shouted. "Fuck it! Fuck!"

He hit down hard on the top of the microwave with his fist. Kelly didn't say anything. She assumed by the lack of David's response that powering up the radio wasn't going as planned. She knew that when David got angry, the best thing was to let him get over it for a few minutes. Running in there holding him or telling him empty platitudes, such as, "Don't worry, everything will work out," only made him more agitated. She gave him space, but she too was upset. That radio was everything.

After a minute of silence had passed, she spoke.

"Check the other electronics."

After a few silent seconds, she heard the movement of objects in the spare room.

David took the Geiger counter out of the microwave, along with the spare cell phone; a flip phone he bought and used often back in 2005, when it was new. The phone needed to be checked first. This was their way out. Sure, maybe the cellular networks were dead at that moment, but they'd be repaired in time. Putting the phone on his lap, he fished the phone's battery out of the microwave and inserted it into the back of this now-antique piece of consumer electronics. He opened the flip phone like a clam shell. Even though they were old school, there was something satisfying about the physical activity of opening and closing a flip phone. He remembered when he used to use the phone daily, how rewarding it was to end a phone call by flipping it closed, either one-handed, or by pressing the top half of the phone against his cheek until it clapped like a plastic clam.

Placing the phone's battery into the back of the phone, he pressed and held the power button. Unfortunately, like the radio, it was unresponsive.

He exhaled. Maybe the battery was dead? Or maybe just flat? After all, he bought it in 2005, and it had been sitting in the microwave for a couple of years. The phone might actually be OK. He needed to cling to that hope, as he reached in to grab the Geiger counter.

David refused to allow himself optimism as he took unused AAA batteries out of a packet and inserted them into the back of the SOEKS detector that he'd bought from Amazon.com a few years ago. But, to David's immense disappointment, the same thing happened with the radiation meter as it did with the radio and cell phone. It was dead, completely unresponsive.

"Why didn't the Faraday cage work!?" David asked himself out loud. "Why didn't it fucking work?" He slumped his back against a tall box of dry-stored food. This was going to be more difficult that he thought.

Ten minutes has passed. That was enough time for David to cool off, thought Kelly. She got out of bed and walked into the spare room.

"Dave, don't worry about the electronics for now. We need to get organized, food-wise. We've gotta inventory our supplies. You start counting what food we have and I'll heat up some water for coffee. And bathing. We're starting to stink and we have to stay clean." Emotionally drained, David nodded.

"I just don't understand why the cage didn't work," he continued. "It must have been a hell of a pulse to go right through the microwave. It looks like it cooked everything inside. We're no better off than anyone else."

"Not true. We actually know what's going on and we can imagine what's happening out there today," Kelly said, gesturing to the window. "Besides, we have food. But we're gonna need to get more water. Check how much water we have stored. In the meantime, I'll make some breakfast."

Kelly was right. This wasn't the time to sulk. David sighed and began unpacking every box in the room, dragging extra boxes out of the closet and emptying their contents into a growing pile in the middle of the room, while Kelly poured cereal into bowls and heated up water for coffee. They still had relatively fresh milk in the fridge, but it had to be used today as the fridge was now at room temperature. Oh well, at least they had coffee. Thank heavens for small mercies.

The two sat on the sofa, munching on cereal, two cups of hot coffee sitting, appropriately, on the coffee table in front of them. Normally the television would be on, but that 42 inch rectangle was now nothing more than an expensive and ineffective mirror.

"I reckon we've got about six months of dry food. Rice, pasta, flour, jams, cooking oil, soap, etc. We've got bags of coffee and a few boxes of UHT milk, too," David said. "Though we won't know for sure how long we've got until we organize a meal plan. Besides, help might already be on its way by now."

A large pot of water was heating up on the stove in the kitchen.

"I'm looking forward to being clean again," Kelly said.

"Yeah."

"Babe. Don't stress out over the radio. We'll figure it out."

David put down his empty bowl and picked up his cup of coffee. The world might be falling apart outside, but at least they still had coffee. The sound of boiling water began to emanate from the kitchen. Kelly got up and headed in the direction of the sound. Turning off the stove, she took the pot off the stove and poured it into a bucket, half filled with cold water, sitting on the kitchen floor. The result was about 4 gallons of hot water, but not too hot.

"You want to go first?" she called to David.

"You go for it," he replied.

Ask anyone who's come back from a camping holiday and they'll tell you that there's no better feeling than showering in your own home. Sure, David and Kelly might not have running water anymore, but they could still appreciate the feeling of washing away two days' worth of grime. Having freshly washed themselves and slipped into clean clothes, they could be forgiven for thinking that things weren't so bad after all. However, that calm was interrupted by movement on the road outside.

"Dave," Kelly called out. "That looks like what's-his-name from down the road."
David walked over to the window and looked out at the street, about forty yards away. Sure enough, one of their neighbors was walking down the street with a bag on his back.

"Should I talk to him?" he asked.

"I don't know. We don't want anyone to know we're here, or that we have supplies. But he's always been friendly. I don't think he's a threat, and he might know something."
Kelly paused.

"Alright. Do it. But don't say too much."
In bare feet, David opened the front door and called out to the neighbor, waving. The neighbor stopped and turned, his hand reaching into his waist. The two stood, facing each other, now about fifty yards between them.

"Are you OK?" David asked, trying to sound reassuring.
He then decided it was safest to play dumb.

"We've lost our power… is yours working?" he yelled.

"Nah," the neighbor responded.

"Wait a sec. I'll come to you," said David, who began walking down the long lawn to the roadside.

David could see the neighbor's hand was concealing something under his jacket, so he made sure he kept his hands freely visible, as to show the neighbor that he wasn't a threat. He approached the man, but stopped at a safe, non-threatening distance.

"I'll be brutally honest," said David, smiling, "I've completely forgotten your name. I'm Dave, by the way."

The neighbor relaxed a little took his hand out from under his jacket.

"Hi Dave. I'm Steve. I live down at 1251."

"Yeah, I recognized you when you walked past. We've got no power or water. Any idea what's up?"

"The whole city's out. It must be a terrorist attack. I just came from trying to get into the mall, but it was a waste of time. The whole thing's been looted and the city's under lock down. There's a few police and army roaming around like lost sheep, trying to maintain order, but they can't really do anything other than shoot at you. I was stopped and explained that I was going to see a client to give legal advice for when the power comes back on. The cop bought it, but I came straight home. It's just too dangerous. I don't recommend going into town. Seriously. Or if you do…"

Steve lifted up his puffy jacket to reveal a pistol in a holster. David smiled and nodded.

"That's about it," Steve continued. "I can't really tell you much more… Do, uh… do you have food?"

"Not really," David lied. "I reckon we've got enough to last this weekend, but we need to get more… Do you have food?"

"Nah, probably about the same as you."

There was no way Steve could know about their stash of food and supplies, and it was essential it stayed that way. Maybe the neighbor was telling the truth? Either way, he was clearly armed and lived only a dozen houses down the street.

"Are you staying?" David asked.

Steve paused and stared down the street.

"I honestly don't know... The thing is, half the city hasn't returned yet after evacuating for the hurricane. So there's probably thousands of desperate, hungry and thirsty people out on the highways, making their way back here. It would be suicide to walk the highways now."

Steve had a good point.

"Are *you* staying?" He asked David.

Three gunshots rang out in a nearby street, causing them both to turn their heads in that direction. David thought for a moment, pondering how much information he should give to his neighbor; a potential ally or potential foe. He mixed his answer with sprinklings of truth and lies.

"Well, we're in the same boat as you. We don't have enough food to stay here but we can't leave either. I guess we'll wait until Monday or Tuesday, when we're out of food, and head inland, away from the cities." He decided to change the subject.

"Is your family OK?"

"Yeah, we're all good. Maureen has the kids thinking it's some sort of game, like camping at home until the power comes back on."

"Alright. Well, if I can help, let me know. I'm sure the power will be back on soon."

Steve continued walking down their quiet, suburban street. David knew that they had to get prepping and prepare for the worst: opportunists, looters and desperate, hungry people.

"I have an idea," Kelly said. "You stay here and count the food and create a meal plan, I'll go to the creek and get water. There's one about a thousand yards from here and getting there is mostly through the woods behind the house. I'll do it during daylight this one time, counting steps and forming a mental path, so that in the future we can collect water at night without light."

David was hesitant as it meant separating. Kelly could see he was uneasy about it, but she tried to reassure him. She was a smart person, and as yesterday proved, not to be trifled with.

"I reckon it'll only take about thirty minutes. I'll show you on the map where I'm going and I'll be careful."

"Alright," David said. "But be very careful. People are getting scared."

"Babe, of course."

Kelly looked at the gun, still sitting on the kitchen counter. A chill ran down her spine as the man's face flashed into her mind, mouth agape, the look of shock on his face as he died from her actions. She shook her head quickly, telling herself that this was no time for what-ifs. She wrapped her hands around the pistol's grip and placed it in her jacket pocket, walking over to David, who was standing in the living room, looking out the window.

"I'll be very careful. Hyper alert. Don't worry. Go count our supplies, babe. Keep yourself occupied."

In the spare room, David took everything out of boxes and put it all into organized groups on the ground. They had twenty 5 lb bags of rice. Twenty of dried beans. Twenty of dried pasta. Twenty of lentils. Dozens of cans of fruit, peas, tomatoes. They had a couple of bottles of sunflower oil. Five bags of flour. Five of sugar and another five bags of ground coffee, plus a box of various instant military meals, known as MREs (Meals Ready-to-

Eat). Of course they also had spices and baking supplies in the kitchen too, which they could use to enhance their meals. In terms of food, they had several months' worth of supplies. David had also stocked up on a few boxes of chlorine tablets to purify water, and a box of butane canisters for their portable cooker. There were miscellaneous items too, which could be used to trade, such as a carton of cigarettes and two bottles of Jim Beam whiskey. The supplies, excluding the MREs, were all rotated regularly, so it was all relatively fresh. For example, when they bought pasta from the store, they put it at the back of the pasta box, and took one from the front. The whiskey and coffee were the most regularly replaced items, as you can no doubt imagine. There were other items too, which they bought never expecting to use, such as a gas mask each and a box of disposable hazmat suits and a few rolls of duct tape. There were also five boxes of 9mm ammunition for their pistol, and stored in the carport there was a five gallon container of gasoline. And, of course, they had their shortwave radio, spare cell phone and a Geiger counter, although those items were now as useless as bicycle pedals on a wheelchair.

David sat down with some sheets of paper and calculated the total quantities of their individual foodstuffs, before creating a meal plan which allowed for variation. Disaster or not, he didn't want to be eating the same thing day after day.

For once, things were looking good. He put the pen down and leaned back in his seat, studying the meal plan, before turning to look over their supplies, taking up the entire floor. David allowed himself a brief moment of pride. They were prepared.

Kelly paused at the edge of the forested area, facing a clearing and a group of houses in front of her. The one good thing about American homes in the suburbs was that they rarely ever had fences. This meant traversing them at night would be silent and quick.

She memorized the number of steps it had taken to get this far and used the three-minute hourglass egg timer in her hand to estimate how long it had taken at a careful pace. This suburban street appeared to be empty with only two cars visible, but she could hear what sounded like one or two adults shouting in a yard not too far away. The creek was somewhere behind the houses in front of her, beyond the trees. The clearing and houses directly in front presented an increased risk of her being seen, which almost caused her to cancel the water reconnaissance trip and return home empty handed, but she needed to continue, count the steps needed and ensure a safe path for recreating this journey with no visible light.

She placed her hand next to the gun in her pocket, just in case, and walked out of the protective embrace of the trees, her heart rate increasing. Kelly walked quickly, counting the steps in her mind.

"Twenty-three, twenty-four, twenty-five, twenty-six, twenty-seven, twenty-eight, twenty-nine, thirty, thirty-one, thi-"

"Hey!" a voice called out.

Kelly stopped dead in her tracks and looked around. A man in a nearby house had spotted her and had his head poking out of his front door, a white Lincoln parked in the driveway. She said nothing, her hand reaching around the grip of the pistol. Neither of them knew what to say, or if either was a threat. Five or six seconds passed.

"Can you help me?" he asked.

Was this a trap? "Trust no one," she thought to herself. Should she run? Before she could do anything, her mouth opened and she called out, "What's wrong?" followed by a sense of regret.

"It's my wife... Can you come here?"

This didn't feel right. She thought for a moment. This was why she wanted to avoid human interaction during a crisis. It's all so full of risk and uncertainty.

"How about you come here?" she yelled.

The man paused for a few seconds, his torso hiding behind the door frame.

"I'm... scared," he called out.

"I'm armed," Kelly said, trying to make her voice sound deeper.

"OK... I'm not."

Was it a trap? Of course he could be lying.

"Please," the man continued. "Are you a doctor or anything?"

"No."

"She needs help... Can you come here? I promise I won't do anything."

Kelly asked herself what David would do in this scenario. Even if he was telling the truth, what could she do? She only had basic first aid training from her last job.

"I'm sorry," she called back. "I can't help you."

"Please!" called the man. "She's not responding. Something's wrong with her."

Kelly was in an awkward position, torn between a sense of basic humanity and fear. For better or worse, she allowed her sense of the former to take precedence.

"Al... alright. But I have a gun."

Kelly took the gun out of her pocket and walked through the empty section in front of her, moving closer to the house ahead, full of the unknown.

"Show yourself. Let's see your hands," she said, now approaching the house with the man in the doorway, her gun now in both her hands, aimed in front.

The man, in his mid forties, edged gingerly into full view and had his hands raised to head height.

"Please. I haven't seen anyone all day. My wife is sick. She's weak. Please, come inside. I don't have a gun."

Was he lying? This was Virginia. He almost certainly had a gun, unless he was one of those anti-gun nuts. Kelly had often joked that they'd be the first to die in a disaster.

"Just stay where I can see you," Kelly ordered.

"OK."

Kelly walked slowly up the steps, the man walking backwards into his living room, arms still raised. She poked her head around the door frame and peered inside. There was a woman lying on the sofa.

"You're the first person I've seen all day," he said. "She had a fever on Wednesday, that's why we didn't evacuate. She wanted to stay."

Kelly issued a command she never imagined herself saying.

"Turn around and place your hands on the wall."

The man complied.

With the gun in her right hand, Kelly slid her left hand across his torso, front and back. She glanced over to the woman on the sofa to ensure it wasn't a trap but the woman remained unresponsive. She checked his pockets and ran her hand down each leg. Nothing was out of the ordinary.

"I don't have gun. I mean, I do, but not here."

That was something Kelly could believe.

"So what's going on," she asked, relaxing a little.

"My wife isn't responding. She hasn't been well since Monday. She didn't want to evacuate and we planned to go to the doctor yesterday but the car won't start. The phone's dead and we've got no power. She's been getting worse each day, and now she's not waking up.

Kelly moved over to the woman on the sofa and placed the back of her hand on her forehead.

"She's burning up."

"She started getting a temperature on Tuesday, but our thermometer's stopped working. I want to take her to a doctor but the car's dead. I can't call an ambulance. Do you have a cell phone?"

"My cell phone's back at home," Kelly lied. She didn't need to burden the guy with the news that it looked like no one in the entire state had a functioning phone.

"You need to take her to the hospital. She has some sort of infection, by the looks of it. Maybe even severe food poisoning."

"Do you have car?" he asked. "I'll pay you, whatever you want."

"Put her in a wheelbarrow or steal a shopping trolley. Just take her to hospital, alright?"

The man thought for a second.

"I have a wheelbarrow."

"Get it. Now."

He walked out the front door and down the steps, around the side of the house. Kelly crouched down and shook the woman lying on the sofa. There was no response, so she leaned in and put her head on her chest. The woman's breathing was terribly weak and the hospital was almost certainly overwhelmed, if it was even still operating. Kelly felt bad for giving the guy false hope. His wife was not going to live.

Kelly looked at the photos on the wall above the sofa featuring the man she'd just spoken to and his wife, smiling, standing on some unknown beach. Next to the photos they had large, three-dimensional words adhered to the wall, reading "Live, laugh, love." Kelly thought that was tacky, but better than the beaten-to-death renditions of "Keep calm and carry on" half the world had fallen in love with. Then she did something she wasn't proud of but couldn't stop herself from doing. She allowed her eyes to scan the room for valuables. Or if not valuables, then things she could trade if the need arose. To both her disappointment and relief, there was nothing noteworthy in the living room. A large stereo and big screen TV, which were both certainly non-functional, took center stage on the opposite wall. She did notice a drinks cabinet, however, which was well stocked with whiskey and other spirits. She turned her head back to the unresponsive woman on the sofa, then back at the booze cabinet, before giving in to her newly found lawlessness, crawling to the cabinet and picking up a small bottle of whiskey, stuffing it down the front of her jacket. The potential looter inside her vanished as quickly as it had appeared upon hearing the footsteps of the man walking up the steps and entering the living room.

"OK. The wheelbarrow is outside. Can you help me place her in it?"
Kelly nodded, and grabbed on tightly to the woman's legs, while her husband grabbed under her arms, lifting her torso. Kelly strained with the weight of this person in her grip. The woman was much heavier than expected, even though she was about the same height and size as herself. It took all their strength to carry her down the steps to the wheelbarrow. With one final heave, they lifted her in, her legs sticking out the back while her head rested on the wheelbarrow's front lip.

"Thank you," panted the man. "God bless you."

"Go to the hospital. Right now." Kelly instructed. "And take your gun."

"OK. Thank you," he repeated, running up the steps and back inside.

Kelly should have been back by now, David thought, anxiously pacing the living room. Out of instinct, he looked at the analogue clock sitting on the wall, but it was stuck at 2:20 PM. It took him longer than he cared to admit to realize the clock was locked at the time of the EMP attack. It was actually closer 1 PM in reality.
He continued to pace around the living room, wishing they had one more gun. He knew he couldn't go out there unarmed. Was Kelly lost? No, that wouldn't be like her. Was she... dead? David immediately hummed a made-up tune, an involuntary defense mechanism when he had intrusive, uncomfortable thoughts. She had been gone an hour; too long for a walk to the creek and back, even if going slowly. It was undeniable that something had happened to her. If only they had some kind of communication device.

"Kelly," David muttered to himself, wandering around the room. He thought how much he took instant communication for granted. Up until two days ago he could just call her at any time, but not now. The disconnect was sickening. He had to do *something*. David walked quickly to the spare room, opening the box which had a hunting knife and a small can of pepper spray. That wouldn't stop a bullet, but it's better than nothing. He clipped it to his jeans and went to the back door. He scanned the surround area behind the house to check the coast was clear before leaving the relative safety of their single-level home. There was no sign of human activity, so he softly clicked the door behind him and walked into the forested area behind their section. He saw something. There was movement. David froze behind a tree, reaching for the pepper spray in his pocket. He wondered how long it takes before pepper spray renders a threat useless. Immediately? After five seconds? He slid his head from behind the tree in the location of the movement, but he saw nothing. Whoever, or whatever it was, was hiding. They'd seen him. Maybe it was a looter? Maybe a hunter? Maybe it was Kelly? "This is fucking ridiculous," he thought. "I've got maybe six months of food behind me and I get killed *now*? On day *two*?"

"Thrrip"

A short whistling sound came from somewhere amongst the trees. It sounded like a bird, but it wasn't. It was their signal.

"Thank God," thought David.

"Thrrip!" he whistled back.

Kelly appeared, gun in hand, from behind a tree.

"You scared the shit out of me," David said.

"That's twice in as many days," responded Kelly.

"What took so long? I was worried."

"I got stopped by a man with a sick wife. Don't worry, I'm fine. She wasn't though. She's not gonna make it."

"What's wrong with her?"

"Not sure. Some infection perhaps, maybe salmonella poisoning. She needs antibiotics."

"Where is she now?"

"I told her husband to take her to the hospital and helped him load her into a wheelbarrow."

David raised his eyebrows.

"You put her in a wheelbarrow?"

"Yeah." She looked at David. She knew him too well. "Before you say it…"

"Bring out yer dead!" he joked.

Despite her ordeal, she couldn't help herself.

"But I'm not dead!"

"'Ere. He says he's not dead!" David responded.

"Well, he will be soon. He's very ill!"

Both of them giggled.

"Oh Dave. "You're a clown, but I love you. You know, humor is an antidote to all ill."

"Maybe. Buuut probably not hers."

Chapter five

Tedium

Eleven days had now passed since the EMP attack. The house next to theirs had been broken in to by looters and they knew that their house could be next. It was clear that there were still people in this city, perhaps hundreds, perhaps thousands. They still heard gunshots in the silent air every day, at differing distances.

Their daily conversations were always carried out in whispers. If it was windy outside or raining, they could enjoy the luxury of using their vocal cords and talking normally, but considering the paper-thin construction of most American homes, they had to keep noise to a minimum at all times. Pots and plates were always managed with both hands and they used plastic cutlery to reduce any clanking sounds which could carry through the walls and outside.

They had a system for whenever they saw someone walking on the road outside their house: get down; shut up. They had to remain hidden if they wanted to survive. In apocalyptic disaster movies, the hero is often seen leaving his place of safety in the midst of the chaos to rescue someone or get something, putting himself at great risk and ending up in a gunfight with evil-doers. This was a version of reality which David and Kelly worked hard to avoid. From the outside, their curtains looked drawn and the house looked empty. Of course there was no car in the carport (that was still sitting somewhere on the side of the road 25 miles away). Inside their living room, however, they had black plastic sheeting covering all the windows of the kitchen and living room. This allowed them to cook food by candlelight or read books on the sofa without the world knowing there were two living beings inside. They only left the house every two or three days for water from the creek, and that was always after midnight.

David had set up a few runs of fishing line around the front of the house with bells attached, harvested from Christmas decorations, while Kelly took photographs of their unexciting lives. She had plenty of rolls of 35mm film, which she stored in the refrigerator; something her grandmother had told her keeps the film fresher, longer. She tried developing some photos once since they'd returned, but the smell of developing chemicals in their tightly sealed house drove David insane.

During the day they read books and played board games, but Monopoly gets pretty boring remarkably fast with only two people. They played card games, such as poker, even trying strip poker once, but when you already have free access to your partner's body at any time, it seemed a little pointless, like sex with extra steps. In the evenings they gave in to their vice: alcohol. They did very well holding back, but eventually the boredom led to them tapping into their own supplies of booze which should have been reserved for trading. With two eager livers, it wasn't long before they'd drained their two trading bottles of whiskey empty and had moved on to tea, which was nowhere near as exciting.

Unlike an action-filled apocalyptic disaster movie, this was a genuinely boring existence, being cooped up indoors and remaining silent. Essential for survival, but as tedious as hell. It would make for a terrible movie or book.

This tedium was broken on the twelfth day with the unexpected arrival of someone at their back door. Kelly was reading an old magazine aloud to David in a hushed voice, when an uninvited stranger began making a clinking noise on the back window, shattering their sense of security and calm. David and Kelly found themselves in a sudden state of high alert, unaware who or what this new threat was. David found himself the closest to the gun and he crawled over to grab it, before hiding in the hallway. Kelly scuttled over and poised behind him. With eyes wide open, David spun his head towards Kelly and silently mouthed the words, "Who is it?".

Kelly shrugged and shook her head simultaneously.

The clinking sound continued, a little louder.

Crouched in the hallway, David and Kelly could hear each other breathing, adrenaline coursing through their veins. David's mind raced. "Was it someone they knew? If it was a looter, they wouldn't knock. Or would they? Was it their parents? No, they're thousands of miles away. Unless they drove here? Does their car still work? No, the gas stations don't work; they wouldn't be able to make it."

David's panicked thoughts were interrupted by the unknown person outside slowly turning the door handle. They kept the door locked, which resulted in the person trying several times more, with each attempt having more energy and confidence.

David motioned to Kelly to stay where she was, and he crawled on his hands and knees far enough that his head was able to see the back kitchen window, closest to the back door. The blinds were closed, and he knew that touching them would be visible to whoever was outside. Something scratched at the door lock. The person was now trying to break into their home. "Why didn't he just break a window and give me a real reason to shoot?"

David wondered, his gun aimed firmly at the middle of the back door.

He had an idea.

Rather than confront someone inside their house and allow an intruder to see their supplies, he scuttled over to the front door and quietly grasped the knob, turning it, with his heart pounding. It opened silently, allowing light to pour into the darkened room. He hoped the change in light wouldn't be noticeable to anyone out the back.

David didn't have time to scan the front yard and street for twenty seconds, as he normally did. He walked straight out, barefoot, around the side of the house, toward the back, going through the carport, his arms stretched out horizontally, the gun pointed towards the ground, with his finger on the Glock's trigger. He was ready to kill whoever was threatening their safety as he leaped around the corner and confronted the looter, side-on..

"Freeze!" Dave shouted, immediately aware he sounded like he was in an 80s police movie. The man shook in fright, and instinctively moved his hand towards a holstered sidearm.

"Move and I shoot!" Dave yelled.

Wait. He recognized this man.

"Steve?" he asked.

His neighbor, whom he'd met just days ago on the street, turned his head slowly towards him.

"Dave."

"What the fuck are you doing?!" David said.

"Dave. Take it easy. Don't shoot. I'm gonna put my hands up slowly. It's all good."

Steve raised both his hands as promised.

"Don't move an inch," David ordered, moving closer to his neighbor and carefully removing the pistol from the holster on his neighbor's waist. He kept his gun pointed at him.

"Steve. Answer me. What are you doing here?"

"Dave. I didn't know you were still living here."

"Well what the hell are you doing? Why are you trying to get inside?"

"Please. I can explain. Just, put down the gun. Please. I'm not a threat. You have my gun."

Kelly was inside, listening intently, pepper spray in hand, not that it would offer much of a challenge against a 9mm bullet. David took a step back and lowered the gun slightly.

"Explain yourself, Steve."

Steve turned in David's direction, opening his palms and extending his fingers to show he had no weapon. He lowered his hands.

"I'm sorry Dave. I knocked first. I thought you were gone and I wanted to see if you have any water. We're all so thirsty at home."

"But you said *you* were *leaving* when I saw you last week," David responded.

"I'm sorry. I lied. I'll be honest with you, OK? It's too dangerous to go out on the roads or near the city and the kids would never make it, so we stayed. I wanted people to leave us alone; to think our house was empty, so we've been hiding at home, waiting for the army or something, but no one's come. It's like the army doesn't exist. We must be at war or something, because there's no help. We're fending for ourselves like animals."

David relaxed a little, but kept his hand wrapped tightly around the pistol grip. Sensing that David was in control of the situation, Kelly called from the Kitchen.

"Everything OK?"

"Yeah. It's fine. It's Steve from down the street. It's safe."

Kelly opened the rear door and came face to face with the failed intruder, the pepper spray in her hand. Steve noticed it and raised his eyebrows slightly.

"You guys only got that? A gun and a can of pepper spray?"

"Well, I guess I have two guns now," David responded, waving Steve's sidearm.

"Look. Guys. I would never have tried to enter your home if I thought you were here," said the neighbor, then trying to lighten the mood by attempting a compliment.

"You did a damn good job of hiding. I mean, I've been all over the neighborhood at night, searching for food and water, and I never saw you guys at all. Never heard anything either. I admit, this week I broke in to all the houses between ours. I only took food and water. Nothing more. That old guy. What's his name. Uses that portable oxygen machine. He lives three doors down from here. He's dead. Found him with his mask around his face yesterday. He's still sitting on the sofa. It scared the shit outta me when I saw him."

"Jerry," David replied.

"That's him. Jerry."

The two stood in silence for a moment. This guy was telling the truth. He had two kids and a wife to provide for and he wasn't a prepper. David actually pitied him. Kids were nothing but liabilities in a crisis situation.

"Steve, I'm gonna remove the clip from your gun and I'm going to place it back in your holster, OK? Just please don't make any sudden movements. Don't freak me out, OK?"

The neighbor nodded.

"I can see that you're just desperate, trying to keep your family alive. But you can't come back here, got it?"

"OK," he replied.

David removed the clip from the gun, aware that there was almost certainly still a bullet in the chamber. He took the risk, placing the pistol into Steve's holster and flipped the leather holder over the top. He then put the clip into Steve's back pocket.

"Thank you," Steve said, nodding.

"It's fine. You just scared us."

Steve's basic biological needs came to the fore of his mind.

"Do… do you guys have any water? Please? I've gone to all these houses and emptied their toilet cisterns but we need more. The kids are seriously thirsty."

David looked at Kelly. It was clear, even to Steve, that they did have water.

"Look. There's no law any more. We have to trade. I can give you a few gallons of water, but we need something in return," David said.

"You name it. Anything."

"We need another gun. Our can of pepper spray would be useless in a shoot-out. Do you have a spare firearm?"

Steve shook his head.

"I honestly don't. I only have this one, and even then, the wife makes me keep it in the safe. Can't have guns readily available when my kids are always getting into everything." Steve then realized this was not helping his plight and he needed that water.

"But I know a guy who does. He's one of those prepper guys. He owes me. I got him off for assault in March. He's guilty of course, but I convinced the jury it was self defense. He owes me big time for that. Just tell him that. He lives in the north of town in the suburbs and I can give you his address. He's cool, he'll hook you up."

Steve paused and looked at both of them. He could see David and Kelly thinking about it, so he tried his hand. "Surely that's worth some water?"

Chapter six

Guns and ammo

Trevon lived on the north of the city, three miles from their house. Three weeks ago, such a journey there and back would have taken around ten to fifteen minutes, depending on the traffic. Three weeks later, after the pulse, however, this journey was most likely going to take an entire day and had a high risk of death.

Kelly and David needed to leave early in the morning if they wanted to avoid the height of human activity. They had to decide between taking the outskirts of the city or going direct through town. The latter would be faster, but more dangerous, and the former would be safer but meant adding two miles to their trip. They decided to take a moderately direct route on the way there, early in the morning, and a longer, safer route in the late afternoon, if Trevon would let them wait with him until sunset.

As they had no working alarm clock but needed to awaken at 4 AM, they used a Native American technique for getting up early for battle, by both drinking a lot of water as they went to bed. This meant that by 3 AM they were fighting disturbingly realistic dreams of going to the toilet; a serious hazard if they had been five years old again.

Climbing out of bed, Kelly was the first to use the bucket in the bathroom to relieve herself, there being no point in using the toilet which had no water to flush. By this stage David had woken up and was putting on his pants, eager for his turn to relieve himself. Using the bucket had become a part of life now, although it meant the last person to use it had to empty it outside. David carried the bucket of warm urine outside into the cool October air and, checking for noises and movement, took it to the edge of the trees behind the house, tipping it closely to the ground as to not make a sound. Over the last three weeks they had become accustomed to living in silence, having long since worn out their jokes about taking vows of silence or living in a self-imposed monastery. Eating, cooking, communicating. Even the act of sexual intercourse had to be done quietly; something which they freely admitted to each other destroyed a sense of inhibition and raw pleasure which they had enjoyed previously.

David replaced the empty bucket in the bathroom and slid on the backpack which was now full of essentials for the journey they were about to undertake, from extra ammunition to a spare roll of 35mm film. Kelly was adamant that if they were about to enter a desolate and dangerous Lynchburg, she wanted to be one of the few who had photos to prove it, and perhaps, if normality one day returned, she would sell these photos for a hefty profit. She wasn't a professional photographer, it was just a hobby she'd had since her dad gave her an old Canonet 28 as a child. Of course, with the advent of digital photography and the quality of cameras built into everyone's cell phone, photography - and the art of being a decent photographer - had lost their value and general standing in society. In the modern era, any stay-at-home mom with a Sony DSLR camera and a spare afternoon was suddenly a 'professional photographer', photoshopping the italicized words "Stacey May Photography," or whatever her name may be, to the bottom of predictable wedding photos.

By all means, photography as an art form was dead. Until the pulse occurred, that is. Now, Kelly was one of a handful in the city, state, or perhaps country, who could document the destruction of an EMP attack and the collapse of a lawful society in a first world city. People new to photography always used to ask her, "What's the best kind of camera to have?" to which the answer was always, "The one you have on you." In this respect, Kelly now had one of the best cameras in the world.

David opened the back door and stood in the door frame, meeting with the cold October air. It made him wonder how they were going to stay warm when the temperatures got below freezing, but that was a problem for the future. Right now, they needed to focus on surviving today.

Kelly walked through the door and closed it behind her with a gentle click, that noise alone being incredibly loud in the deathly still morning air. Kelly turned to David and held his face in the darkness. This was it; the thing they vowed not to do. Time to head into the center of the city. David leaned in and kissed his wife. They held that position for a few seconds, the feeling of warm breath on each other's faces. At that moment it wasn't too late to turn back and go inside, but before she had time to weigh the pros and cons once more, David whispered to her.

"Let's go… and no matter what happens, remember that I love you."

Kelly took a breath.

"I love you too. I love you so much."

The two silhouettes walked toward the treeline at the back of the house, measuring each step carefully and feeling for trees. They'd made a conscious effort to stick to a set path each time they walked into the wooded area behind their home, studying and counting the trees and contour of the low hill upon which the trees sat, memorizing their approximate locations while making sure no twigs or branches lay in their path.

Every footstep was loud in the calm of the morning air, despite their slow, methodical movements, and it took them almost ten minutes to travel a few hundred yards to the clearing on the other side. So far so good, but now they were about to enter uncharted territory, walking on roads in front of houses and crossing a freeway, on the other side of which was a commercial area full of probably looted business and, perhaps, armed and desperate citizens.

Aided by their soft-soled sneakers, they walked silently in the center of a residential street, being two dark humanesque shapes on full alert. The lack of streetlights helped them remain undiscovered as they passed empty homes, once full of laughter, families and stories. Where were the owners, Kelly wondered. Were some still inside? Had they fled? Were their bodies sitting inside rotting, like that of their neighbor Jerry?

Kelly was in the lead, having memorized their old city map the night before. David, with the gun in his right hand, followed.

Kelly raised her hand and flipped it forward a few times, indicating they were heading in the right direction. Over the bored days and nights at home, they had created a series of hand signals to use in situations where they couldn't talk. Perfect for if one of them heard a noise outside and needed the other to hold the gun.

The highway overpass formed a black concrete bar across the dark morning sky, coming slowly closer, step by step. They needed to pass under it and down the main road toward the mall complex. David noticed that there was a surprising amount of rubbish on the roads; something that used to annoy him. Littering was a sign of a person with no care for the planet or their own self respect. He never understood it. Now, however, he understood if people dropped cans and smashed bottles on the road. I mean, who are we keeping it clean for, he thought. They walked under the overpass, with Kelly indicating that they needed to move to the side of the road and be careful as they were clearly exposed.

It was still dark, but there was more light available now; enough to make out the expressions on each other's faces. This made them more visible, but it also helped them see debris and rubbish on the roads and sidewalks as they tried desperately to go undetected. They weren't fighters, heroes or renegades, throwing caution to the wind for movie-like action scenes. They were survivors, opting to take the path of least resistance at all times, or not to take the path at all.
The business on the right had its front window smashed with glass fragments lying on the ground in front. The sudden cracking sound of Kelly's shoe standing on a flat shard of glass was enough to send a blasts of ice-cold adrenaline through their chests. David and Kelly both froze absolutely still, knowing that anyone in the immediate vicinity would have heard that noise if they were listening for it. The deafening sound of silence soon replaced the sudden noise, with nothingness filling the early morning air once again, long enough for Kelly to make a decision. Rather than rolling the dice on another forward step, Kelly signaled to David to back up. The two took long, careful steps backward, until they were clear of the appliance shop front. Kelly gave the "go around" signal, and they gave the appliance store a wide berth, even though it meant walking onto the road. David fought the natural urge to explain the pointlessness of looting an appliance store after an EMP attack.

The sun was somewhere over the Atlantic, heading closer by the hour, evident by the clouds above which started to gain determinable shapes. This meant that Kelly and David were becoming visible and they were now only halfway to their destination. They walked silently down alleyways wherever possible, with Kelly using this increasing amount of light to take photographs of the destruction. David didn't complain, but he wasn't thrilled with her stopping them both for the tenth time to photograph hastily erected and hastily abandoned roadblocks made of bricks and car tires.

They soon found themselves walking through a small parking lot behind an office building with its ground floor windows busted out, obviously looted. Coming up against a tall chain-link fence, it was determined that the only way to continue in their chosen direction was to walk down the driveway and continue on the main road until they could walk discreetly behind more businesses. Scanning the surroundings, she gave the "Go" signal with her hand and they approached the main road, dotted with empty cars, their doors open and their windows smashed. Kelly adjusted the aperture setting on her Nikon camera to suit the low light before focusing it to the vehicle in the foreground.

Click.

She took a photo, wondering how it would look once developed. The road ahead looked clear, save for another roadblock up ahead. She couldn't really tell in the low light, but there might even have been movement behind it.

Standing at a corner, the cold, brick wall of an office block against them, David watched their surroundings, his back to Kelly as he scanned the office windows above them and the driveway behind them. Kelly tapped his shoulder, causing David to turn to her quickly.

"Hazard," was the hand signal she gave David, followed by her shrugging her shoulders in uncertainty and pointing to the roadblock about a hundred yards up ahead. Kelly stepped aside and David moved forward a few inches, poking his head around the corner of the office block and looking down the road. It was lighter now, but still too dark to see clearly. They stood there, staring in the same direction like meerkats in a nature documentary. Kelly turned to David and shrugged, to which David answered with a shrug of his own. Using skills only seen in *Who's Line is it Anyway*, Kelly used her hands to indicate that they needed to go down that very road, past the hazard. He showed the pistol to Kelly and indicated that he would go in front, to which she nodded.

They had been standing at that corner, against the wall, for about three minutes before David finally gave the "Let's go" signal. They stepped out.

Neither of them made a sound as they paced carefully towards to the roadblock, sticking close to the buildings on their right, pulling into every driveway and hugging the corners for a moment to ensure the case was indeed clear. The moments when they found themselves on the roads were when they were at their most vulnerable, and they knew it, even though the city appeared deserted in the early morning light. The roadblock ahead was about three feet in height and spanned half of the width of the street, comprising mostly bricks, tires and debris. She might have simply been imagining the movement she thought she saw earlier. After all, in low light your eyes can play tricks on you. Therefore, if they'd estimated it correctly, they would arrive at Trevon's house at about 6 AM; avoiding the brightness of daytime.

The roadblock was about 50 yards ahead of them now as they carefully turned into another driveway separating two looted businesses. They needed to get past that roadblock and stay on this street in order to avoid walking around the mall, which, with its high windowless sides and expansive outdoor parking lot, would offer no protection from unsavory individuals. These streets were their best bet; their path of least resistance.

David was now in front, his head poking around the corner of the business, scanning the road, with Kelly behind him. He gave the all-clear and they continued slinking in the direction of the roadblock, his Glock aimed forward.

There was a difference of about a third of a second between the flash of light emanating from above the roadblock and the sound of a gunshot which blasted loudly across the morning air, corresponding with a chunk of the brick wall to the right of David's arm exploding in a cloud of dust. A gunfight erupted, with David instinctively firing his gun back at the roadblock several times. Kelly pulled him by his backpack, dragging him around the corner from whence they'd came while he unloaded five more shots in the direction of the orange muzzle flash. David almost tripped over backwards during the three seconds it took from the first gunshot, to them running down the driveway for safety. It was unlikely he'd hit the person who fired at them, the antagonist almost certainly hiding behind the roadblock as soon as David returned fire, but at least it bought them those three vital seconds to escape. The two jogged as quickly and quietly as possible across the parking lot and through an alleyway to a smaller road running parallel to theirs. Up ahead of them was the front entrance to the mall, its glass doors smashed. It would be suicidal to go in there, but maybe the shooter at the roadblock was coming for them? Maybe the shooter wasn't alone? It was guaranteed that anyone within a mile had heard the

gunfire. They certainly couldn't go back in that direction
and running down the side of the enormous mall offered
nowhere to hide. They had no other choice. Panting, and
with his hand shaking, David frantically pointed at the
mall entrance and Kelly gave a rapid nod of her head,
both of them terrified. They ran.

The first strange thing David noticed about the mall
entrance was that someone had swept the broken glass
from the doors to one side. Surely it wasn't mall
management, he wondered. He wasn't sure if it made him
feeler safer or more at risk, but regardless, it allowed
them to enter the pitch black interior of the shopping mall
undetected. The second thing he noticed about the
shopping mall as they felt their way inside was the smell
of urine and feces. Did this mean there were people
inside it? David believed with certainty that there were.
The third and most troubling thing they noticed about the
mall is that it was completely dark. They couldn't see
anything more than a few feet in front of them. They
knew the layout of the mall by heart, of course, spending
many a Sunday afternoon here, but this was no longer the
mall they once knew. From what they could see in the
dark, the sporting goods store on the right had been
ransacked. Aware that they couldn't go forwards into the
pitch black, and that they couldn't give themselves away
by turning on their flashlight, David took Kelly's hand
and led her past a large empty box and and what looked
like a basketball on the ground, heading into the sporting
goods store, if only to hide out until they felt the threat
had gone or until more light had begun to shine through
the mall's partial glass ceiling. David tripped over
something and fell onto an empty display, the shelf
scraping coldly into his left arm. Kelly crouched down
next to him. He touched his arm and felt its stickiness,

before bringing his invisible fingers up to his mouth, the metallic taste of blood now on his tongue.

Both scared, they sat on the floor of the store, silently. They wished they could see what mess lay before them. Unfortunately their wish was about to be granted, a voice somewhere nearby speaking clearly.

"Move and you're dead, d'you understand?"

Neither David nor Kelly answered, holding their breath, frozen with fear. A light as bright at the sun blasted their eyes. It was a flashlight, held by someone in the store, maybe twenty feet away.

"My gun is aimed at you. You move and you're dead. Tell me you understand."

Kelly answered first.

"We understand. Don't shoot."

The flashlight occupied their vision, the device's holder stood as frozen as they were. He spoke again.

"You're gonna let go of that gun in your hand and you're gonna chuck it over here, understood?"

There was no way out of this. They were at the mercy of whoever held that flashlight, and presumably, a gun. David placed it down on the ground and with a flick of his forearm, scuttled it across the floor. It went somewhere in the direction of their new captor.

"You got any other weapons?" he asked.

"No," David replied.

"What are you doing here?"

"We're going across town to trade."

This information, whether the truth or a lie, seemed to relax the unknown and as yet unseen man.

"You trade?" he asked.

"When we have to," David replied.

The flashlight jiggled around, moving closer. It moved towards the ground, a few feet in front of them. The sound of moving fabric indicated that the man had reached down and picked up their pistol.

"Tell you what," the man continued. I'm going to turn this off to save the batteries, and we're gonna talk."

"OK," said David, not having much choice in the matter. The flashlight switched off.

"What've you got in that backpack?" the voice in the darkness asked.

David wondered how much information he should reveal, but if the voice did indeed have a gun, there was no point in lying by omission.

"Stuff to trade. A bag of rice-"

"Don't need rice. Or any food," the voice interrupted. "I cleared out the supermarket already."

David continued.

"Coffee?"

"Got coffee."

"Cigarettes?"

The voice didn't immediately respond, which was a small sign of optimism.

"Smokes are worth more to me than food right now, but I still have plenty. Gimme something more."

"That's all we've got," David said, his brief flirt with optimism extinguishing as quickly as it had appeared. "We've got a box of ammo. 9mm."

"Got any meth? Or booze?" asked the voice.

"We've got booze. At home," David lied.

The three of them sat in silence, their eyes adjusting to the gradual increase of natural light appearing in the mall's concourse.

"I'll tell you what. Give me the cigarettes and this gun, and I'll let you leave. You come back with booze and I'll give you your gun back, and maybe we can trade some more."

"But…" David stammered. "We don't have another gun… and it's suicide outside."

"Not my problem. You came in here to my store, uninvited. You're fucking lucky I don't end you both here and now. There's nothing stopping me. There's no police. No law. *I* am the law," the voice responded, sounding like the villain in a shitty action movie.

"I've killed people already, that's how I'm still alive."

"So… you'll let us go?" David asked.

"Yep. I'll let you go. But I'm keeping this gun as insurance. You bring me a bottle of booze; whiskey, rum, brandy, whatever, and you get your gun back. Oh, and the cigarettes. Give me those, too. Be fucking grateful."

"OK… Th… thank you," David said, realizing how pathetic it sounded.
He'd just lost their only form of protection as well as any bartering power they had.

"Thank you again. We'll come back to trade tomorrow, but for now, can you get us through the mall? To the other side?"
The silence which followed in the grainy morning light seemed like a positive sign. The voice, which was beginning to form a face in the darkness, gave them an answer.

"Alright. Fine. You'll be safe with me. There's another guy at the other end of the mall. He's not as nice as me. He shoots first and asks questions later, but stick with me and you'll be alright. Let's see that backpack."
The flashlight turned on again as David slid the backpack off his shoulders. He pushed it over towards the face, who reached down and turned it upside down, spilling its contents onto the floor. Kelly, who had been silent during these last few minutes, had her hand firmly on the pepper spray in her jacket pocket. She estimated how long it

would take to spray it in the man's direction, and whether that would allow her enough time to tackle him, allowing David to get their gun back and shoot the man dead. She'd killed before, and in this situation, sitting on the floor of a looted sporting goods store at gunpoint, she was more than willing to end the guy's life.

David disrupted her angry fantasy with forced pleasantries.

"I'm David, by the way. And this is Kelly."

The mystery face, his eyes becoming somewhat visible, studied the two people sitting on the dirty floor in front of them.

"You're bleeding, David," came the reply. "I don't want you bleeding in my store."

The man, holding all their possessions and their means of self defense, pepper spray aside, instructed them to get up.

"David. Raise your arms up."

David complied. The man moved closer and frisked him, running his hands over his fleecy jacket and down each leg. Kelly, assuming she was next, discreetly took the pepper spray out of her pocket and pushed it down the front of her pants, the tiny aerosol sitting behind the button fly in her jeans, before raising her hands preemptively. The man frisked her too, taking longer than was necessary to touch and squeeze her breasts.

"Alright. I'm gonna take you to the other side of the mall and you're going to go and get me a bottle of booze. Then you get your shit back. Actually, I want two bottles. You understand?"

This was getting ridiculous, David thought. They didn't have any booze at home; they'd drunk it, and this power-hungry moron wanted more.

"Yes sir," David said.

The three of them moved towards the exit of the sporting goods store, stepping over boxes. The man put David and Kelly's pistol somewhere out the back of the store and ushered them out. He turned around and reached up, pulling down the storefront security grille to the ground and locking it with a key. It made both David and Kelly wonder what else he had in there of value.

Looking through the mall's entry doors, it was visibly lighter outside and for the first time they noticed two human bodies in the parking lot, a few yards away, lying face-up in the morning light. The mystery voice from the darkness was now a person in front of them. He noticed them staring at the corpses outside.

"They didn't want to trade," he said, ushering David and Kelly into the bowels of the mall, gesturing with his pistol.

The three set off into the dimly lit shopping mall, the pungent smell of excrement hanging in the cold air.

"What's your name?" Kelly asked, trying to form an artificial bond, in the hope it might help insure their safe passage.

"To you, I'm God," he answered arrogantly. "I giveth and I taketh away."

Loathing his obnoxious arrogance, Kelly tried to win him over with literal praise.

"Thank you again for your grace," she said, earnestly.

She noticed David's eyes on her. She knew exactly what he was thinking, but thought it best to ignore his glance, lest their chaperone figured out that she was hamming it up to placate him. If they survived the day, they'd laugh about it later.

They walked past what used to be a cafe they both enjoyed visiting. On many occasions they'd sit there, watching the world go by, cappuccinos in hand, after watching a movie. Now, the chairs were knocked over and the counter, once full of cakes and muffins, was dark and empty. David and Kelly weren't typical mall people, but they liked this mall. It was *their* mall. At least it used to be.

Eventually they approached a clothing store on the other side of the mall, near the far entrance. It was one of those predictable clothing stores, catering to 'tweenagers'. The kind of store which played generic electronic beats through its speakers and had absurdly thin, anorexic mannequins out front, as if Auschwitz prisoners were somehow teleported into modern clothes and forced to stand in this shop's front window in unnatural poses. Such stores preyed upon the insecurities of Instagram-obsessed girls, taking their idiot parents' money in the process. This meant that when Kelly and David saw this store with its windows smashed, its bright lights turned off and its sickly mannequins thrown into a pile, it offered a guilty sense of satisfaction.

"Hey, CJ," the face called out.

"Yo," a voice from inside responded.

"It's me. Got a couple of traders here. They're just passing through."

"'Aight," came the reply from somewhere inside the virtual concentration camp.

Empty clothing racks and upturned tables from a nearby cafe formed a maze-like barricade inside the former clothing store, with a figure soon appearing in front of them.

"Where you two headin'?" the figure said, standing up from behind his barricade. He was a big guy, solidly built, maybe about 40 years old.

"North of here, about a mile or so," David replied. "Going to get a gun."

"I've got their gun back in the store," said their self-appointed god.

"Insurance," he added.

"You two ain't gonna last five seconds out there without a gun," the big guy said, almost playfully, showing his own weapon, an impressive-looking handgun, but one with less precision than a toddler in the NBA.

"Yeah, well, your friend took our gun," Kelly replied, becoming agitated.
Their self-appointed god laughed.

"I'm going back to my store. You guys better come back with my booze if you want your gun and your stuff back. You know where to find me."
God turned around and walked back through his kingdom, leaving David and Kelly alone with this new threat.

"So you wanna trade something?" the man asked Kelly.

"Your friend took it all. We've got nothing to offer you. We're just leaving."
They just wanted to get out of that mall, even if it meant taking a chance with death outside in the increasing morning light. Besides, they were probably about halfway to Trevon's house. They could run like mad and hope for the best.

"You should come back here behind the barricade and wait till tonight, when its dark. It's safer. I'll protect you."
David interjected.

"We're fine. But thank you. We'd better get going. Come on, Kel."

"I wasn't talkin' to you," CJ said to David, his voice firm.

Kelly and David looked at each other, ready to run to the mall exit, but before they could act on the urge, CJ lifted his gun in their direction, his faux amiability replaced with coldness.

"Hey, girl. Come here."

She stood still, a thousand thoughts racing through her mind, while David felt every hair on his head stand on end. With the gun aimed at them, they couldn't be sure of escape without one of them dying right then and there, in a shit-smelling mall, at the hand of an immoral psycho.

"Girl. I said come *here.*"

Kelly looked at David, both standing in the doorway to this former clothing store. They mimicked each others' facial expressions, which were both pure fear. Not fear of death - at least, not yet - but fear of something else. Something that might warrant suicide. Thoughts now raced through David's mind, making him light-headed. He would fight for his wife, but what could he do now, standing alongside her with no weapon, and a barricade between him and the fucking asshole with the gun? He could do nothing. He couldn't believe this was real. Surely it wasn't.

"I ain't gonna ask you again. Move your ass. Get in here now, bitch."

Kelly turned back to David, whose eyes were beginning to water. This wasn't real, he thought. He shook his head gently, staring at his wife. They were a calm and rational couple, but this kind of situation was well out of their control. Five seconds passed and the man appeared at the front of the store, gun pointed straight at Kelly.

"I'mma need her," said the man, pushing Kelly into the doorway and into the store. "Chill, man. I ain't gonna hurt her."

"Please don't," David begged, pointlessly. His eyes were watering as the love of his life was led around the side of the barricade, where they managed to make eye contact one last time. With tears in her eyes, Kelly mouthed the words, "It's OK" to David, but they both knew it wasn't. It really wasn't.

It was dark at the back of the store, behind the second barricade, but Kelly could make out the body of a girl. She was dead, with dark bruises on her neck, and naked from the waist down. She looked in her mid teens. Kelly felt dizzy, wanting to throw up.

"Pants off," instructed CJ.

Kelly hesitated, resulting in the man placing the hard and narrow barrel of the pistol against her temple.

"Kelly," David cried out, choking tears. "I love you!"

This caused Kelly to cry herself, but CJ wasn't there to console. With his left hand he grabbed Kelly's left breast and squeezed it harshly, emitting an animalistic grunt.

"Take your fucking pants off or I'll finish you, like her," he said, nodding to the bluish, half naked corpse lying a few feet to their right.

Kelly had to make a choice between uncertain life and certain death.

Kelly complied.

Dear reader,

Life is not like a Hollywood movie. Sometimes terrible things happen to good people through no fault of their own.

Life is often greatly unfair, with all of us being mistreated at the hands of others at some point in our lives.

The death of a loved one, rape, infidelity and betrayal cause pain in a way that physical damage cannot. Such terrible misfortunes leave permanent bruises on the soul, destroying those affected from deep within.

It's not fair and it shouldn't happen.

But it does.

In the dark of the store, the corpse of a girl lying alongside, Kelly pulled her jeans and her underwear down to her knees. It was a difficult task as her hands were trembling, but she managed. Was this the same fear the girl next to her had felt? It was hard to imagine as her face looked so peaceful in the cold embrace of death.

With her body exposed from the waist down, Kelly was instructed to lie on the floor, which she did, while sobbing tears of both fear and anger. The floor was cold on her buttocks as she sat, then lay on her back. The faster she did this, the faster he would finish, and the faster she could leave. She imagined herself running away. Running as fast as her legs would take her. Running forever.

Placing the pistol under his arm to free up his hands, the man undid his pants and and underwear, his erection protruding. Somehow this entire scenario seemed to stimulate the man further. Kelly didn't understand. It didn't make sense to her how someone could be sexually aroused through sheer power and control. It was disgusting.

There was nothing romantic about this next scene; completely different to the intimacy Kelly had shared with David. With Kelly on the ground, the man got to his knees and climbed on top of her, holding her wrists with his hands, his penis aiming toward her. With penetration inevitable, Kelly made the decision that she would not just *submit*. She would rather die than let this beast inside her.

With a fierce, angry scream, she threw her knee up as hard as she could, crushing the testicles hovering inches above her thighs. This stunned the attempted rapist just long enough for him to loosen one of her arms from his grip, allowing her to grab her pepper spray. She pressed down hard on the top of the small canister in her hand, releasing a jet of its contents into his eyes and mouth. The man was still frozen in shock from the knee to his balls two seconds earlier, but he soon gasped for breath, inhaling a lungful of pepper spray. Spurred on by the scream, David found himself unthinkingly climbing over the barricades between them, not fearing death, only wanting to protect his partner. The rapist was in agony, coughing in pain, but he was also a strong man. He and Kelly both fumbled for the gun which had fallen to the ground somewhere beside them. He had the advantage of strength, but Kelly had the advantage of eyesight.

"David!" she screamed, as she pushed the gun away with her hand, the rapist still on top of her, his fading erection serving as a metaphor for this particular sexual conquest.

The rapist let go of her wriggling arms in order to squeeze her throat.

David was now over the barricade and scrambling towards them on his hands and knees.

"Gun!" Kelly gasped, sounding like Gollum.

David couldn't see it. He scrambled his hands across the surface of the floor and looked around in a panic while Kelly hit the coughing attacker's head fruitlessly with her free arm. It was pointless. He was too strong.

The shape of the gun caught David's frantic glances, spotting its silhouette on the floor between bottles of alcohol and boxes of medicine. He fell forward to grab it, Kelly now unable to talk as the air was squeezed from her very being. David clawed at the pistol and spun around, clambering to his feet, kicking the man in the head as hard as he could.

"Get off her!"

Why didn't he just shoot him? Either way, the rapist saw the gun and froze. The rapist decided that this was not worth dying for.

"Get off her now!"

The wheezing attacker paused for half a second, then let go of Kelly's neck, allowing her to gasp heavily for air. In the darkness David could see the man's eyes were wet and his nose was dripping with snot, caused by the capsaicin in the pepper spray. His gaze was fixed firmly on David, Kelly still squashed beneath his weight.

"Shoot him!" Kelly gasped.

But David didn't fire. If this were a movie, he'd probably say something heroic and pull the trigger, but this wasn't a movie. He'd never killed a person before. He didn't know what to do.

In the stand-off, the bigger picture began to form in his mind. There was no police force any more. No more laws. This beast before him just tried to rape his wife. He was the law, now. He was the judge, jury and executioner. David's adrenaline-fueled mindlessness was quickly replaced with cold, vicious anger.

He pulled the trigger. Again and again and again; dry thunderclaps emanating from the handgun, blood splattering from the man's chest. The force of bullet after bullet slashed through his torso, ripping up his organs. The impact of each piece of lead pushed the rapist off his victim and onto the floor. His half-naked body flopped backward about as he struggled, gurgling blood. David shot him again. The bastard. "How dare he!" he thought. He fired the gun once again. And once more.

"Stop!" Kelly called out.

David's teeth were clenched hard, his mouth slightly open. He'd become an ape in human clothes, a lust for killing spread across his face. He had just killed a man and it felt good. Fucking good. Silence descended into the cold, concrete store.

"It's over," Kelly said, kicking the rapist's dead legs off her own. "It's over. Thank you, David. Thank you."

She was panting, and covered in blood, her eyes watering from both emotion and pepper spray which had misted down onto her own face. She started to hastily pull up her pants.

"We've gotta go. Right now," she said.

Reality hit David, snapping him from his primal mindset. They climbed to their feet and began to run around the double barricades and out of the shop, turning towards the mall exit near them, but then David grabbed Kelly, freezing them both in their footsteps.

"We have to go back the way we came," David said. "It's suicide going out this way."

He darted his eyes around, aware that at any moment, 'God' would probably appear to cast judgment.

"Here," David said, pointing to the cell phone repair booth in the middle of the mall concourse.

He grabbed Kelly's hand and pulled her towards it, climbing over the counter of the rectangular booth.

"Come on! Hide!" he said.

Kelly clambered over behind him.

Breathing heavily, they huddled on the floor in the corner of the booth. With a shaking hand, David put his index finger to his lips, pleading for silence. They tried to control their breathing and waited.

Sure enough, moments later they heard footsteps. The footsteps were fast, then they'd stop. Then they'd hear running again, followed by silence. God was darting from entrance way to entrance way, tactically pausing in each one for safety, getting closer one store at a time.

"CJ?" he called out, sounding like he was now three or four stores away.

Another brief spurt of fast footsteps were heard, followed by silence. The footsteps were closer now, but they were quieter. God was on full alert.

Kelly and David, breathing through their open mouths, stared vacantly at each other, waiting for God.

Sitting with his knees to his chest, David grasped the gun in his hand and a sudden feeling of dread ran through his mind.

"How many bullets are in this thing?" he wondered. He didn't know. The footsteps were very close now.

"CJ!"

That time it sounded like he was standing right next to them. The most deafening silence followed for ten, perhaps fifteen seconds, before they heard quick footsteps again, going right past their heads. Acting on impulse, David tightened his chest and raised his torso above the counter, aiming the gun at the back of their self-appointed god, just ten feet away.

He squeezed the trigger.

One shot rang out, followed by nothing. The impressive-looking TEC-22 pistol had jammed in his hands. He ducked down next to Kelly, their faces locked in fear. The dry crack of a gunshot was replaced with deafening silence. Kelly looked at David and he looked back at her. He knew what she was wondering. The truth is, he didn't know if he'd hit him or not. Was god lying dead on the ground, ten feet from them? Did he miss and god was now waiting there, his gun aimed back in their direction? It was a stand-off.

Approximately ten or fifteen minutes had passed since he had fired the gun. He was too scared to try and unjam the pistol due to the noise it would make, giving away their location to the man who called himself god.

It wasn't until they had sat in that booth, in the middle of the shit-scented mall's main thoroughfare for almost twenty minutes, that David came up with an idea. It was risky, but it was worth trying.

David quietly removed one of his shoes and gave it to Kelly to throw out of the booth in the opposite direction, away from the clothing store where she had escaped rape and death. This would serve as a distraction long enough for David to jump up, surprising god, demanding that he dropped his weapon. They had to try it. How much longer were they to wait if they didn't?

David prepared himself mentally, jammed gun in hand, while Kelly raised the shoe over her shoulder, ready to hurl it with all her might.

David looked at his wife and mouthed, "Ready?" to her. Kelly nodded.

Using only the shape of his mouth, he mimed the words, "One.... two... three!"

Kelly threw the shoe away from the booth and against a door frame 40 feet away, while David jumped up, gun in his hands in the direction they'd last seen god.

"Drop your gun! Drop it and I won't shoo-"

David stopped and exhaled, his blank expression morphing into a weak, open-mouthed smile.

'Kel. I got him."

She rose up next to her husband and looked at where his jammed gun was pointing. Richard Dawkins was right. God was indeed dead.

Kelly refused to go back into the clothing store for understandable reasons, so David went in there alone, grabbing eight bottles of Jack Daniel's Tennessee Whiskey from CJ's stash and stuffing them into two large plastic shopping bags. Kelly, meanwhile had taken the handgun off their now-deceased god and checked his pockets. By chance, his wallet was in his left pocket and Kelly couldn't help but find out the true identity of god.

"Dave. Did you know god's real name is Ronald Douglas?"

David laughed from inside the former clothing store.

"That sounds like the lovechild of Ronald McDonald and Michael Douglas," he shouted.

Kelly laughed for the first time in quite a while. It felt good.

"I was thinking, we should go get our backpack

and see what goodies Ronnie has stashed away back in the sporting goods store."

David walked out with his new collection of booze. If they could get this home, they'd be set for weeks.

"Sounds good. Let's go."

They made their way through the mall, with Kelly's newly acquired pistol at the ready, unjammed and prepared to shoot anything that moved. There were no more rules. From here on, they killed to survive.

Back at the sporting goods store, they walked into the back, finally able to see how it actually looked in slightly better light. God wasn't kidding: he had perhaps a ton of stocked dry foods. He had medicine too.

"Check this out, Kel. He's got antibiotics, what looks like medical marijuana... Painkillers... Iodine tablets... Shit, and gold too. Jewelry. You name it."

"Jesus. He must have cherry-picked from every store in this place," said Kelly, her eyes adjusting to the bounty which lay before them.

David found a large school bag and poured boxes of different drugs into it, filling it to the brim, to the point it would barely close.

"You wear this; I'll take the backpack," he instructed.

As well as loading up as much as they could carry with drugs and booze, they'd also found a selection of weapons in a large cabinet in the lunchroom at the back of the store. Not only did they reacquaint themselves with their trusty Glock 19, but they helped themselves to a clichéd but undeniably cool Desert Eagle, as well as a Springfield Super Match M1A and a few hundred rounds of ammo.

Whatever came their way, they were armed and ready.

They dropped the store's front shutter and locked it with god's key, moving to a nearby store to wait until nightfall. They'd scrapped their initial plan to meet with Trevon as it was no longer needed. They had the extra gun they wanted, and much more. Their plan now was simple: go home.

Waiting in the back of an empty store until nightfall was certainly boring, but it was a small price to pay for increased safety. It also gave them a chance to talk through what had happened that day and vow to take no prisoners from this point on.

Chapter seven

Passing the time

Signs of human activity had dropped significantly over the weeks which followed. The number of gunshots ringing out in the still air had all but vanished, and the closest they had to an intruder was a once-domesticated dog walking into their fishing line alarm system.

While dedicated to each other, the lack of human interaction did have a negative impact on Kelly and David's relationship, with the two of them being forced into each other's personal space day after day.

David tried to occupy himself by attempting, unsuccessfully, to make a crystal radio from a plastic tube, copper wire taken from their string trimmer's electric motor and resistors taken from their washing machine's small circuit board.

Kelly kept herself busy with her photography, developing the photos she'd taken over the past few weeks, some of which were brilliant. She'd also moved the washing machine outside and connected it to her bicycle with a tight loop of rope, allowing her to get exercise while their clothes sloshed around in soapy water.

Being in close quarters with each other, day after day, was what spurred them to keep in contact with Steve and Maureen, their neighbors from a few houses down the street, visiting them twice a week for board game evenings and forming their own reading club, where they would sit together in their living room while one person would read a book aloud, allowing the others to sit back and form an audience. Depending on the type of book, their neighbor's kids, ridiculously named Braxley and Portia, also took part. Those listening in the room would often lose themselves in the story, with no mobile phones to distract them, the book being as close as they could get to watching a movie. They had also shared food and recipes together, as well as personal information, revealing a lot about each other's lives. Steve was a criminal lawyer, though not a high-flyer, and Maureen was a stay-at-home mom. Braxley was a typical boy, being a pain the ass a great deal of the time and getting himself into mischief, while Portia was a little know-it-all. Even though Kelly and David were never very comfortable around kids, they learned how to get along with Steve and Maureen's little terrors, although truth be told, they would probably visit their neighbors more often than twice a week if it wasn't for their kids.

Dishing the dirt after an evening of reading, cooking over a camping stove and talking, Kelly and David would often mock the kids' names, comparing them to the name of a pharmaceutical company.

It was on a Tuesday, or perhaps Wednesday (day names didn't matter anymore) when Steve and David hatched a plan to go back to the sporting goods store in the mall for more supplies. They'd just finished rigging up a rudimentary communication system, using the telephone lines in the street and the phone jacks in each other's kitchens, creating a closed circuit between their homes. It was very basic, involving a car battery, a 12 volt lamp and a push button on each end, which resulted in the lamp flashing in their opposing kitchens. They didn't know Morse code, so they came up with their own version to send simple messages, albeit painfully slowly.

Unfortunately, on more than one occasion Steve and Maureen's kids would push the button for fun, creating chaos in Kelly and David's kitchen as they tried to figure out what the hell was trying to be said.

They had enough food supplies and chlorine for cleansing water, but booze was already becoming short in supply. Not only that, both families were bored.

Steve and David played rock, paper, scissors to decide who was going to be given the task of telling their wives about their newly hatched plan to go on a mission to get more supplies. Standing out the back of Steve and Maureen's house, they closed their right hands into fists and shook them three times.

David had rock, Steve had paper.

"Best out of three?" David asked.

"No way!" Steve replied.

David took a deep breath.

"Alright then. I'll float the idea tomorrow at Oprah's Book Club. Who's gonna be reading what?"

"We're starting a new book. Maureen's gonna choose it and it's her turn to read," Steve replied.

"Please don't let it be a romance novel," David pleaded, shaking his head slowly.

Steve let out a chuckle.

"Dave, you just bring the whiskey. After that I don't mind if she reads the damn phone book."

"Mooooom!" yelled Portia from inside the house, her high-pitched voice going straight through the walls. The smiles on David and Steve's face were immediately replaced with serious expressions as they met each other's gaze, then looked around their surroundings. The kids knew damn well never to raise their voices.

"I'll take care of this. See you tomorrow," Steve said to David, opening the back door and going inside. The kids were told on a daily basis that voices traveled in the still air. Those damn brats are gonna get them all killed, David thought to himself as he walked into the shared forested area behind their homes, heading to his own house.

Maureen had a cheeky smile on her face as she walked into the living room, carrying tonight's book, hidden under her shirt. She knew it might not be everyone's cup of tea, but perhaps she could convince them otherwise.

"Everyone ready?" she asked.

The audience in their living room was genuinely concerned, clutching their glasses of whiskey in their hands. Over three months they'd already read the 'good' books they collectively owned, such as as George Orwell's 1984, Colson Whitehead's The Underground Railroad and Slaughterhouse-Five by Kurt Vonnegut. Heck, they'd even walked into questionable books such as Eat Pray Love by Elizabeth Gilbert, and completely useless books, such as The 7 Habits of Highly Effective People by Stephen R. Covey. It was common knowledge, at least in that room, that they were starting to scrape the bottom of the bibliophilia barrel.

Maureen scanned the room, filled with concerned faces illuminated by the candle on the table next to her. She was *loving* this, evident by the smile on her face. The two kids looked around at the faces of the adults, not understanding why the adults were so tense during what they perceived as a benign situation.

She pulled out the book, spun it around to reveal its cover, and held it proudly against her chest.

"Oh *no*," Steve said first, followed closely by Kelly.

David was the furthest away and couldn't quite see the name of the paperback in her hand.

"What is it? Someone please… just rip off the band-aid."

Maureen responded with a smile a mile wide.

"What I Did For a Duke by Julie Anne Long!"

David didn't know this book, but could tell from everyone else's expression that it can't possibly be something worthy of Shakespeare. Steve helped to confirm his fears.

"It's one of those trashy women's romance novels from the supermarket."

Steve closed his eyes and audibly groaned. The kids thought this was hilarious.

"Can't we just read the phone book?" David asked.

Maureen tried to reason with the unruly mob in front of her.

"Come on. It's not that bad. You'll *like* it. Just give it a chance. It's the beautiful story of the Duke of Falconbridge who falls in love with Genevieve Eversea in order to break her heart as an act of revenge. But then he discovers his love for her is real. It's a beautiful story, I promise! You'll love it, just give it a chance!"

Sighs and groans filled the room, peppered with giggling from the kids.

David didn't have the fortitude to endure a single page of that book, taking this as his chance to nip it in the bud with the radical idea he'd hatched with Steve the day before.

"Before we start," David began. "I have an idea I wanted to float with you."

The room waited as David took a sip from his glass, before looking over to Steve, who gave him a discreet nod. He decided to drop Steve in it, so at least they'd sink together.

"Steve and I came up with an idea yesterday."

Steve's mouth tightened. In the dimly lit living room, it almost looked like Steve was frantically shaking his head at David. Too late, bud. We're in this together, David thought.

"We were thinking... about going to the mall to get supplies."

"No. Absolutely not," came the response from Maureen. "You told us what happened at the mall. It's suicide in there. If you even make it there alive!"

"I understand your concerns," David said calmly. "I really do. But it's different now. There's much less activity outside. You don't hear gunshots much anymore. And if that store shutter is still intact – and we have the key - it's an absolute gold mine of supplies."

"And condoms," Steve said, without thinking. That piece of information sent the room into silence. Condoms weren't something Kelly or David ever considered as valuable. They certainly didn't need them.

"I mean... We're all adults here," Steve added, ignoring the two non-adults in the room. "Maureen's run out of 'the pill', and... it's been a while for us." That was information neither Kelly or David needed to hear, because immediately it created the unpleasant image in their minds of Maureen and Steve fucking.

"Plus, we can probably get more food and medicine. And books," David added. Kelly finally spoke up.

"I don't know if this is a good idea, babe."

"I know," David said. "Just hear me out. You guys would stay here. It'd just be me and Steve going at night. I remember how to get there and where the roadblocks are. Plus, this time we'd be better prepared than when you and I went there." The room sat in silence. The prospect of books, condoms, booze, soap, weed, different foods and medicine appealed to everyone in some way, but such an endeavor was dangerous. Perhaps even more dangerous than ever, given that it was now late November, two and a half months since the EMP attack. This meant the leaves were off the trees, reducing the chance of camouflage.

Kelly was conflicted. She wanted to be with her husband and to take part in anything new to break the boredom, but the thought of going near that mall made her very uncomfortable, given what had almost happened there weeks before.

But, in their current lives, they were all just existing, repeating meals and tasks, day after day. She wondered how much longer this would go on for, and if they would live out the rest of their days in their house in a permanent state of high alert.

"You know what?" Kelly asked. "You guys should do it."

David was slightly taken aback by this. He knew that their relationship had taken a hit from their lack of personal space, but was this her way of getting rid of him? This feeling frightened him, but he told himself that he must be imagining it. Kelly loved him. Right?

"I thought you wouldn't be on board with this idea?"

"Well, I wasn't at first. But I've had a minute to think. We do need more supplies. I mean, we have the essentials, but we can all agree we're going nuts here," she said, looking around the room. David looked concerned.

"I was a little scared you were trying to get rid of me," David asked her, apprehensive of her answer.

Kelly looked at him sincerely.

"Babe. You know I love you. Yes, it's been hard emotionally for us, but they're in the same boat," she said, gesturing towards Maureen and Steve.

Maureen nodded.

"It's been tough on all of us," said Maureen. "We always admired you two for being so strong throughout this disaster. If I'm honest, it's been hell in this household. It's really testing our marriage."
This was the first time the four of them had spoken openly together about the emotional toll the situation had had on their marriages. They wished they'd had this conversation weeks ago.

"Our bedroom is dead," Maureen admitted, causing Steve to stare at the glass in his hands.

"Well, ours has taken a hit too," said Kelly, making David equally uncomfortable.

"We still do it," David hastily replied, worried that he would appear as less of a man. "But not as much as we used to."
Steve let out a breathy, almost sarcastic laugh.

"At least you guys still can," he added. "Even if we wanted to, Maureen's off the pill, and getting pregnant could be a death sentence for both mother and child."
The kids were sitting silently, aware that the adults were talking openly about a taboo subject.

"Should they be hearing this?" Kelly asked Maureen, gesturing with her head towards Portia and Braxley.

"It doesn't matter," Maureen answered.
She was right. It was just sex; a part of life, and life as they knew it no longer existed anyway. Maureen didn't know if they'd even be alive in a year from now. She turned to Steve.

"You know I love you with all my heart, honey."

"I know," Steve replied, before sitting in silence for a few seconds. At least both couples were in the same boat, he thought. Then Steve's demeanor changed unexpectedly.

"I have an idea," he said, standing up. "Give me the candle for a minute."

Steve picked up the candle in its holder and walked out of the room, shielding the tiny, flickering flame with his hand. A heavy darkness descended on the living room, with the only source of light coming from the direction of their bedroom down the hallway.

"Got it," came Steve's voice from another room. In the pitch black of the room, Kelly briefly entertained the horrifying thought that Steve might want to try swinging to spice up their marriages.

Steve's face soon appeared in the hallway again, holding their only source of light, coming closer with something in his other hand.

"Honey," he said to Maureen, handing her a book. "Read this tonight."

As Maureen turned the book over, revealing its cover, David quietly prayed it wasn't the Bible.

"Oh. That's good," said Maureen. "The Five Love Languages by Gary Chapman."

This time it was the kids who groaned.

"Good idea," Kelly said, reaching over in the darkness and squeezing David's hand.

Chapter eight

Looting

Steve and David were dressed warmly in woolen clothes and thermal underwear as they walked between the same office buildings that had nearly taken one of their lives some weeks earlier.

They'd left home sometime after midnight and had planned to get to the mall alive, assess whether or not there was still anything left in the sporting goods store, take all they could carry in their backpacks, and get home in one piece, all before sunrise.

The path they'd drawn out the day beforehand listed all the threats and obstacles David and Kelly could remember, and who would be carrying which gun.

David was leading in the front, with his borrowed Desert Eagle drawn, while Steve followed close behind with David's recently acquired Springfield M1A rifle. They estimated the entire journey would take them about three hours if they were careful.

Kelly and Maureen, meanwhile, needed to keep themselves occupied. In Maureen's house, they decided to stay up and bake a simple raisin cake together to pass the time and stop their minds from wandering to their husbands, sneaking through the center of a lawless, Godless city.

"We should write down this recipe, just in case it actually works," Maureen joked.

"You're more optimistic than I am," Kelly responded.

They had no cookbooks which dealt with baking after an apocalypse, and they couldn't light a fire outside in the calm nighttime air as its flames and smoke would be visible for all to see.

"So, how much flour d'you think we should put in? How many cups?" Maureen asked.

Kelly liked to bake cookies occasionally, but she was never going to appear as a guest on The Kitchen.

"Uh… yes?" Kelly responded, laughing.

"Three cups it is," Maureen responded, dropping the powdery white contents into the bowl.

"I'll add the same amount of sugar," she continued, pouring the sugar into the measuring cup, then into the bowl.

Kelly opened the bag of raisins sitting on the counter and handed it to Maureen, just happy to have something to do with her hands.

"Just pour the whole thing in," Kelly suggested.

David and Steve had their backs against an office block, scanning the empty space between themselves and the mall entrance. There was no movement, but that didn't mean there was no one there. Anyone who'd made it this far would have learned not to be seen if you wanted to live. Movement meant a person or an animal, with either being potentially useful, either for food, information, or both. There was a half moon in the sky above them, which illuminated their faces every time it appeared from behind a cloud. This meant their movements were controlled by the heavens above. They both looked up at

the outline of a cloud moving closer to the weak, half
moon hanging above them.
Just a little longer...
Almost there...
Almost...
David gave the signal, tapping Steve's shoulder. They
drew their weapons in front and ran across the parking lot
towards the mall entrance, giving the dozen smashed up
cars in front of them a wide berth, not knowing who or
what could be inside them, before arriving to the outer
wall of the shopping center and standing against it, frozen
in time, as the moon made another unwelcome
appearance. The entrance to the mall was just to their
side. They just had to wait for the moon to give its signal.

Baking powder was not something preppers tended to
have in their stockpiles, which suddenly made it one of
the most valuable items of the moment.
  "What else can we use?" Kelly asked Maureen,
an avid baker.
  "Oh, baking powder's just sodium bicarbonate
and cream of tartar together," Maureen responded
chirpily.
  "I did not know that," Kelly said, actually
impressed. "So you're the chemist in this operation."
  "Nooo, just when it comes to baking. Besides,
we're not cooking a traditional cake in the oven, so we
won't be using a rising agent anyway."
  "So how are we going to bake it?"
  "You'll see," Maureen said, smiling. "Go fill up
this pot with water. Don't use the good water, either. Just
use creek water."
Kelly gently frowned in confusion, but Maureen told her
not to worry.
  "You'll see," she repeated.

Steve took the road flare out of his back pocket and handed it to David, who knew approximately where to throw it, once they were inside the mall. This would illuminate wherever it landed, creating a distraction for anyone nearby while hopefully allowing them to sneak towards the sporting goods store on the right.

David made the first step, walking like a cat, into the interior of the mall. The cold air made it harder to smell the stench of feces, but not impossible. He and Steve crouched down behind an information board near the entrance, close to the entry of the sporting goods store. Thank God, he thought, looking at the closed shutter of the store. It was still locked down, although the shutter appeared bent and damaged in the dull, grainy moonlight streaming in behind them.

David took the cap off the cylindrical flare, exposing the igniting compound. Going purely by touch, he pulled the flare's cap in two, feeling for the abrasive texture of the scratcher. He tapped Steve's shoulder, giving him the "Get ready" signal. Steve closed his eyes tightly and stood up, aiming the rifle around the sign, into the darkness, prepared to kill anything that moved. With his eyes also closed, David then hit the cap hard against the top of the flare. It began hissing with a red flash, the brightness visible through his closed eyelids. David stood up and threw it hard into the darkness, the shadows of tables, debris and door frames dancing as the flare charged through the air. It hit a storefront door frame with a clunk and rested, hissing in the distance, illuminating the concourse of the mall some forty yards away. David then ran over to the sporting goods store's shutter, fishing out the key in his pocket, while Steve had opened his eyes and now aimed the rifle in the direction of the flare, fizzing loudly. His hands fumbling, David couldn't get the key into the shutter's keyhole.

"Shit," he said, dropping the key.

It bounced off the shutter grille, narrowly avoiding the key slipping inside the shop and out of his reach forever. He clawed at the ground and grabbed it hard, bringing it back up to the keyhole, about a foot off the ground.

"Come on!" whispered Steve, focusing his gun intently into the mall.

David managed to unlock the grille and tried to pull it upward, but it was jamming. Someone had tried desperately to get through the shutters and had bashed at the tracks on either side of the door frame, warping it and preventing it from opening up. David pulled hard, with the structure clanking and rattling loudly. He pulled again, this time forcing it up by about ten inches off the ground, but that was all he could manage.

"Steve!" he called, dropping his backpack off and pushing it under the shutter, sliding in afterward.

Steve ran over, rifle in hand, and did the same, while David poked his Desert Eagle outward, through the slats in the grille. If anyone was in the mall, they had now certainly heard them.

The familiar hiss of a butane cooker broke the silence of kitchen, with Kelly placing a large pot of cold creek water on top of the flame. They used paving stones as a method of extra support for the pot, aware that little, single-burner camping stoves were never designed to hold the weight of three gallons of water.

"You're going to boil the cake?" Kelly asked.

"Now you got it," Maureen replied.

"In creek water?" asked Kelly, a little incredulous.

"Don't worry, I'll boil the heck out of it first," she said, careful not to say the word 'hell', even though the kids were in bed, asleep.

"I, uh… I have my reservations about this," Kelly commented.

Maureen laughed.

"I'll boil off any bugs. I'm just sick of everything tasting like chlorine."

"Oh, I'm with there you there," Kelly replied. "Though the chlorine does hide the taste of mud!" Maureen took the candle burning in the kitchen and walked to the hallway, leaving Kelly alone with the pot of cold, dirty water and a blue butane flame. She didn't like being alone, even for a moment, while her husband was somewhere in the depths of hell. Maybe with a broken leg, or taken hostage, or worse. Maureen returned with a pillowcase in her hand.

"Alright, Maureen, you sure have my attention. I have no idea what you're planning."

With his pistol in his right hand, David turned on his flashlight and scanned the messy store frantically to make sure they were alone and, equally importantly, to see if the supplies were still there. He moved towards the back, where everything was hidden, stepping over boxes and sports junk that no one wanted to loot in those early hours following the pulse. Steve moved backwards into the store, Keeping the rifle aimed towards the front.

"Dave?" he whispered loudly.

There was no answer.

David didn't hear him, being too busy out the back, jamming food into the two backpacks at his feet. The supplies were all still there, everything was still intact.

"Dave?!" Steve said, louder.

"Just keep guard! Gimme a minute!"

"Hurry up, man!" Steve answered back, nervous. Running purely on adrenaline, David threw all manner of things into the backpack, quickly filling it up. He hastily moved onto the other backpack and began filling that too. Steve then saw noticed something. Some movement. It was someone moving inside the mall, getting closer, darting between obstacles, their face becoming visible by the light of the road flare, still burning angrily further down the mall. Steve and David had agreed to shoot dead any threat, no questions asked. But was this a threat? Steve didn't know, but he didn't want to come home a cold-blooded murder. He was a dad; not a cold-blooded killer. It *had* to be self defense. He shouted clearly across the mall.

"If you come any closer I will shoot you!" David heard this and packed the backpack furiously, filling it up to the brim, but knocking the first backpack over, some of its contents spilling onto the floor. He scrounged around the floor, stuffing it all back in. A voice called out from the direction of the flare.

"Take it easy, man! I just wanna trade. You got the key for the store. I wanna trade with you!"

"No trading! Stay where you are. If I see you I'll shoot you! I promise you that!" Other than the sound of plastic rustling at the back of the store, there was no sound from the direction of the flare. A few seconds passed, before the male voice called out again, clearly desperate.

"Come on, man! Don't be like that. I need food. I'll trade. I'll do anything you want. I'll suck your dick. Anything. Please!" Steve was shocked.

"Stay where the fuck you are!" Steve shouted back.

Carrying both heavy backpacks in his arms, David moved as quickly as he could from the back of the store toward the front, knocking into things in the darkness.

"Let's go!" David said, heading towards the shutter.
Steve moved with him, poking the barrel of the rifle through the shutter and aiming it towards the guy near the flare, while David pushed the backpacks and his pistol underneath the shutter. David slid underneath and to the other side, picking up his gun and aiming it in the direction of the flare. Now it was Steve's turn. Steve removed the rifle from the shutter and got down on the ground, sliding underneath it on his back.

"Come on, man! Please! Don't do this! I'll do anything!" came the voice.

"I said don't fucking move!" said Steve, on his back, sliding out and putting on the backpack.

"Where is he?" David asked, unsure where to aim.
Steve got to his feet, now outside the store, and hoisted the rifle butt back to his shoulder, scanning for the source of the voice.

"Close the shutter!" Steve ordered.
David pulled down hard on the shutter and it crashed against the ground. While David was jingling the key frantically in the shutter's lock, Steve noticed movement behind a collection of planter boxes, much closer than he had seen the man before.

"Stop!" Steve yelled, to no avail.
Steve aimed at the boxes and pulled the trigger, causing an explosion of sound to echo through every corner of the building. David fumbled with the lock, his ears now ringing from the gunshot. A figure stood up slowly from behind the planter boxes, clutching its throat.

"Oh my God, I got him," Steve said, the sound of regret in his voice.

The injured man made a gurgling sound and staggered a couple of feet toward one of the mall's the planter boxes, before collapsing. They had to get the hell out of there immediately.

"You're putting it in *that*?"

"You betcha," Maureen replied, opening up the pillowcase and scraping in the sticky contents.

She'd added cooking oil and cinnamon to give it a little more flavor, but ultimately there wasn't much else to this cake, other than flour, sugar and raisins.

Maureen squeezed the end of the pillowcase into a ball and used a piece of twine to tie it closed.

"You're gonna cook the cake in a pillowcase in water?" Kelly asked, now more curious than incredulous.

"It's how my grandma used to do it. Or at least that's what she *said* they did back during the depression. But you know how it is with grandparents; saying absolutely everything was done harder back then."

Kelly screwed up her face and tried to imitate the voice of an old woman.

"In my day we used to walk fifty miles to get to school."

"In the snow!" Maureen replied.

"Barefoot!" added Kelly.

"And naked!" Maureen answered, both of them now laughing.

This bland, pillowcase shaped, muddy-water cake was proving to be a great distraction from the dark thoughts constantly trying to enter their minds.

With the water boiling, Maureen lowered the pillowcase into the bubbling water and put the lid on the pot.

"Now we wait."

The waiting was the painful part, as it meant they naturally worried about their husbands. Kelly tried to distract them both by talking about food.

"I'll tell you one thing I really miss: Lasagna."

"Oh, don't get me started. I lie awake at night fantasizing about food," said Maureen.

"You do that too?" Kelly asked.

"Every night. I would kill for a pizza, dripping with melted cheese. Or a steak."

"Mmm," Kelly replied. "I haven't had pizza in months. I've forgotten what it tastes like."

"And chicken. And turkey. Oh, and ham."

"Bacon."

"Oh, stop. I'd forgotten about bacon," exclaimed Kelly in delight.

Weighed down by their looted treasure, and fearful of running because of the noise it would create, it had taken David and Steve almost an hour to get back to their suburb. Once they'd reached the end of a nearby street, they slinked quietly between two dark houses and into the forested area behind their own homes. They were almost home, two innocent murderers in a lawless land.

The sound of the rear door opening sent a shiver down the spines of the two women in the kitchen. Maureen blew out the candle immediately, plunging them into darkness, while Kelly picked up the gun resting on the kitchen bench. Kelly ordered Maureen to stay there, while she moved towards the hallway at the back of the house. She heard a quiet whistle, a chirping sound, coming from down the hallway. It was their signal.

"David!" she called.

"We made it!" he responded.

"Steve?" Maureen called out.

"Hi honey, I'm home!" came the response, with an invisible smile in the dark of the night.

Kelly, David, Maureen and Steve stayed up until the morning light, their spoils of victory spread across the living room floor. It wasn't until they'd drawn the blinds and Kelly had removed the black sheet off the window that they could truly assess what they had obtained some hours before. With a pen and paper, Steve and David noted everything they'd collected.

"OK, so... We got... One bag of pool chlorine, a Glock G29 compact handgun, four packs of ground coffee, thirteen chocolate bars, two bags of powdered milk, two bottles of whiskey, another two of rum, two bottles of brandy, a container of weed, a box of cigars, a bag of dried fruit, two jars of peanut butter, another two of chocolate spread, and the pièce de résistance: five boxes of condoms!"

Maureen and Steve looked at each other, coy smiles on their faces. David threw a box of condoms across the room to Steve, offering one of his worst jokes to date.

"Now you can't say that I don't give a fuck!"

Braxley and Portia appeared in the living room.

"D'you guys want raisin cake for breakfast?" Maureen asked.

They looked at the haul on the living room floor, then back at their mother, nodding. The moist cake, still warm and surprisingly not tasting like mud, went down well. It was dense, but compared to the bland foods to which they'd grown accustomed, this was heaven in a bowl. The cake had the added benefit of keeping the kids silent for another ten minutes at least; their mouths full. For the first time in a long time, everyone could just live in the moment.

Chapter nine

Uninvited guest

It was going to be a long winter. An early dusting of snow had fallen over Lynchburg in early December and the nighttime temperature occasionally slipped below freezing.

"So much for global warming," Kelly said to David, both bundled up like arctic explorers inside their own home. The jovial atmosphere of days gone by had begun to dissipate. Dark moods and common arguments were becoming more common, fueled by boredom. Kelly scanned the living room and sat on the recliner.

"It's been three months today," she said to David, sitting on the sofa, buried under a comforter.

He heard what she said but stared at the floor, ignoring her presence. Their conversations had withered away lately, typically replaced by silence. Silence in a silent world.

Kelly raised her Nikon camera in his direction, focused it to his face and clicked the shutter, being on her last roll of film.

"Don't," David said.

"What?" Kelly asked.

He didn't answer.

"You're in a shitty mood," she stated.

He chose not to respond to her, sensing that another argument would be inevitable, regardless of what he said.

Kelly wanted to engage in conversation, even though neither had anything to say that hadn't already been said.

"Do you want to talk about it?"

"Of course I don't want to talk about it," David thought, but he said nothing.

"David. Neither of us are happy right now, but we need to communicate."

David continued to stare the floor. He wondered why she didn't just go into another room and leave him in peace. Kelly found his silence a little insulting, feeling like she was putting all the effort into keeping their collective sanity. The two sat in silence again, in some sort of conversational Mexican standoff where no party could possibly win. After another minute of dead air, Kelly spoke.

"David, if we don't communicate-"

"Shut up. Please. Just stop talking." David snapped.

Normally he would never talk to his wife like that, but she was being ridiculous. Didn't she have somewhere to be? Something to do? Why was she in the room, her sole purpose being to annoy him?

"Don't talk to me like that," she responded.

David pressed his molars together, breathing through his nose. He wanted to get up and get in the car and drive away. He wanted to be somewhere warm. Away from this house and his nagging wife. Kelly, ever the savior, tried to turn the conversation around.

"We'll have drinks tonight with Steve and Maureen. That'll cheer you up."

"I'm fucking sick of Steve and Maureen. I'm sick of their stupid, bratty kids. And they're sick of us."

Without another word, Kelly got up and walked out of the room. She stopped at the living room doorway, turned around and lifted her Nikon to her face. She aimed it at David who was pouting on the sofa.

Click.

"Get the fuck out of here!" David yelled, breaking their no shouting rule.

Kelly turned and walked down the hallway, into the spare room, closing the door behind her, tears forming in her eyes.

It was going to be a long winter.

"Hey guys," whispered Maureen, opening the rear door of their typical suburban house, albeit without power or water.

Something was different. The smell in Maureen and Steve's house was heavenly.

"What are you cooking?" Kelly asked.

"Goose!" Maureen replied, enthusiastically.

Without saying a word, David walked past them both and went to the living room, picking a spot on the sofa across from Steve.

"Where did you get a goose?" she asked.

"It was a gift from God," Maureen responded, smiling. "I found it next to the road yesterday."

Kelly's initial look of surprise drained away immediately.

"Roadkill? We're having roadkill for dinner?" she asked.

"Well, no, not really. It obviously wasn't hit by a car. It died from natural causes."

"Natural causes? Like a stroke?" Kelly asked, dubious about their main course bubbling away in oil in a saucepan in front of them. Maureen shrugged.

"I mean, don't get me wrong," Kelly continued, "it smells delicious, but what if it's diseased? We can't get sick; there are no doctors."

"I thought of that, don't worry. I've been frying it for forty minutes. Anything bad has been certainly been killed off. This goose is perfectly safe to eat, I promise."
In the living room, Steve and David weren't talking much. There was nothing to say and their kids never said anything of consequence, so there was no point in engaging them either.

"Wanna drink?" Steve asked.
David nodded.
Steve opened the top of a bottle of Captain Morgan rum and poured some into a dirty glass, there being no point in having spotlessly clean glassware anymore. He got up and handed the drink to David.

"It's been too long now," Steve said.
David nodded for a long time.

"Three months today," David finally said.
The two sat in silence, the only sound being the frying goose in the kitchen and an occasional scrape of a utensil in the pot. They used to have a fair amount of fun in this house, reading and drinking and, when the kids were asleep, smoking weed. It was boring now; methodical.

"I thought I heard a plane yesterday," Steve said. "I went outside but... I dunno. Maybe my ears were playing tricks on me. They have to send help by now. It's been too long."

"Three months," David repeated, flatly, staring at the floor, nursing his rum in his cold hands.

"You know, Dave. I don't think I can survive the winter," Steve said quietly.
He stared at David for a moment, before whispering in his direction.

"Do you ever think about just running away?"
Of course he had. The last few weeks had been intolerable. Kelly was in a permanent foul mood, and so

was he, although his pride prevented him from taking his half of the blame.

David took a deep breath and exhaled. He couldn't leave Kelly alone to fend for herself. They were a team and he loved her, but their marriage was at breaking point in this perpetual hell.

"It's never mentioned in prepper handbooks," David said.

"What is?" Steve replied.

"What a disaster does to your marriage."

Steve nodded.

"Sometimes I envy Jerry. He got out easy."

David hadn't forgotten about their dead neighbor, but never spoke of him.

"I buried him yesterday," Steve continued. "Out the back of his house."

That was unexpected news.

"You should have come got me. I could have helped."

"It's OK. We hang out enough as it is. I just wanted to be alone, away from all this, you know?"

David nodded. He understood perfectly.

Kelly and Maureen were having a similar conversation of their own.

"I do everything around the house now. Washing the clothes, cooking the food, everything," Kelly complained. "He just mopes around like a useless zombie."

Maureen nodded.

"He's no better," she replied, pointing an oily spatula in Steve's direction. "He just yells at the kids - well, not yells - you know what I mean, and he doesn't speak to me unless it's to complain. I do the laundry, I do the dishes, I cook the food, all by hand, and he just sits there."

The two sipped on rum, huddling close to the frying goose pieces in the saucepan, trying to absorb the food's warmth as it bubbled away.

"Can I tell you a secret?" Kelly asked, continuing before Maureen had the chance to say yes. "I sometimes think of just running away, you know?"

"But where would we go?"

"Ha," Kelly chuckled. "We? So you've thought about it too?"

Maureen seemed a little embarrassed, but Kelly was right.

"Yes, I've thought about it. But the kids, you know? I can't leave without the kids."

Maureen moved the piece of goose around the pot, the oil sloshing over it.

"Kelly... Do you..." Maureen's question trailed off.

"Do I what?" Kelly asked.

"Do you... ever regret not having kids?"

Kelly knew the answer, but didn't want to hurt Maureen's feelings.

"You're a wonderful mother. But kids aren't for everyone. They weren't ever in our plan."

Maureen stared vacantly into the bubbling pot.

"I just... sometimes I wonder if it was all worth it."

She pushed the goose around with the spatula.

"Maybe it's just a case of the grass is always greener, but lately I've been questioning my choices in life."

"Maureen, you're not alone. It's perfectly natural, given our current situation."

"I know. I just sometimes... I think that... I missed out on a lot. I could have traveled the world. In college I dreamed that I'd see Europe. That I'd make love to some romantic French or Italian guy. Maybe Europe is all still OK? Maybe life is normal there. Not like here." Kelly nodded but didn't answer. What could she possibly say? She couldn't turn to Maureen and say "yes, you screwed up. You got knocked up by a boring lawyer. You had kids and missed out on travel, love and adventure." Of course she couldn't say that. After all, she was in the same situation.

"You still have time," Kelly said. "This situation can't go on forever. Help must be on its way. I mean it has to be. China or Russia or… I dunno, *Australia* must surely be coming to help us out by now. Any minute we're gonna see tanks or troops or something. This can't last forever."

The smell of the cooked goose was mouth-watering as Maureen placed a piece each on everyone's plate, hot oil pooling around each morsel. A scoop of cooked, white rice sat on each plate alongside the goose, with Maureen trying to hide its natural blandness with some dried herbs stolen from one of their neighbors several weeks ago. With the six of them sitting around the table, Maureen said grace.

"Come, Lord Jesus, be our Guest, and let these gifts to us be blessed. Amen."
A half-hearted "Amen" murmured around the table. Despite being dragged to church as children, neither David nor Kelly were very religious. Maybe they were alone in the universe, or maybe there was a higher power, they didn't know. If there *was* a higher power, however, they both would like a word in private with him or her, after enduring the last three months.

"Bon appétit," Maureen added, giving the green light for everyone to pick up their knives and forks in order to satiate their salivating mouths.

"Mmm," said Kelly, the first to put a piece in her mouth.

It was the most delicious thing she had eaten in weeks. A real, home-cooked meal with real meat.

"Oh, yeah. Well done, honey," Steve added.

"It's good," said David, enjoying it immensely, but keeping his words to a minimum.

No one spoke during the meal, all overwhelmed with the feeling of oily, cooked meat washing over their taste buds. Maureen was rightly pleased with herself for finding that goose before the animals got to it. She was a prim and proper housewife, but not scared to roll up her sleeves to pluck and gut a waterfowl for dinner. The kids were both grossed out by the procedure, of course, but given the lack of entertainment available, they even pitched in and helped prepare the goose, covering it in herbs.

The combination of goose and rum gently lightened the forlorn mood, and after dinner they sat on the sofa, talking about life before the pulse.

"You know what I miss the most?" asked Maureen. "Music."

The room nodded.

"Music was everywhere," she continued. "You couldn't escape it. But when it's gone. Lord above, what I wouldn't give to hear Huey Lewis and the News just one more time."

"Do you know my guilty pleasure?" Kelly asked. "Yanni."

"Oh, gosh. There's a name I haven't heard for ages," said Maureen. "He did that beautiful aria, what's it called?"

"Yes!" Kelly said, smiling. "It's called Aria!"

A moment of silence washed across the room, replaced with Maureen unexpectedly beginning to hum the chorus of Yanni's song. Kelly smiled and joined in. They didn't know the lyrics, but the melody was all that mattered. The living room came to life again that evening, the two women humming all they could remember from a happier time, the mood eliciting tears from Maureen's eyes. On the second time through the chorus, Steve began to tap a gentle drum rhythm on the coffee table and, fueled by the great Captain Morgan, even David felt the magic in that cold living room, allowing his embittered heart to open, music soothing the savage beast within his soul.

After Maureen and Kelly brought the song down and faded it out with softened humming, the four adults in the room quietly clapped, tapping their fingers on their palms, for what was undoubtedly the most beautiful three minutes of the last three months.

"Your turn, Dave," said Steve. "Give us a song." Dave pondered for a moment, before adjusting his pose on the sofa, impersonating someone driving a car. He shook his head around a little to get into character, and smiling, whispered, "Hiya Barbie! Hi Ken! You wanna go for a ride?"

Kelly reached over and hit his thigh, causing giggles around the room.

"Be serious," she pleaded.

"Alright, alright," he responded, his response giving himself an idea for a different song. Tapping his thighs, he began moving to his own beat, warming up to the intro.

"My baby don't mess around, 'cause she loves me so, this I know fo' surrre."

Maureen was lost, but Kelly started nodding, deciding to join in the next line.

"But does she really wanna, but can't stand to see me walk out tha' dooor."

Steve and the kids knew this one, even if they didn't
know the words, so they joined in, humming at the very
least.

"Don't try to fight the feeling, 'cause the thought
alone is killin' me right nooow."

Now the room was swaying, a mixture of humming and
soft singing.

"Thank God for Mom and Dad for sticking to together
like we don't know hooow."

With the room swaying, the mood light as a feather and
chorus just a single breath away, an almighty thump
impacted the roof above their heads. The room froze,
smiles instantly replaced with fear.

Steve signaled everyone to be silent, blowing out the
candle and placing his index finger to his lips.

"Someone must have heard us," he whispered.
"They might be trying to draw us out. Stay here, stay
down."

Steve got up quietly and grabbed his pistol from on top of
the living room shelf. David had his sitting on the table
next to the sofa. With guns safely in hand, Kelly huddled
down with Maureen and the kids as the two men felt their
way along the walls to the back door.

Steve and David paused by the door, giving their eyes a
moment to adjust to the pitch black outside, before
slowly turning the handle. The stillness of the nighttime
air allowed them both to listen intently for any sounds,
but the early winter night was lifeless. For all they knew,
there were guns pointed at them right now.

In the living room, Kelly and Maureen had the kids lying
in front of the sofa, down and away from the window to
improve their chances in a shoot-out, if need be.

David tapped Steve's shoulder and leaned in close to his
ear.

"Circle the house. I'll wait here."
Steve tapped David's shoulder twice; a sign of agreement, walking onto the now-overgrown grass, careful not to make a sound. David went closer to the treeline to listen for footsteps or breathing while Steve circled around to the front of the house, clockwise. Whoever it was, they had to be within projectile-throwing distance. With his gun aimed straight in front, David scanned the forested area behind the house while Steve continued towards the first corner of his home, each footstep being calculated and deliberate, acutely aware of the geography of his castle.
David waited, poised next to a tree at the back of Steve's section, listening intently, aware of his heart thumping hard in his chest. They've made it this far, they couldn't die now, he thought. The moment he heard any noise he was going to blow it away with his Desert Eagle.
Steve, meanwhile, edged around the front of his home straining his eyes across his darkened lawn and down towards the road, every tree forming a sinister shape in the grainy darkness. He crept, catlike around the front, eyes darting in all directions, reaching the third corner of his rectangular house.
He heard a noise.
It sounded vaguely like movement and breathing, just around the corner. He hoped it was David, but surely David wouldn't be dumb enough to come around the side of the house towards him while they were both armed in the dark. Steve had to trust David's sensibilities as he slid up against the edge of his house. Steve's head poked slowly around the corner of the house, his gun concealed. The treeline behind the house slowly came into view as his head slid further outward. With one eye, he scanned all he could see, but saw no movement. However he heard a noise again, sounding like a person breathing,

somewhere low, against the base of his house. As smoothly and quickly as possible, he moved the gun over to his left hand and slid further against the corner, allowing enough space for his left hand to slide out and extend, aiming at the intruder hunched up against his outer wall. It was hard to see, but it looked like a child. Are they using children to lure people out now, he wondered, not knowing if he should shoot, aware that whoever sent the obviously terrified child must be armed and watching. With his pistol aimed at the child, he took a breath and gathered the fortitude needed to protect his family.

"Don't. Move." he whispered.

The child continued breathing, wheezing.

"I won't hurt you," Steve whispered. "But don't move. Do you understand?"

The child didn't respond. What the fuck do I do now, he asked himself. He tried interacting with the child-sized person again.

"What's your name? I'm Steve."

There was no answer, just frightened breathing. Now what, he wondered.

David was aware that Steve was taking too long to loop around the house and he became worried, three or four minutes now passing. David backed away from the forest's edge and, gun still aimed towards the tree-filled darkness, walked sideways towards the first corner of the house, following Steve's route. After a minute of careful pacing, he saw Steve's silhouette against the far corner. He edged closer, not wanting to frighten Steve, who had clearly seen something. He crept closer, whispering "Steve" when he was just a few feet behind him. Steve jumped a little, but then backed towards him, turning to face David.

"It's a kid. He's not responding. He might be hurt."

"Decoy," Steve whispered back.

This meant that the actual perpetrator was somewhere out there in the darkness. They knew when they were outmaneuvered, with both deciding to retreat the way they came, backing into the house, quietly locking the door and feeling their way back to the living room. Steve's foot met with Kelly's waist as he slid back into the room, whispering to the group.

"People are outside. Can't see them. Kelly, Maureen, arm yourselves. Portia, Braxley, get down and don't make a sound."

Kelly got up and felt on the kitchen counter for the Glock 19, which had become hers since David had adopted the Desert Eagle. Maureen stumbled into the kitchen, opening the dishwasher with a click, retrieving the Glock G29 compact handgun which David had acquired at their midnight trip to the mall. Everyone took up positions around the living room, crouching on the floor, waiting.

They'd lost track of how long they'd been poised in a state of high alert in the living room. It was a sudden snort from Braxley snoring that gave everyone a hit of adrenaline and reminded them they were in a life and death situation. It was probably around 1 AM at that point and no activity had been heard for about three hours. It was a stand-off. David crawled over to Steve with an idea.

"We can't all stay up like this. We can take turns being on alert, OK?"

"Agreed."

"Alright, I'll stay awake as long as I can. You all move to the middle of the room and sleep. I'll come get you in about an hour."

"OK."

The sound of crows in the winter air replaced the morning silence as the first light of the day appeared in a paper-thin horizontal line under the back door. Steve, who was supposed to be on guard duty, was fast asleep, sitting against the hallway door frame. David bolted awake from a dream that got a little too close to reality, reminding him of the danger they were in, causing his system to flood him with adrenaline. It truly was the worst way to start the day, but much more effective than coffee.

David opened his eyes to see Steve sitting against the living room doorway, legs outstretched, mouth open, deep in a world of dreams. "This is what happens when you hire a lawyer to protect your family," he thought. He crawled over and touched Steve, who bolted awake in much the same way he had, 30 seconds earlier.

"What's happening?" Steve asked.

"I was about to ask you," David replied.

"Oh. Guess I dozed off a bit.'

"Ya think?"

"You reckon that kid's still outside?" asked Steve.

"We gotta find out," David answered, waking up Kelly and Maureen to watch the kids and get back on high alert.

The room organized itself and David and Steve approached the back door. They looked at each other, nodding seriously, both aware that such a Rambo-like gesture meant absolutely nothing. David instructed Steve to stay on the look out, while he was going left, around the side of the house. Steve nodded, slowly turning the doorknob, releasing them both into the crisp morning air. As David approached the corner of the house, he wondered if the child was still there on the other side. After all, if it was indeed a decoy, it would either have wandered back to its captor hours ago, or died of hypothermia. David braced himself and, holding his torso straight, slowly allowed one eye to peer around the perimeter of Steve's house, in the direction of the child. His eyes focused on the foreground in front of him. It took around one second for the object before him to translate into signals which his brain could interpret and recognize. He raised his eyes slightly upward, scanning the lawn and area down to the road, but it was empty. David dropped his eyes down again, focusing his attention on the object in front of him. He visibly relaxed and dropped his shoulders, breathing a long and world-weary breath, before turning around to Steve, who was facing the forested area behind the house, gun extended.

"Hey, Inspector Clouseau," he called out.
Steve turned to him, confused.
"Come here, you fucking dingus."
Steve began moving over, still on edge. David began to shake his head at Steve, sighing once again.
"Put your gun down, Steve. You're not gonna need it."
Steve approached the edge of the house and peered around to see what had taken three years off their lives through stress. David helped him out.
"It's a goose."
"It's a goose?" Steve asked.
"It's a goose," David confirmed.
"It's a goose!" Steve repeated, allowing himself a breathy laugh, mostly out of frustration.
David dropped his head down, exhausted, then moved towards the bird, touching it with his foot. It was a goner. Steve bent down and picked it up by its neck, inspecting it, before taking it inside.

"It's alright, everyone, no cause for alarm. It's a goose."

"A goose?" Kelly asked, confused.

"Yep, a goose," said Steve.

"What? It was a goose?" Maureen asked.

"It was a goose," David confirmed.

"Well... That's great!" said Maureen, perking up.

"That's... weird," added Kelly.

Maureen boiled water and put coffee in the French press, the dead goose sitting on the kitchen counter. Despite enduring a night of uncertainty and stress, there was still humor to be had.

"So I guess the butcher is still doing deliveries after all," Kelly chimed in from the sofa.

"That was a fowl attempt at humor," David shot back.

"Don't give up your day jobs, guys," said Steve from the sofa, feeling a little guilty that the feared child decoy turned out to have feathers.

'I dunno, I thought the jokes were pretty good," Maureen chimed in from the kitchen, adding "Me *goose*-ta those jokes."

"Well, they're not quacking me up," Steve added, immediately aware that ducks quack, not geese.

After they'd exhausted every possible goose-related pun, perhaps as an involuntary stress-relieving mechanism, the four adults and two children pontificated how the goose had come to hit their roof. No theory was considered too far-fetched as they searched for answers.

"Two geese in as many days, though. That's pretty weird," said Kelly.

"But they're migrating, no? Don't they migrate around this time of year?" asked Steve.

"Yeah, but when do you ever see them dead?" David asked.

"Well... Geese don't live forever," Maureen added, not entirely unhappy with the idea of another delicious serving of goose.

She wondered if this one would last long enough in the cold outdoor air to be cooked for Christmas, two weeks in the future.

"But they don't normally fall out of the sky," David responded.

"Maybe it was hit by a plane?" Steve added, optimistically. "Do you think they're sending planes now?"

"If a plane hit that goose it would be a mess, but look at it," David continued. "It's got a bloody beak, but otherwise it's fine."

The group sat in silence for a moment, pondering, while Maureen filled up four cups with hot coffee. They might be living in the Book of Revelation, but at least they still had fresh coffee.

"It must be sick. Why else would it be bleeding on its beak?" proposed Kelly.

"That could be from hitting the roof," Maureen suggested.

"If it *is* sick... Is anyone feeling unwell from dinner?" Steve asked.

Everyone looked at each other, for some reason scared to answer the simple question. Perhaps out of fear they'd all been poisoned.

"No," David said first.

"I feel fine," Kelly added.

"Me too, said Maureen.

"Good, me too," said Steve. "You guys feeling fine?" he asked Portia and Braxley. The kids were tired, but feeling normal.

"Well, that's all good then. This coffee tastes like pennies, though," Steve joked, adding, "So, goose for Christmas, then, huh?"

Chapter ten

Christmas

Christmas day was twelve hours away, but you'd not know it by looking out the window. The suburb was silent and the lawns overgrown and not a single home had Christmas decorations. Though the mood in David and Kelly's house was beginning to be positive again, if only briefly, caused by the distraction of preparing for a Christmas get-together with Steve and Maureen.

A week prior, the two had decided to decorate the inside of the house; something they were both acutely aware was fairly pointless, but at the very least it gave them something to do and created an atmosphere of expectation. Anything to break the monotony.

David and Kelly had tried to mend the cracks in their relationship by talking each evening about what personal issues they were having and how they could create plans to work through them, but this wasn't an easy task, given that the issues were shared.

Distractions, therefore, became essential to their survival. In the spare room, David continued tinkering on his homemade crystal radio, sadly without success, apart from hearing an occasional crackle, while Kelly converted the spare room to a darkroom in the evening, enlarging and developing her rolls of film from the last few weeks. She'd been busy photographing anything and everything since the pulse, with her plan being to hold a photo exposition if normality ever returned. She'd also

been busy developing and enlarging a photo for
Christmas day at Steve and Maureen's house, with the
plan being to give the photo to their neighbors as a
Christmas gift.

David had also turned his hand to baking, creating
Christmas pot brownies in a makeshift oven outside using
bricks, a risky thing to do, with smoke from the fire
visible to anyone who walked nearby. This risk meant
that Kelly was employed as both his bodyguard and
spectator while he encouraged a small fire to burn in the
winter air behind their house.

The colder, northerly winter winds also meant a few dead
birds lay around their section every now and then,
something to which they had became accustomed, with
scavenging cats and other animals quickly removing the
dead creatures like nature's vacuum cleaners.

Kelly had also been keeping a journal of their lives,
something she thought might compliment her photos
when, or if, life ever returned to normal. The biggest
problem she faced was trying to find things to write
down. Daily life was mostly reading books, eating and
sharing chores such as washing clothes or dishes.
Tomorrow, December 25, offered them a welcome reason
to shake up their routine.

In the living room, David took a bite of a pot brownie
which he had baked earlier in the day. It was a little bland
and he'd added a touch too much baking soda, making it
slightly bitter, but it wasn't the worst thing he'd ever
eaten. He put the rest in his mouth and chewed, happy
with its moistness, thanks to the cooking oil which took
the place of butter. He thought about how much he
missed cheese and dairy products; with powdered milk
offering a pretty poor replacement for the real thing.

"It was milk, then it wasn't, then it was milk again," he thought, amusing himself with his philosophizing. Or perhaps that was just the weed.

Once night had fallen, Kelly got busy developing her last roll of film, which she had filled up with photos two weeks prior. She knew there were probably some decent photos on the roll, but part of her was also a little reluctant to see them, as they were taken during the lowest point in their relationship so far.

David knew not to open the door to the spare room while Kelly was working on her photos, as the light, even from a candle, could ruin the process. In the current boredom of their lives, he wanted to see how the process worked, but obviously couldn't. Although he once joined Kelly in the room while she narrated what she was doing in the pitch black, something which David found hilariously pointless. David, who still disliked the smell of the developing chemicals, was now finding himself excited whenever Kelly produced developed photos, hanging on a line over their bathtub. It was a welcome relief to see something new in the house.

Kelly placed her first, freshly developed negative into the enlarger and placed photographic paper on the base. David had replaced the enlarger's 110 volt lamp with a 12 volt lamp taken from a car headlight, powered by a car battery. It did the job remarkably well, and produced fine photographs, though once normality returned, Kelly told herself that she would take her negatives to one of the few remaining photo stores to have them all professionally enlarged.

Each photo she removed from the tray filled with chemicals took her back in time to the moment the photo was taken. She lifted up the next photo, dripping wet with fixer solution, and hung it on the length of fishing line which David had installed in the spare room. The photo dripping in her hands was of David's face. It was just before he yelled at her. This wasn't a photo she wanted to keep, but she realized its artistic value, amplified by the situation in which they were living.

"All done," Kelly said, carrying wet photos down the hallway to the bathroom, hanging them up over the bathtub.
David got up, candle in hand, and walked into the bathroom as Kelly delivered another two photos, using clothespins to hold them up. David held the candle a little closer and leaned in, looking at the faces staring back at him.

"This one's cool," he said, his face inches away from a photo of himself mixing pot brownies in the kitchen. "But there are no photos of you," he added, aware that she was always behind the camera and not in front of it.

"They're a bit dark," he added.

"Yeah, I know. I think my chemicals are getting stale. Or that car battery is getting flat."
Kelly was a perfectionist when it came to her craft of photography, so the darker photos annoyed her, more than she was letting on.

"Merry Christmas," Maureen announced, opening the rear door and inviting Kelly and David inside.

"Merry Christmas," Kelly responded cheerfully, a large, flat gift in her hand, wrapped in a blanket.

"We come bearing gifts," David added, four pot brownies on a plate in his hands.

"Hey, come on in, guys," Steve announced from the decorated living room.

"Make yourselves comfortable," Maureen continued. "The goose is almost done."
David squeezed past them and headed to the living room, shaking Steve's hand.

"Can I help with anything?" Kelly asked Maureen.

"It's pretty much all done here. Grab yourself a drink. And you can fill mine up while you're at it."
Kelly poured some brandy into Maureen's glass.

"Cheers!" they said, clinking glasses and talking of the day's events.
Steve and David did the same in the living room, while Braxley and Portia amused themselves, drawing pictures on paper by candlelight. It almost felt like a normal Christmas.

"Oh my God. This is delicious," said Kelly, putting another a piece of oily goose into her mouth. "I don't know if it's possible, but it's even better than last time!"

"It's really good, Maureen," David added. "Thank you for going to all this trouble."

"Oh, it's nothing," Maureen responded. "It gave me something to do today."

"It's not bad," said Steve. "Tastes a bit like pennies, but not bad."
David let out a chuckle.

"It does *not* taste like pennies," Maureen added, somewhat offended.
David tried to change the subject.

"I've got an after dinner surprise. You all saw the brownies, but there's something else we're gonna enjoy after this meal, which is delicious, by the way. Don't listen to Steve."
Maureen smiled in appreciation.

"Thank you, Dave. Now, what's the surprise?"
she asked.

David was no good with keeping surprises a secret, so he
announced it at the dinner table.

"I brought over four cigars. I've been hanging
onto them since Steve and I went to the mall."

"Oh, dude. You're a legend," said Steve, who
imagined the sweet taste of a hand-rolled tobacco leaf
and dense smoke on his tongue.

Normally none of them smoked, but considering the
rarity of cigars, it was something they were going to
enjoy, no matter what.

"And I have something special for you both,"
Kelly added.

"And a little something for you guys too," she
said, turning to Portia and Braxley. The kids were excited
with this news.

Steve put down his fork and picked up his glass, golden
brandy swirling at its base.

"I wanna make a toast," he said. One at a time,
each of the four adults picked up their glasses and held
them off the table. Steve looked around at his dinner
guests.

"Here's to good friends. And the future."

"To good friends and the future," the table
chanted back, clinking their glasses.

Braxley and Portia were hyperactive after dinner,
something to which Maureen and Steve were immune,
but something which made David and Kelly
uncomfortable.

"Sit down, guys," David told the kids, climbing
over the the furniture.

Normally, in modern America, telling another person's
unruly child to be quiet or calm down would be a great

insult to the parents. Of course it never used to be that
way, but parenting in the Land of the Free had somehow
become less about teaching right and wrong in a
functional society, and more about child worship. Parents
bowed and swayed to their child's every whim, creating
entitled, free-range brats, as a visit to any mall food court
could attest.

Fortunately, Steve and Maureen had become so close to
Kelly and David, that they didn't mind them
reprimanding their kids. If anything, it meant they didn't
have to.

"I wanna brownie!" Portia demanded, her shrill,
eight year old voice getting on Kelly's nerves.

A wicked thought entered her mind. She wondered if she
could get away with tearing a chunk of pot brownie off
her own and giving it to Portia. "Would that harm her? Is
that legal?" she thought to herself, realizing the absurdity
of the question the moment it appeared as a notion. There
were no laws anymore, not even moral ones. She kinda
did want to see a stoned kid, though. Especially one with
such a stupid name. It would be hilarious. Kelly thought
for a second. "No," she told herself. "Grow up."

She stuffed the rest of the brownie into her mouth, to
Portia's disgust, her eight year old face screwing up into
a pout.

"These are for adults," Maureen told her. The girl
crossed her arms and walked over to the presents on the
floor.

"Can we open the presents now?" she asked.

"Yeah, can we?" added Braxley, looking up from
his drawing; a rocket ship flying past a crater-filled
planet.

"Yeah, whatta you guys think?" Steve asked the
room. "Presents then cigars?"

"Sounds like a plan to me," David said, the two women nodding.

"Oh, Kelly," Maureen said sincerely. "It's great. Really, really great."
The two kids clambered over the sofa to get a better look at what Maureen was holding. It was a large photo of their family, taken two weeks earlier. The individuals in the photo weren't doing anything remarkable, just sitting on the sofa, but the fact that it was an actual photograph in her hands, taken after the pulse, made it incredibly special.

"We used to take photos for granted," Maureen said, staring into the photograph. "They were like music. They were everywhere. Now they're so precious."
She looked up at Kelly.

"I remember when I was a kid, when someone in the family would go on a trip somewhere, they'd come back and we'd sit together in their living room, passing the photos around in a circle."

"We did that too!" Kelly replied.

"Hmm," Maureen pondered. "You know, photos seemed to have more value back then. But then digital photos and Facebook came along and... I don't know, we just got saturated with photos. Everyone has a camera in their pocket."

"Not anymore," Steve added.

"Exactly!" Maureen continued. "Photos are valuable again. At least until normality returns."
Maureen passed the photo to Steve, who studied it. He reached over and picked up the candle to see it better.

"I'm sorry it's so dark," Kelly said. "All of my photos from that roll of film came out dark. Some were a little splotchy too. I guess my chemicals are going stale."

"It looks good to me, Kel," Steve replied.

"I love it. I really mean it. Thank you so much," added Maureen.

"And this is for you guys," Kelly said to Braxley and Portia, handing them a Snickers bar each from her bag.

"Ohhhhh, what do you say?" Steve asked his children.

"Thank you," they replied in unison, holding their Christmas gifts in their hands, better than any Playstation game or toy, given the circumstances.

"Can I eat it now?" Braxley asked his mom.

"Alright, but don't get hyped up," said Maureen, the kids tearing open the wrappers and stuffing their faces.

"Eat it slowly," Steve said. "Make it last."

The flame of the candle washed over the end of the cigar as Kelly sucked in breaths of air, using only her mouth. Clouds of smoke became visible and the end of her cigar glowed red as she passed the candle to Maureen, the four of them standing out the back of the house. The visible flame from the candle put them at risk of being seen from anyone in the forested area near them, but they were all armed, just in case. It had become a rule that any time one of them had to go outside, whether to empty the piss bucket or do the washing, they had a gun with them. The nutty, sweet cigar smoke rolled over their tongues.

"Mine tastes a bit off," Steve whispered. "Like smoking a galvanized nail. Where did you store these?"

"In the pantry," David whispered. "Though the house has been sealed up to try and keep the cold out, so the cooking has made everything pretty damp."

"Mine tastes alright," Kelly whispered in the still night air, the sky full of stars.

"The stars never used to shine this brightly," Maureen whispered. "There was always so much light from street lights and the city."

The four of them looked up. A pale white dot moved across the sky.

"Satellite," Steve said, pointing with his cigar. They followed it with their eyes until it slowly disappeared out of sight, behind the trees. Maybe it was a communications satellite and people somewhere on the planet were using it to talk to each other. Or, maybe no one was was. Either way, it was a reminder of their isolation.

Chapter eleven

Revelation

Kelly organized her photographs chronologically, writing the date and approximate time of when each photo was taken on the back, in pencil. To save her limited supply of photographic paper, she only enlarged the ones she felt were the best or the most dramatic. This meant she had around a hundred photos which would have to remain trapped as negatives, until the rescue happened, whenever that might be. If at all.

"Babe, you busy?" Kelly asked David.

"Oh yeah, flat out," he said, sarcastically.

It was a silly question.

"I could use your help. I'm organizing my negatives. Let's go outside."

With a pen and a sheet of paper in hand, Kelly collected her shoe box of negatives and stepped into the back yard, the winter air just as cold as it was inside. David came out behind her and they sat down on a couple of lawn chairs, the daytime sun shining above them, and a frozen bird, lying dead in the overgrown grass beside them. Kelly held a negative up above her head, squinting at it.

"This was during the first week," she commented. "Your hair looked good, babe."

She passed the strip of negatives over to David who began studying the first one, featuring himself, green skinned with two white eyes and bright white hair.

"Even as a negative I looked better then. I've lost weight."

He paused, studying that moment in history, looking at a younger, naïve version of himself.

"Have you got the negatives from yesterday?" he asked.

Kelly looked into the box on her lap, touching the strips of negatives.

"Here it is," she said, passing it to David.

"Shit, I looked grumpy," he said, looking at himself on the sofa when he was staring angrily at the living room floor.

"Oh, you *were*," replied Kelly, picking up her pen.

"These ones are pretty pale," he added.

Kelly stared at the negatives in her hand, taken some weeks prior. She paused, absorbing what David had said.

"Pale?" she asked.

"Yeah, this one," he said, pointing to the second negative in the strip. "It's kinda whited out."

"That's weird," Kelly responded. She studied the other negatives in the strip. They were also more pale than normal. This was the first time she'd studied them in bright daylight.

"I never noticed that before. I thought it was the fixer that caused the photos to be dark."

"What does the fixer do?" David asked.

"It's used in the last stage of developing. You dip the finished photo into it and it removes the silver halide from the paper. I thought it had gone bad."

"I don't follow," said David.

"Well, I thought the photos I made a couple of days ago were dark because the fixer had gone bad. But it's the negatives that've gone wrong, not the positives.

They must have been exposed to light. What a pain in the ass."

Kelly studied the negatives, running her eyes over them all.

"It doesn't make sense," she continued.

"What doesn't?" David responded.

"The bleaching. It's even."

"OK," David said, getting bored with the conversation, seeing as photography was never a terribly interesting topic for him, pornography aside.

"I mean, if light got in there somehow, like if I opened the back of the camera, or if daylight came through the curtain during developing, maybe a few frames would be ruined, but not the whole lot."

"Well, it can't be daylight that's the problem if you always do your developing at night."

"Yeah."

"Maybe the original roll of film was bad?" David suggested.

"That's never happened before," Kelly replied. She studied the negatives closely, annoyed that she'd lost some good photos for an unknown reason.

"Photoshop," David said. "When we get rescued, you can fix the photos with Photoshop."

Kelly wasn't really listening.

"Look here," she said. These ones have splotches."

David leaned in, looking through the negative.

"I don't get it. I was so careful," Kelly said, a defeated tone in her voice. "Somehow, light radiation has got in there before I could develop the negatives."

It was the combination of the words 'light' and 'radiation' together that stuck out in David's mind. It was like the word 'tunafish'. He always thought it was pointless to add the word 'fish' to the end of the word 'tuna'. Of course it was a fish, he thought. It's hardly going to be a 'tunabird'. He chuckled to himself, the dead bird in front of them unable fly like a living bird or swim like a tunabird.

Kelly continued to study the negatives, while David pondered light, and where it sat on the scale of electromagnetic radiation. Visible light, after all, is a form of electromagnetic radiation, just like radio waves. Yet, the light we see occupies just a tiny part of the entire spectrum. Visible light sits below non-ionizing radiation like microwaves, and above harmful, ionizing radiation, such as X-rays or gamma rays from nuclear waste.

At that very moment, some dots began to join in David's mind. This was quickly followed by a sudden chilling sensation which washed through David's very being.

His eyes changed from staring vacantly at the trees to being intently focused. David quickly looked down at the grass, studying the small bird lying dead on the ground. He frowned in frustration, thinking a dozen thoughts at once, but none of them good. He got up from his chair suddenly and stood in the sun, moving towards the dead bird, looking at it intently. This sudden movement surprised Kelly, and she looked up at him in confusion, but David looked deadly serious.

"The birds," he said flatly, his eyes moving in deep thought.

Kelly had stopped fishing around in the shoe box for another line of negatives to compare and stared at her husband, who was now acting erratically.

"The birds," David repeated, scanning the lawn.

"What about the birds?" she asked.

David spun around to face Kelly.

"They're dead."

Kelly frowned.

"Yes. Your point being?"

It was evident on David's face that was wasn't trying to be funny. A few seconds of silence followed.

"You're scaring me, Dave."

His eyes darted around. He turned back to the bird on the ground, then spun back around to Kelly. He was breathing quickly.

"Get inside."

He jumped forward towards Kelly.

"Get inside!"

David ran for the door, Kelly getting up too, her box of negatives in her hands.

"Get inside!" he shouted again, Kelly now rushing in behind him.

"Babe, talk to me," she said, standing in the hallway.

"The birds," he said, now panicking.

"David, what's going-"

"The film," he said, talking over her and pointing repeatedly at her negatives. "Can radiation affect film?"

"Well... Maybe. I guess so," answered Kelly.

"Chernobyl," he said, still pointing at the box of negatives in her hands. "After Chernobyl, the workers wore radiation badges. They were made of film. Like, normal camera film."

Kelly stood in the hallway, processing this information.

"Are you saying the birds have been killed by radiation?"

David stared at her, scared to say yes. Kelly's eyes looked down the hall to the spare room.

"My God. My photos. The bleached negatives. And Steve! Steve said he tasted metal. Pennies. Remember?"

"Yes. And the cigar," David added. "He said it was like nails."

"Shit. I thought he was joking," Kelly replied.

"Me too. But remember that Chernobyl documentary. They said that some people tasted metal after the meltdown. People who had liver problems."

"Jesus Christ," Kelly said, both of them standing in the hallway, unsure of what to do.

"But where's it coming from?" Kelly asked.

"I don't know!"

Filled with thought, they stood motionless.

"Wait. The power station," David said. "How far away is the closest nuclear power station?"

Kelly stared at the wall, thinking.

"North Anna nuclear power station. About a hundred miles north of here," she answered.

"My God," David said. "It all makes sense. I never thought of it. The pool. The spent fuel pool. They store all the used nuclear rods in the water to keep it cool… Jesus. It's been months. The water must have all evaporated or boiled away by now."

"Of course," Kelly responded, nodding, her mouth ajar. "But why are we only seeing dead birds now?"

"I don't know. That first goose. Maureen said she saw it, what, three weeks ago? Geese migrate for winter and they must have flown over the power station." He looked back at Kelly.

"Winter," he continued. "In winter we get northerlies. The wind changes and blows down this way."

"Shit," said Kelly. "The Geiger counter!"

David shook his head hurriedly.

"It's fried."

"Try it again anyway!"

David was now starting to panic.

"OK. Uh… OK. I'll try it now. You… get in the bath! Wash yourself, right now! Don't touch your

clothes. Wash every part of you and rinse off with emergency water. I'll try the Geiger counter."
Kelly stood in front of him, not quite believing this was happening.

"Go!" David shouted.
Kelly bolted into action and ran to the bathroom, taking off her clothes, while David darted into the spare room. He dropped to the ground and opened the disused microwave with the Geiger counter sitting inside. Fumbling with batteries again, he pushed a fresh set into the back and turned it over, holding down the power button on the front. Nothing happened.
The sound of splashing water came from down the hall.

"Fuck! It's freezing!" came a shivering voice, gasping for air.

"It doesn't work!" David shouted. "It's still broken!"
David dropped the Geiger counter on the ground and started removing his endless layers of winter clothes as he ran into the bathroom. He had to wash any radioactive particles off himself, if any were on him. Kelly was standing naked in the bathtub, shivering, rubbing a bar of soap over herself frantically. Even in a crisis, David found himself aroused at the sight of her naked body, something he hadn't seen for days due to the temperature inside the house. Kelly frantically worked a soapy lather over herself, the suds collecting on her breasts, her nipples hard and pronounced due to the cold. She was beautiful. David tore at his pants, dropping them to the floor.

"Seriously?" She said, incredulously. "You're getting hard *now*?"
David didn't respond, aware there was no time for intimacy. He climbed into the bath and poured icy water over himself, causing his lungs to fight for air.

"Soap," he said.

Kelly passed the bar to him. She reached down to the bathroom floor and sparingly poured cold water over herself, washing soap from her hair and face, the suds sliding between her legs on their downward journey. David rubbed the soap over himself while Kelly got out, shivering. With numb hands she tried to dry herself with the towel hanging on the rail.

"Get dressed. Wear clothes that have been stored for ages. Nothing that's been hanging outside," he instructed, while he began rinsing himself.

"Where are we gonna go?" Kelly asked, standing with wet hair in the bedroom, putting on clothes. David rushed in and started getting dressed himself.

"I don't know. But we have to get away from here."

"What about Steve and Maureen?"

"I don't know," David repeated, shivering.

"We have to tell them!"

David's hair, poorly cut by Kelly the previous week, was longer in some parts than others and it was still dripping wet. He rubbed it vigorously with the towel.

"I don't want to scare them," David said.

Kelly pulled jeans up over her thermal leggings, fastening up her button fly. She reached for another sweater to put on top of the sweater she was already wearing.

"But they have to know," she continued. "Signal them. You know you have to tell them."

David sat on the bed, trying to put on a pair of socks with cold, numb fingers.

"We can't take them with us," he said.

Kelly knew he was right. The kids would slow them down. But they couldn't just *leave* them.

"But they have to know. They need to know," she demanded. "Tell them now."
David jogged down the hallway to the kitchen and connected a wire on their rudimentary communication system to the positive terminal on the car battery sitting on the counter. He pushed the button frantically for ten seconds and waited.
The 12 volt lamp next to him sat dead. He didn't want to rush over to their house, partly because he didn't wish to be outside for a second longer than necessary, but also because he couldn't bear to see Steve and Maureen fear for their kids' lives.
He pressed the button frantically again, pushing it about forty times. Finally, his lamp illuminated, a beautiful, long glow, which meant they were ready to receive a message. David grabbed the piece of paper which had their version of Morse code, and tried to push the button as calmly as possible, his hands shivering.

"What're they saying?" Portia asked, watching her mother with a pen and paper, ready to write.
"Nothing yet, sweetheart," she replied.
"Oh, here we go."
The lamp pulsed, followed by a pause, then a couple more flashes, and another pause.
"S... T... A... um, what's that one. Dot dot dash?"
Portia studied the paper.
"G."
"Good girl. You're a smart one," Maureen said, patting Portia's head.
"I... N... S... I... D... E..."
"What are they saying, mommy?"
Maureen's face was one of confusion.

"Honey," she called out to Steve. "Come here a minute."

David called out to Kelly, who was busy filling up the backpack with essentials, still unsure of where they could go.

"I told them to stay inside. They flashed that they got the message. Do I tell them about the radiation?" Kelly ran past David and into the kitchen, opening the pantry, looking for their last two chocolate bars.

"I don't know," she said, getting out of breath. "I've got to get the map."
David waited by the lamp and push button in case they replied. Kelly rushed past him and ran into the spare room, grabbing the crumpled map of Virginia off the shelf. She turned and hurried back to the kitchen, putting it on the counter.

"It'll be faster if we take the bikes, wherever we go," Kelly said.

"The suits. Go put on a hazmat suit," he told Kelly. "And get the masks."
Kelly disappeared into the spare room again opening boxes in search of the bright white hazmat suits they ordered off Amazon a couple of years ago.

"Found them," she called out.

"They're not replying," said David.

"OK. Then come and put on a suit."
David darted down to the spare room and put on a bright white hazmat suit, leaving only a hole where their faces poked through.

"We'll be seen from a mile away wearing these," he said, staring his neon white sleeves. "Didn't they have black ones?"

"Honestly, it wasn't high on my priority list when I ordered them," Kelly replied. "Just be glad I didn't order the bright yellow ones."

"We're gonna have to change these often," David said. "Stuff spares in the backpack. And get the guns and ammo."

"Guns are already in the living room."

"Good. Now grab anything useful."

Kelly and David rushed from room to room looking for anything which could be useful when preparing to leave the relative safety of their home.

"Do you think we've got everything?" Kelly asked.

"I dunno, I dunno," David responded, nervously. "But we need to figure out where we're going."

Dressed as white as snow, the two ran down the hallway and toward the kitchen, where they came face to face with Steve, armed with a kitchen clever. All three of them yelped in surprise.

"What the fuck are you guys doing?!" Steve shouted.

"What the fuck are *you* doing?" Kelly yelled back.

Steve looked at the two, dressed in white hazmat suits. A couple of seconds passed as they all looked at each other.

"You said you had meat!" said Steve, now confused.

"...What?!" David replied, shaking his head and screwing up his face in confusion.

"A stag. One of you messaged that you'd caught a stag."

Kelly looked at David, whose forehead was furrowed in confusion.

"I told you to stay inside!" David snapped back.

Now it was Steve's turn to be confused.

"Guys. What the hell's going on?" he said.

No one spoke for a moment. Kelly knew she had to say something.

"Steve. The birds. The dark photos. You said you tasted metal. We've figured it out. It's radiation. It's got to be. The nuclear plant must be melting down."

"North Anna?"

"It has to be."

"But that's, what, a hundred and twenty miles away."

"The wind is blowing down this way."

Steve paused, taking it all in.

"My God. Are... Are we in danger?"

"We don't know," David answered. "My Geiger counter doesn't work. Kel and I are getting the fuck outta here."

"Jesus Christ." Steve looked around the room, shock being replaced by fear. "Where are you gonna go?"

"We don't know. We were going to plot a course right now."

"You're going in the daylight?"

"I guess so. We have no choice. We're gonna take our bikes now as I don't think we can't ride at night."

"Go home, Steve," Kelly said. "Go look after your family."

"And stay inside, no matter what," David added. "Don't drink any water. Seal up your doors and windows. Go and shower and throw away the clothes you're wearing."

David remembered something.

"Steve. Hang on."

David rushed down the hall and into the spare room, grabbing boxes of iodine tablets.

"Take one a day. Everyone in your house takes one a day, got it?"

Steve nodded, then paused, unsure of what to do next. It was all too much to take in.

"Go!" David ordered. "I'll signal you when I know where we're going."

Steve turned around, intending to leave.

"Wait," Kelly said. She stepped toward Steve and hugged him. David stepped in and hugged them both, the three of them embracing in the cold, silent kitchen. It might be the last time they ever saw each other again.

Chapter twelve

Flee

Kelly studied the map intently, using a ruler and a pen to draw lines, while David spoke to Steve via their improvised communication system.

"We can't go inland; too many crazies. And it's too dangerous to go north. Can't go south either as we'd be in the path of the fallout," Kelly said.

It was the first time David had heard the word 'fallout' used outside of a documentary, computer game or band name.

"It's gonna take two or three days. That's two or three days' exposure if the wind keeps blowing this way," she added.

"Where are we going?"

She paused. This was the first time she'd slowed down in an hour.

"You're not gonna like it," she said.

"Tell me."

"Well, I've looked everywhere, and our safest route is east."

"OK. How far?"

Kelly looked up at him and they met each other's gaze.

"All the way."

"To the sea?" David asked, his eyes widening.

Kelly nodded.

"Fuck me. How far is that?"

Kelly read out her notes.

"I reckon we've got to ride our bikes about a hundred miles. After that, we take creeks and rivers for another hundred or so."

David stared at Kelly blankly.

"It's too far. We'll never make it."

"It's far, but it's the only way out of the path of the fallout with the winds blowing this way."

"Two hundred miles?!"

"Do you have a better idea?" Kelly asked.

They stared at each other, before David turned around and looked at the button in front of him. He messaged the word "W… A… I… T…" to Steve and, disheartened, slumped down to the floor.

"We'll never make it," David said, a voice coming from the kitchen floor. "We can't carry that much food or water, and even if we did, someone will kill us both."

"I don't have any other alternative."

"What if we stayed here? Maybe the radiation's not that strong?" David asked, knowing full well that it can't be safe if it's affecting camera film.

Kelly paused.

"David. Maybe it was just a one off caused by the wind, but maybe it's not. I mean, if it's affecting film, and if Steve could taste it, then it might already be too late."

They sat in silence for a couple of minutes, both aware that they could be being irradiated in their own home at that instant.

David climbed to his feet and leaned towards the push button on the kitchen counter, pressing it a few times.

The light illuminated almost immediately afterward.

David began pressing the button, pulsing it slowly with his index finger.

"G… O… I… N… G… T… O… S… E… A…"
About a minute passed before the light came back on
solidly, meaning Steve and Maureen had received the
message. They could only imagine the fear in that
household right now. It took another minute before a
response appeared in their kitchen, letter by letter.
"G… O… D… S… P… E… E… D…"

David brought their bicycles into the house and loaded
them up with as much gear as they could hold. They'd
taken iodine tablets to protect their thyroid glands, but
had no idea if it was pointless or not. David was anxious,
wanting to get out of the house right away, but it was
Kelly who suggested they wait until it got dark,
considering their paper-white overalls. It made sense,
even though it meant gamma radiation could already be
altering their DNA and sending them to early graves.
Kelly didn't mention it to David, but she hoped that, if
they did die, someone would find her negatives and
journal, and would write a book about their experiences;
their triumphs and tragedies, their love and loss.

At around 6 PM, with their hazmat overalls and gas
masks, they closed the door to their house, leaving it
unlocked, and pushed off down the street. With their
stomachs full of water, peanut butter and dried fruit to
offer hydration and calories, they were now at the mercy
of whatever lay ahead.

Riding quickly through the suburbs, avoiding the dark
metal boxes in their way which appeared to be vehicles,
they headed southeast towards Rustburg. Using nothing
but the light of the stars, they were going to try and travel
the ten hour bike ride through the night, as impossible as

it seemed. It would only take one problem to throw their plan into chaos, and it was inevitable that, on such a journey, problems would be abundant. David wanted to save two miles by riding on the highway northeast through Lynchburg, with the flatter, smoother roads also saving half an hour of travel time, but Kelly advised it was probably safer to take the side roads instead. Yes, it would take longer and the roads would be twistier, but they wouldn't have to ride through a gridlocked 'ghost highway', full of vandalized cars, broken glass and the threat of desperate, armed people.

It was two full hours by the time they'd joined up to Richmond Highway, having traveled just twenty meager miles. Their masks constantly fogged up and they were already exhausted, but at least the highway was smoother and their journey from here on was more downhill than up; dropping down around six hundred feet in altitude to get to their destination: a river, named Deep Creek. Once on the highway they were thankfully able to ease the exertion of their riding a little, moving at a slower pace, using the oncoming lane, which was almost empty of cars.

For a brief moment, near the unusually named township of Farmville, David and Kelly felt like they might actually make it to the river in one night. The burning pain in their legs had morphed into a manageable, chronic ache, and they were now beyond halfway to their destination. The combination of exhaustion and a brief flirtation with the thought of potential success spurred David to take off his mask and breathe in the icy nighttime air, if just for a moment. After all, he thought, it's like smoking one cigarette: it might harm you, but it won't kill you. Kelly saw David breathing the crisp, potentially poisoned air and felt immediate jealousy. She wanted to tell him to put the mask back on, but realized such a demand would be more to quell her sense of envy than to protect David's health. She gave in and removed her own mask, joining him in his guilty pleasure.

"God, the air feels so good. So clean," Kelly said, immediately aware that it probably wasn't.
It was also good to be able to finally talk to one another.

"It's good to actually see again," David said, following the dark path in front of him, the night sky forming a stunning ceiling of black velvet and glitter.
It was almost beautiful.
Their riding had slowed as they took in the scene above them, David's head aimed skywards, as he rode straight into an abandoned car.

"David!" Kelly cried out as David tumbled onto the road, wheezing in pain.
He didn't wear a helmet; there was no way to do so while wearing the suit and mask. Kelly dropped her bike to the ground and ran to him, her legs feeling like jelly.

"Are you OK?" she asked, as all people do when they don't know what else to say to someone who's hurt themselves. David crawled around on the ground, wheezing, wincing in pain.

"David," Kelly said, holding him.
Unexpectedly, he started crying. It was a strange sight for Kelly to observe; the silhouette of her husband, sobbing. It was also strange to hear the sound of crying in David's voice because he so rarely cried, like most men. It became clear to Kelly that David was hurt, but more emotionally than physically.

"Let it out," Kelly whispered to him, his body shaking with tears. She reached over and brushed his cheek with her hand.

"We'll be OK," she added. "I love you... And we're a team."

She wanted to ask if he was hurt badly, aware of the noise they'd generated over the last two minutes, but chose to let him get whatever burden he was carrying out of his system. In the minute that followed, Kelly wondered why he'd started to cry now, of all times. Was it his pride which had taken a hit? It's odd, she thought, because he seemed happy at the time of the accident. Perhaps it was the straw that broke the camel's back. Crying's healthy, she thought. Why didn't David do it more often. She even wondered if that was why men died sooner than women, or why they killed themselves more, or why they were more violent than women. The solution was simple, she thought. Tears. They wash away the pain in one's heart, even though they were socially unacceptable, at least for men.

David calmed down, his emotional outburst causing him to feel embarrassed. As he often did, David employed humor as defense mechanism.

"I didn't get his license plate."

Kelly let out a gentle laugh.

"Are you hurt?"

David reached up and rubbed his scalp.

"I hit my head... On the car's hood."

Kelly ran her fingers through his hair and felt for any blood or damage. There was a sizable bump, but his head was dry.

"I think," David said, pausing. "I think my ego took the biggest hit."

"It's alright, babe," Kelly replied, softly.

She paused, before saying something that would cause David to be embarrassed again.

"I never see you cry."

David looked down. Talking about his emotions, for most males, caused him to retreat into his shell or divert the conversation with humor.

"Can you still ride? Is your bike OK?" Kelly asked.

David ran his fingers over the bike, feeling the tautness of the chain. He squeezed both tires with his fingers to ensure they still had air in them, and briefly spun the wheels.

"Shit," he said.

The front wheel was bent.

"Is it bad?" Kelly asked.

"The front wheel is buckled. It still has air and it spins, but it's curved to the side."

She didn't ask the obvious question, whether or not he could still ride it. That would become apparent soon enough. David spun the front wheel again, its rim audibly rubbing against the brakes each time it turned.

"If it still rides, I gotta remove the front brakes. If I don't, everyone will hear me," he said, reaching over to open the bike repair kit in a zipped pouch under the bike's seat.

He took out a bunch of hex keys and felt in the dark for the socket which would allow him to unscrew the braking caliper mechanism. He fumbled for about thirty seconds, unsuccessfully.

"I can't find the damn hole."

"That's a first for you," Kelly joked, her turn to employ humor to lighten the mood.

It worked, causing David to chuckle quietly in the starlight, the frame of a cold bicycle on his lap.

"Got it," he announced, turning the key a dozen or so times, followed by the sound of a small nut hitting the highway asphalt. He reached into his bag to find the roll of duct tape they'd brought with them, tearing off a piece which he used to hold the brake caliper out of the way of the wheel's spokes.

"We should try moving," David announced.

"Hang on. Not yet."

Kelly crawled closer to David and turned around, leaning up against the abandoned car which had offered them both pain and an unexpected moment of bonding.

"I love you," she said, squeezing his hand.

"You know I love you too, babe" David answered. "You're my everything."

Their breathing calmed and the night sky above them glistened as they drank water and scooped out the remaining peanut butter from the plastic jar with their fingers.

Kelly couldn't quite see how badly David's bike was damaged, but it was evident by his pale white silhouette wobbling rhythmically that it was not an enjoyable experience for him. If they weren't fleeing for their lives, it would be a hilarious sight. Unfortunately this damage had slowed their progress to a jogging pace. They had their masks back on, and had changed into new hazmats suits.

"This is fucking impossible," David whispered to Kelly, riding behind him.

With David unable to move quickly, it was better for him to be in front.

"Just take your time," Kelly whispered back in a muffled voice, aware that they were falling behind schedule, and sunrise was just a few hours away. Providing they even made it to the river, Kelly was also justifiably concerned about what they'd do when they eventually got there. They couldn't wade or swim through the freezing water. They'd have to float, somehow, on something.

This worry shifted to the forefront of Kelly's mind, when the horizon in front of them began to glow gently, the sun burning its way towards them from somewhere over the Atlantic. The clear sky of the night had also begun to be replaced with clouds. Kelly was becoming concerned that they should have been at the river by now, but still had an unknown distance to travel ahead of them.

"Hang on," Kelly called to David.

The two of them came to a halt on the tree-lined country road that had replaced the highway. A road sign was just ahead.

David removed his mask, the cold, possibly poisoned air filling his lungs. God, it felt good to breath again though, he thought.

Kelly unzipped the front of her white suit and reached inside, removing the crumpled map of Virginia and turning it towards the horizon. It was still too dark to see the map clearly.

"I need to see where we are. It's getting light and we're gonna have to hide."

David realized that this meant they weren't going to make it to the river today. They'd have to be irradiated with gamma rays for another day. Was the pain in David's head caused by the accident some hours earlier, or was it cancer growing in his brain, he wondered.

Kelly looked around, checking the tree-lined road ahead and the bushes on either side, before holding up a cigarette lighter to the map and clicking a tiny flame into life. There wasn't much gas left in it.

"OK, it's not bad. That town ahead has to be Crewe," she said, her eyes just inches from the tattered wad of paper in her hand. "We should go around it to the east. The river has to be just the other side; maybe another couple of miles."

"But it's getting light. And we're in white. It'd be suicide. Should we hide here in the bushes or do you really think we'll make it before sun up?" asked an exhausted David.
Kelly paused, allowing the flame to vanish, her eyes not prepared for the darkness which replaced it.

"We've seen no one all night," she continued. "Maybe everyone's gone. Or dead. We should at least try. Masks on."
Kelly wiped the moisture from the inside of her gas mask with her finger and slipped it over her head, putting her weight on the bike pedal. She began to propel forward, past David, who did the same. They were so close they could taste it. Or was that the radiation?

"The river!" Kelly whispered loudly, pulling her bike to a stop, atop a small road bridge, a creek below them.
David wobbled up alongside, cold yet wet with sweat. It was now around 5 AM and the wintry gray sky was brightening. Panting, he removed his mask.

"Now what?" David asked, his eyes peering at the outline of the creek in the early morning light.
It was a damn good question. Kelly looked around. If only there was a boat prepared for them, full of blankets and food and drink. What a dream that would have been. She noticed the silhouette of a house on the other side of the road, down a long driveway.

"I don't know. Maybe we can hide there," she said, pointing to the house with a barn alongside.
David turned and stared at the direction in which she was pointing. There was indeed a house and a barn, but was it safe?

"Guns," said David. "And take these things off."
He pointed to his white overalls.

Kelly and David walked their bikes down the gravel driveway, sticking to the grass on either side to minimize noise. The dark clothing they had been wearing underneath their hazmat suits gave them a little more safety in the darkness, but not for long. There was a house, but they decided that the barn should be their destination. Kelly was silent, but desperately hoped that a miracle could occur and that they could find a boat inside with a working engine and a tank full of gas.

Approaching the wooden barn, they met an issue which had to be overcome. The large, wooden barn door had a padlock on the front, but the latch to which it was attached was affixed to the wooden frame with regular screws. David scanned the horizons and peered at the house nearby, while Kelly drew out her Swiss Army knife, selecting the Phillips head instrument. Raindrops began to patter the ground around them as she pressed hard, turning each screw an inch at a time.

"Rain," said David, a worried look on his face.

"Yes," said Kelly, busier with more important things.

"The rain might be full of radioactive particles from the sky and dropping them on us," he added.

"Shit," Kelly said, now understanding his sudden fascination with precipitation. She increased her speed, turning the six screws faster.

People aside, their two newest foes, rain and daylight, both began to increase in intensity. David kicked himself for suggesting they take off their hazmat suits, with potentially radioactive rain hitting their heads and clothing.

Undoing the final screw, the latch came away from the door frame, allowing the door to the barn to open with a

gentle creaking sound, fortunately masked by the rain.
The two stepped inside, pulling the door closed.
The high ceiling towered above them as they craned their
necks in all directions looking for something to get them
moving on the river. It took but a moment for their
collective hearts to sink with disappointment. There was
a modern-looking tractor, about a hundred bales of hay,
commercial farming implements and various tools.

"This is useless!" David whispered out loud, the
rain hitting the metal roof high above their heads. Kelly
felt responsible for wasting their time, taking them here.

"I didn't mean it was your fault," David said,
realizing how it could be construed as though he was
blaming her. "You did great getting us here, but we can't
ride a dead tractor down the river."
Kelly stood still, a thousand-yard-stare on her face. David
paced around the dirt floor, the sound of the rain now
heavy above them. He looked at the tools. There was
nothing they could use to float on a river. He turned back
to Kelly.

"Look. You did fucking brilliantly getting us
here. We can only be safer here than back at home.
We've moved a hundred miles. A hundred fucking miles
in the blackness of night. That's some Master and
Commander level navigating."
The compliment was nice, but Kelly was too upset to
accept it. She'd pinned her hopes on there being some
magical pot of gold waiting for them at the river. Some
resolution. She'd put too much weight on this destination
offering salvation.

"Kel, let's just stay here today. We can't go out
in the rain anyway."
David pointed to the columns of hay forming a wall at the
back of the barn.

"Let's get rid of these clothes and go lie down."

Kelly nodded. She had to admit that she'd done well getting them here, but she also had to realize when they were defeated. She took her sweater off, revealing another underneath.

"We only had very brief contact with the rain, so maybe we're OK?" she asked, not wanting to have to get naked in the freezing air.

"Let's just get down to our thermals, grab the foil survival blankets and get in the hay," David responded. "It'll be much warmer in there."

David pulled down a few bales of hay and Kelly tore at them with a large garden fork, creating a prickly but soft mattress on the ground, being their last physical act in an exhausting night. Covering themselves with hay and their foil blankets, they lay down and held each other for warmth.

David was the first to awaken, briefly confused by his new surroundings. The rain had stopped and daylight was visible through gaps in the barn's walls. He looked at his wife, sleeping peacefully, hay stuck to her hair. What could they do, he wondered. He scanned the barn's contents again, fruitlessly, the gentle sound of water trickling somewhere outside, behind them. This was stupid, he thought. They couldn't wear the same clothes they'd arrived in for fear of radiation contamination and they couldn't go out in just their thermal underwear under fresh hazmat suits or they'd freeze to death. They were trapped in a barn near the river they had fought so hard to reach. He looked at the tractor, its giant rear wheels sitting high above their heads. He briefly entertained the idea of taking the inner tubes out from the giant tires and floating down the river in them, but they would also certainly leave them exposed to the radioactive elements while getting them soaking wet in the process, almost certainly giving them hypothermia. What about the house, he wondered. Maybe there was something they could use in there. He had to try.

David climbed out from underneath the hay, and put on a pair of farmers overalls hanging on the barn wall, before putting on his shoes and mask and picking up his pistol. Prizing the barn door open, he scanned the landscape. Overcast skies and fenced, wet fields spread out before him, once home to grazing cattle that had almost certainly been shot and eaten by looters. The house was about 40 yards to his left. For the first time he could see that its front door was wide open. Either the owner was home and loved the feeling of freezing air or its owners were gone and their house had already been looted. If it was looted, David pondered, why didn't they also loot the barn? Maybe there was someone home after all, protecting their property. He had to find out.

Making sure there was no sign of visible human activity on the road, he walked quickly over the grass and to the edge of the house, placing his back against it. He didn't want to stay outside in the radioactive air for a second longer than necessary. David raised his head up to the house's living room window, aware that doing so could get it blown off. His eyes absorbed the image before him. It was a ransacked home. Looted.

David moved around the front door and carefully slipped inside, gun aimed in front. His shoes paced softly on the cream colored carpet, made dirty from muddy footsteps, making it evident that he certainly wasn't the first to come here. Going from room to room, it quickly became apparent that there was nothing of value. Sure, there was plenty of furniture and many modern, unusable appliances, but nothing useful for their current apocalyptic situation. Another wasted venture. The kitchen pantry and fridge were empty, even the bathroom cabinets were bare. Though, in the bedroom there were still some clothes, which they desperately needed. It wasn't a complete waste, David thought, suddenly feeling like he was in a computer game, going through a map and collecting things of value for an upcoming quest. God help him if this game had a final 'boss' to defeat, he wondered.

David put on the clothes in front of him, covering the farmers overalls he was already wearing. The clothes were made for a larger man than himself, older too, judging by the beige and brown colors and patterns. He picked up another pair of pants and a sweater for Kelly, and made his way back to the barn, going around the back to lower the chance of detection, before opening the door to see Kelly awake, the rifle aimed straight at him.

"Oh," David said, surprised.

"David," said Kelly, putting the gun down. "Where the hell were you? I woke up alone and freaked out."

"I was at the house. I got you some clothes."

"Is there anything useful in there? Like, maybe a 40 foot yacht in the living room?"

"The whole place has been looted. It's empty."

Kelly didn't reply to this bad news, getting up and removing her water bottle from her bicycle's drink holder. David did the same with his own bottle, sitting down next to Kelly on the hay, placing the clothes on her lap.

"Jesus. Forget crazies with guns, I'm more scared of being caught by the fashion police," she said, again finding humor in a dire situation.

"We're gonna need more water eventually," said David. "I heard rainwater trickling when I woke up, going down the gutter into a tank behind the barn, but we can't drink that."

Kelly gestured to the tractor, a few feet away.

"What about if we floated down the river on those tires?"

"Already thought about that. The only benefit to that idea would be that we'd die of hypothermia before we died of radiation exposure."

He was right. Chances are, if there was a boat, even an inflatable dinghy, it would have been stolen weeks ago. Kelly scanned the barn, the silence only broken by the rhythmic tapping of water droplets dripping down the gutter outside. A light went on inside her mind. David noticed her facial expression begin to change and his eyes narrowed a little in curiosity. Kelly then got up and put on the clothes David had brought her.

"You're thinking of something," David said, giving Kelly a sideways glance. "What are you thinking?" Kelly looked serious. She wasn't sure yet, and didn't want to give David, or herself, false hope.

"Just stay here a minute," she said, putting on a fresh hazmat suit and slipping her mask over her face. Kelly scanned the perimeter from the barn door for a few seconds and walked out. Through the gaps between the wall's wooden boards, David could see her moving around the side of the barn. She was back inside just thirty seconds later, removing her mask to reveal a cunning smile.

"The water tank," she said.

"We can't drink it," David replied, worried that she was starting to forget the seriousness of the invisible radiation quite possibly buzzing around them.

"No," she continued. "We can use it like a boat."

It took David's imagination a few seconds to join the dots, but, by God, she was right. She explained her simple plan, though it wasn't necessary. It was ingenious.

"It's plastic. We can drain it and cut the top off it."

For the first time since that moment just before he crashed his bike into a car some hours before, David felt genuinely optimistic.

"Let's do it," he said, getting up.

Kelly turned on the tap at the base of the large tank, spilling its contents onto the grass at the back of the barn. It was almost full, so it would take a few minutes to drain. David, meanwhile, was rummaging through the tools in the barn, finding a large wood saw. He went outside to see Kelly peering inside the tank, through a hole in the top, about the diameter of a dinner plate.

"We'll definitely have to chop the top off," Kelly confirmed.

"Yeah. I mean, we've both lost a lot of weight, but unless we Kate Moss it up, and throw up every meal from the last three months, we ain't squeezing through that hole," added David.

With the water drained, Kelly and David pushed the tank onto its side and rolled it around the side of the barn, getting it safely inside, away from any prying eyes that might be traveling on the road.

"We'll have to clean it. It had radioactive water in it," David pointed out.

But what would they clean it with, he wondered.

"I guess we just need to get the particles off," he added.

Using all the chemicals and liquids they could find in the barn, they washed and rinsed the tank, inside and out, rubbing it with hay, before hacking at it like mad with the wood saw he found.

"Babe. We can use these as paddles," said Kelly, holding up a spade and a shovel.

"Good good good," said David. "Get the stuff off the bikes and get ready to go."

With the coast clear, David and Kelly rolled the topless water tank up the long driveway toward the road, stopping every now and then to check for signs of human activity. It took at least five long minutes to move the device to the bridge and slide it down to the water's edge.

"Don't touch the water," David said to Kelly, climbing into the tank, their bright white overalls standing out against the wet bushes around them. Kelly rocked the tank, walking it on its edges further towards the water, before climbing in herself.

"It doesn't feel very stable," she said, the tank rocking around them, its edge still in contact with the ground.

The freezing water swirled around the outside of the tank, the two of them bottomed out on the ground.

"We're grounded," Kelly said, looking over the edge with a shovel in hand. "Try wiggling it."

The two of them bobbed about in their dark green, plastic vessel, while Kelly pushed the shovel against the embankment. Suddenly, the tank turned around, caught by the moving water, setting itself free from its earthly mooring.

"We're moving!" David yelped.

"We're fucking moving!" Kelly responded.

Trying desperately to keep the tank from tipping over, Kelly pushed at the ground with her shovel. The large green cylinder bobbed and swirled in uncontrolled circles toward the center of the stream, beginning its lengthy journey to a larger river, its two bright white occupants on their knees, churning at the water with their garden tools.

"This might just work," said Kelly, allowing herself a brief moment of pride.

The morning's heavy rains were initially unwanted when they started falling, perhaps some eight hours ago, but their effects were of great help. The normally foot-deep creek was now twice that depth and the increased body of water meant they were moving at two or three miles per hour, sometimes faster, sometimes slower. It was going to be a long and uncertain journey, but it was definitely faster than walking, plus it also meant that they didn't have to expend any energy as the river did all the work. Kelly and David had agreed that, once they get to a larger body of water, in the unlikely event that they found an actual boat, they would abandon their homemade craft and take that instead. But after three hours on the water, there was no sign of any boat, or any human activity for that matter, allowing a very welcome sense of calm to descend. They took turns paddling, although there was very little actual control involved. The main job of the paddler was to simply keep the tank away from the riverbanks and fallen tree logs which occasionally blocked the path, while the flow of the water did the gruntwork.

With each mile they traveled, the creek gradually increased in width and volume, which told Kelly that they were on their way to another, larger river. However, she had no real way of knowing where they actually were; a problem which grew as the sun set. David, who was on his knees, shovel in hand, crouched down to voice his concerns to Kelly, resting on the tank's floor.

"It's getting kinda dark, Kel," he said, stating the obvious.

"I know," she replied, holding back the urge to say, "Well, duh."

"How far do you think we've traveled?"

"Yeah, I was thinking about that myself. I honestly couldn't say for sure. We've lost track of where we are on the map, but if we're going at about two miles per hour, then it would be about seven hours from where we started to reach the Appomattox River."

Crouched on the floor of the tank, David did some guesstimating.

"We've been going for about five hours now. Maybe six. We might even get there before it's completely pitch black."

The large plastic tank, about the size of a compact car, briefly scraped against the ground, its momentum turning it clockwise and and setting it free from its brief, earthly grasp. David popped his head up to scan the river ahead through his foggy mask, only to be whipped in the face by a leafy branch.

Kelly saw it all and laughed. The whole situation was ridiculous.

"Look at us," she said, a pained smile on her masked face.

"Two neon-white rejects from a Beastie Boys video in a chopped off water tank, floating down a river, completely lost."

Realizing the absurdity of their situation, David let out a good laugh. It really was a sight to behold.

Sleep that night was erratic and unsatisfying, with both travelers being perpetually cold and cramped in what was little more than a glorified bucket. They were moving but the tank was effectively out of control unless both of them were paddling on opposite sides, as a single paddler caused the craft to simply turn around in the water like a spinning record. Given the overcast darkness of the night, they both gave up on trying to avoid rocks or logs, meaning that the tank would bang into unseen objects regularly, causing the walls to jar with an unpleasant noise, immediately releasing both crewmates from the embrace of sleep. Conversation was their only tool to alleviate boredom, and given the gravity of the situation, it wasn't very jovial.

"Do you think Steve and Maureen are OK?" Kelly asked.

In the many hours of boredom, David had wondered the very same thing.

"I honestly don't know."

"Before we left, we told them not to drink the water."

"I know," David replied. "But they had no choice. I can only hope they used our bottled supplies."

"Maybe they fled as well?" Kelly asked, deluding herself.

David turned to her in the darkness, causing the tank to wobble around.

"I don't want to be pessimistic, babe, but…"

"I know," Kelly replied. "I only hope they survive."

"You awake?"

Kelly was staring at David, the morning light in the far east of the cloudy sky growing brighter. He stirred, ripped from a rare moment of slumber.

"Hm."

"Look where we are."

David opened his eyes, looking up at the cylindrical walls of their plastic prison, immediately reminding him that he was floating on a river in a giant teacup. Kelly was on her knees by his side, in her bright white overalls and gas mask, map in hand. Noticing the lack of trees passing above, he got to his knees to take in the view.

"Lake Chesdin," Kelly said.

"Is that good?" David asked.

"Yes and no. It's good that we finally know where we are…"

"But?"

"But, there's a dam at the other end of this lake. That means the current is gonna crawl to a halt soon, so we're gonna have to paddle in daylight, then if we get to the dam, we're gonna have to roll this thing around the dam and down the other side to the continuing stream," said Kelly.

David sighed.

"This nightmare would make an epic movie but a mediocre book."

Kelly laughed.

"Yeah, but it'd have to be in the fiction section. No one would believe we've survived this far."

It took the entire day to traverse Lake Chesdin to reach Brasfield Dam; a journey of around ten miles. The current of the river had been replaced by still water reflecting the darkening skies above. Lifting the tank out of the water wasn't as bad as they imagined, thanks to a boat ramp on the southern end of the dam, but getting it safely to the other side was a challenge, given the height of the dam. In the end, David opted to just let go of their craft, causing the dark green cylinder to roll and bounce forty feet to the shrubs below. The tank survived, and the two travelers continued their onward journey, but they had new problems: the shallowness of the river on the other side of the dam meant the bottom of the tank constantly scraped against river stones, something incredibly difficult to solve in the dark. Kelly and David rocked back and forth dozens of times to try and free up their craft, having to climb out and maneuver the tank manually on several occasions. There were also growing signs of human habitation, with the roofs of houses visible on the hills above the river.

"I reckon we're probably getting close to Petersburg," said Kelly, staring up at the dark shapes of power lines in the night sky.

"Hmm," David replied, aware of the increased risk of human interaction.

"We're going to need an actual boat, sooner or later," Kelly added.

"True. But there's a problem with that idea: propulsion. Even if we could find a boat, we can't paddle a boat out to sea with a spade and a shovel."

Kelly stared at the dark sky, before an idea suddenly entered her mind.

"Remember back when we were trying to get home after the pulse, we heard a lawn mower. Some really basic engines must still be working, right?"

David didn't want to disappoint her, but he'd already considered that idea the previous day.

"In theory, yes," David said. "But... even if we could find one that works, think of the noise. We'd be heard a mile away."

David was right, Kelly thought. It would be suicide, but it would get them there faster.

"Alright. But what if we used an electric motor and batteries?"

David had already thought of that too.

"Well, in theory, that would work. But unless you have the battery pack from a Tesla car, we'd have to use a regular car battery. That would get us maybe a mile before it went flat."

Kelly suddenly felt like she was battling with an enemy, not a husband.

"Well, I'm trying to come up with ideas to get us out of this mess," she responded, crestfallen.

"I know, babe. You're the brains behind this vessel which has already moved us, like, forty miles. That's an achievement, so don't worry. We'll figure something out."

The sound of the stream babbling over stones replaced their strained attempts at conversation, and they found themselves only talking to each other when issuing commands to free their grounded water tank; something which happened on a regular basis for hours until they'd made it closer to Petersburg, with the river deepening.

Being back in places of human habitation put their nerves on edge, with their guns always at hand. Bridges connecting the city of Petersburg passed overhead, their ugly gray undersides offering an unrestricted view into their plastic tank for anyone who might be walking across. It was when they were close to towns and cities when conversation stopped, out of fear of being heard and due to stress. And, it was as they were passing through Petersburg that evening, that they both heard the unmistakable sound of a human male voice.

Kelly shot a glance to David who crouched down into the fetal position, covering himself with his foil emergency blanket. Kelly copied him, and they slowly drifted under another dark bridge. If there was a person on that bridge they would have certainly seen inside the tank, but was it visible that there were two people and supplies inside?

"There's something in there," the voice said.

It sounded like it came from the end of the bridge, or maybe just under it. David and Kelly froze still. It was unlike her, but at that moment she prayed to God for mercy.

Fifteen seconds passed, maybe twenty before a gunshot rang out and a bullet hit the plastic tank, a clean round bullet hole appearing in the darkness above Kelly's shoulder. Kelly held back the urge to scream.

"Are you OK?" She whispered to David.

"Yes," he lied.

It had felt like the searing hot bullet had hit his calf muscle and entered his leg.

"Don't waste the fucking ammo! It's just rubbish!" a different voice yelled from near the bridge. An inch of water began to pool on David's side of the tank, mixing with his blood as they drifted a few more yards. His lower leg felt like it was on fire.

Kelly prayed silently, asking God to keep them safe. David began to pray himself, hoping God would let him live. Two atheists on a sinking ship.

"I'm getting wet," whispered Kelly, the encroaching darkness making it harder to see what was happening.

"The tank!" Kelly whispered. "David. I think we're sinking."

"Kelly."

"What is it?"

"Please, don't get upset. But... I've been shot."

"What? Where? Are you OK?"

"My leg. And I don't know. It hurts pretty bad."

Like most men, David was the type to claim he was dying of Ebola whenever he had a cold, as if no other human had suffered like he was suffering, so when he was acting so calm about being shot, she knew it was serious. The water was now four inches deep inside the tank and rising.

"I'm bleeding pretty bad. It hurts, Kel. The bullet hit the tank too."

David removed the foil blanket and looked at his leg in the evening darkness. The white leg of his overalls appeared dark on one leg, near the back of the knee.

"You're gonna be OK," Kelly said, as if she were in a movie. The words never seemed to offer any comfort in films, so it was unlikely they would offer comfort in reality. "Just hang on, my love. I'll paddle us to shore." Kelly got up, carefully, looking behind her. The bridge was drifting out of sight, around the curve of the river. She picked up the shovel and started paddling, but it only caused the round tank to turn in circles.

"Babe, I need you. Don't give up on me. I need you to paddle," she begged.

David wrapped his fingers around the jagged, sawn-off ridge of the tank and pulled himself upward and out of the six inches of icy water in the base of their craft, the movement causing a dull, buzzing agony in his injured leg. With one knee propping him up against the tank wall, he dipped his spade into the water and churned at the river just a few inches below. They formed a rhythm of paddling with equal force, preventing the tank from spinning too much in either direction, and moved closer to the bank, constantly moving with the flow of the stream. The tank was sitting deeper into the water with each passing minute, and the five minutes it took to move their increasingly un-hydrodynamic vessel toward the shore, resulted in it sinking lower into the dark, murky river. The water was reaching their waists by the time it touched the ground. David was losing blood and he had stopped communicating.

"I'll help you out," Kelly said. "Hold onto your backpack."

Kelly ran her arm through one of the shoulder straps on her backpack and climbed out of the tank, causing it to tip over and water to rush in and flood it completely. David gasped in the freezing cold water, and clung to Kelly as the tank toppled over, submerging it almost completely. Splashing in the water, Kelly pulled David through the shallow mud, him hopping on one leg, until they reached solid ground. They collapsed on the bank, soaking wet and chilled to the bone. Kelly searched around frantically and saw a row of buildings near the water's edge, knowing she had to go there for shelter, even with the risk of confrontation.

"I need you to stay with me," she whispered. "We gotta try one of those buildings. Get your gun out." Holding each other's torsos, Kelly guided David over a flat, concrete area, him hopping on one leg. They were now clearly visible to anyone nearby in their white, wet hazmat suits. With one hand, Kelly ripped her mask off and discarded it. She thought that if David was going to die, she would too. The first building looked like it used to be a business, but it had been looted bare, with only a counter remaining in the front, its entry door wide open. Kelly escorted David inside and placed him down on the floor, causing him to wince in pain

"I'm sorry, babe. Wait here."
With her gun drawn, she crept to the back of the business, looking for a room where they could hide and she could use her flashlight to help stop David's bleeding, but she found nothing that blocked their view from outside, with all the exterior windows being smashed. She went into the bathroom, noticing it had a separate room for the toilet. It was small; just a few square feet, but it had no exterior window. She rushed back to David, trying not to alert anyone in the conjoined building of their presence. Hoisting him to his legs, resulting in a gasp of pain, she

dragged David into the tiny, dark room. Closing the toilet room door, she dove into her backpack and rummaged in the pitch black, trying to find her flashlight.

"Stay with me babe," she begged David, who was propped up against the toilet, clearly in shock. Grasping the flashlight, she fumbled with the switch on the side, immediately showering the tiny room with bright white light, piercing their eyes. She'd never seen David's face in shock before; his eyes open and glassy but his expression vacant. She aimed the beam of the flashlight at his leg, the white hazmat suit a mottled blend of muddy brown and blood red.

"Jesus," she said, pulling at the trouser leg. This caused David to wince and grunt, feebly.

"I'm sorry, babe," she said, tears in her eyes. Her husband, the cause of so much love and joy, was slumped pathetically against a toilet, the life force draining out of him. What a pointless way to die, after they'd come so far. They'd survived death and disaster, only to fall victim to a fatal gunshot wound from an unknown attacker. What a waste of life, love and potential.

Kelly searched her pocket for her Swiss Army knife, the flashlight firing its bright light in all directions as she retrieved it, pulling out its largest implement: a knife. Putting the flashlight in her mouth, Kelly tore at the dirty pant leg with the blade, hacking up the the fabric, revealing David's wet and blood-soaked thermal leggings underneath. She realized that pulling the thermal legging up to the knee would be faster than trying to cut it, so Kelly prepared to slide it hard in one swift movement, mentally readying herself to confront the gore it concealed. David moaned in pain as she did this, causing her to apologize to her husband, tears in her eyes. There was blood all over his calf, which she needed to clear up to see the entry and exit wound, and to determine if his shin was shattered or if he'd bleed to death right there and then.

Kelly unzipped her own hazmat suit down to her waist and removed the sweater David had given her before they left on that stupid raft. Part of it was still dry. She rubbed the sweater over his calf, clearing the blood away.

"Babe, it's OK," she said, feeling around his leg for the exit wound.

Blood trickled down his leg toward his shoe. It looked like he might live, she thought. It might not be the end.

"Please, God," she whispered, desperately. Aware that she needed to clean and bind the wound to stop blood loss, she opened her first aid kid, taking out a plastic tube of saline solution, biting the top off and squirting its contents on David's leg. In the chaos of the moment, it struck her as strange that a gunshot wound can look so benign from the outside with the true damage remaining unseen beneath the skin. Problem was, she couldn't find the exit wound. Kelly leaned in, trying to be calm, looking all over David's hairy calf, trying to find where the bullet had exited. His shin was intact, so where did it go? She pawed at his leg, causing him to wince in pain.

"I can't find the exit wound," she said, frustrated. She adjusted the flashlight's position all around the leg, desperately.

"It looks like… It looks like… I don't know. It looks like maybe the bullet... Maybe it hasn't gone in." Maybe she'd watched too many movies, but she gradually began to hope that David's dramatic gunshot wound wasn't actually that bad, at least from the outside. She squeezed the calf muscle gently and studied it closely. The bullet had taken a chunk off the back of his leg, but there was no entry wound. It was more like a deep slash, and while it would certainly hurt for a while, it definitely wasn't going to kill him. She didn't know whether to laugh or cry.

"How bad is it?" David whispered.

Kelly, out of frustration, did something she probably shouldn't have.

"Oh, babe. You're gonna die," she said, flatly.

"What?" David responded, not sure what to make of this news. He seemed to perk up, mostly by surprise. Kelly was saying he'd be fine only a few minutes ago, so how could he be dying?

"It's true, I'm sorry babe," she continued. "The truth is, we're all gonna die one day."

David's shock was starting to wear off and his brain was beginning to recognize the dull burn of pain signals firing from the damaged nerve endings his leg.

"Are you... Joking?"

Kelly slumped back against the toilet door. Her husband needed a bandage, but he wasn't going to die that night in that toilet room.

"It's a flesh wound, Shatner."

"A flesh wound?"

"Yes. Nice acting though."

"Acting?" David said, angry. "I thought I was going to die. I was fucking *shot!*"

Kelly breathed in, exhaling heavily, relieved.

"You were. And it's just a flesh wound. I'm glad you're OK, babe, but I just *know* I'm going to hearing about this for the next thirty years. 'Oh, I can't do the laundry, I was *shot*' you'll be saying. God help me."

David was relieved by the news but greatly offended with its delivery. For once, he didn't know what to say, and the two sat in silence for a few seconds.

"Here," Kelly perked up, handing him some alcohol wipes and a bandage. "Fix yourself up. Auditions are at 9 AM tomorrow."

She loved that man, but God, if he wouldn't be the death of her.

It was a long, cold night, trapped in that room, no bigger than a closet. Kelly had retrieved their foil-like emergency blankets, and David had his head rested against Kelly's breasts, the two of them still damp from the river the night before. Kelly snored for a brief moment, waking David up with a fright. If normality ever returned to their lives, he promised himself that he'd drag Kelly to a doctor to fix her God-awful snoring. Most nights were like sleeping with a damn Harley-Davidson. It was pitch black inside the toilet room, making him wonder what time it was. This caused him to instinctively feel for his wristwatch that was no longer there; sitting somewhere back in that motel in Bedford. He woke up Kelly, touching her face. God, it was good to feel her face, he thought. Kelly began to stir, entering the land of the conscious.

"We gotta get out of here, babe," he said. "We can fix the hole in the tank and continue, if it's dark." Kelly thought for a moment. She just wanted to be somewhere warm. What she wouldn't give for a damn hot shower and fresh clothes.

"Alright," she said. "But let's eat something now. It might be our last meal if there are crazies outside."

Peering around the toilet door in the morning light revealed a ransacked office with a dead plant on the front desk. There were fishing sinkers, hooks and a couple of life preservers on the ground. Creeping forward, David limping on his damaged leg, revealed an enclave of similar single-level businesses on the water's edge. A couple of empty boat trailers sat on the concrete out front.

"There's a boat trailer," Kelly whispered, pointing across the lot, suddenly optimistic. They edged forward toward the front window of the business, hoping that perhaps some higher power had indeed granted their wish and delivered them a boat in the middle of the night. A quick scan of the yard dashed those hopes.

"It's a dock," David whispered, pointing toward the river's edge. "There's a boat ramp."

"A fat lot of good it'll do us without a boat," Kelly added.

"Why can't we catch a break?" David said. It wasn't fair. They'd survived almost four months of chaos, shortages, attacks, death and radiation, only to be stranded, 80 miles from potential freedom. They had to find a way.

"Look, they have to fix boats here. Let's see if there's anything left in these buildings that we can use to repair the water tank and float away," said Kelly, even though the thought of getting back into the HMS Gazebo was the last thing she wanted.

"Dave, you look through this building, I'll go next door. And please be careful."

"Alright. You too. We might not be alone." David hobbled around the office, collecting anything he could find which looters had ignored, picking up some fishing line and a reel which sat on the floor. Kelly, meanwhile, slinked into the building joined to theirs. It was Kelly's immediate return which surprised him, her face looking like she'd seen a ghost, or worse. David tightened his shoulders, suddenly fearful.

"Come with me," she said.

David complied, with both of them creeping closer to the adjacent building, shards of glass crunching underfoot. Kelly led David past the looted shopfront and through the large open door of the building's workshop, her turning around to read David's expression. He paused in the doorway, his eyes focused intently on what they had sitting before them. It was a combination of intoxicated joy, followed by a dose of reality crashing and burning before them. Kelly turned to David, her eyebrows raised in anticipation, but reading David's face caused her brow to come crashing down, much like the damaged sailboat which sat on the workshop floor before them. Turning his gaze between the patchy red and white hull and his wife's eyes, He shook his head a little.

"Maybe we can fix it," Kelly said. "If we can, it'll be safer than the tank."

David stared the the mess before him. The little sailboat appeared to have been in for major repairs, but had no mast and lay on its side. It was no better than their plastic tank.

"But… It's broken," David whispered. "I mean, look. It's on the ground."

David pointed to blocks of wood, strewn around the base of the unpainted hull.

"Someone's already tried to steal it. Look," he continued, pointing to the blocks. "It's on the ground and there's no way we can move it without a trailer and some way to lift it. It's gotta weigh a ton. It… It looks like shit."

Perhaps the optimist out of the two, Kelly wasn't ready to raise the white flag just yet.

"Maybe we can make a mast and a sail?"

David exhaled through his nose, a look of pain on his face as a breeze blew some leaves into the workshop.

They'd come so far, he thought. Maybe there's another boat?

The good news was that they were alone, at least in their immediate area. The small group of businesses by the water's edge were all related to boat repair and fishing, with nothing of any value left by looters and little cause for anyone to return. The bad news was that there was little in the way of materials left to repair their tank in order to continue floating down the Appomattox River. David wanted to repair the hole in their water tank, something that could be done in minutes with a piece of finely-carved cork and duct tape, whereas Kelly wanted to try and get the de-masted sailboat somehow fixed, onto a trailer and into the water, something that could take weeks, if at all.

"But we could be out of here in twenty minutes if we just fix the tank," David pleaded.

"David. That thing will kill us both. Besides, do you think we're gonna find a better boat in Norfolk, further down the river? When - if - we get that far alive, I do not want to be stopping. It'll be too dangerous. If this boat floats, we can sail right past and out to sea."
David put one hand on his hip and pointed the other hand at the sailboat.

"Sail right past? Without a sail? There's no mast."
Kelly knew he was right, but there's no way she was getting back in that damn plastic bucket. She had an idea, which relied on her knowledge of David's personality.

"OK. How about we compromise," Kelly said, not asking.
David looked at her, dubiously.

"Compromise? Like, I take the tank and you take this piece of shit? Good luck lifting it up."

"There's no need to be a dick," Kelly said.

"OK. Look. I'm sorry." David replied, bowing and sweeping his arm, as if on stage. "Please. Tell me your great idea."

Kelly exhaled. Did he have to be so dramatic?

"David, give me one day. We still have a couple of bottles of water. So, give me one day to try to fix this thing. If we can't fix it in one day, we get back in the tub."

David shook his head.

"Kelly, we'd need a week. And we need a sail. And ten people to lift it up."

Kelly lifted her hands upright, index fingers raised, punctuating each word with hand movements.

"Just. One. Day."

Kelly's strategy was simple. Like so many guys, David was often reluctant to do chores, but once he became involved in the task, he wouldn't stop until it was done properly. Back when times were happier, he'd often put off cleaning the bathroom or dusting the house, but when he finally did, he'd end up pouring a good hour into it, not stopping until it was perfect. Attempting the same strategy with a broken sailboat was bold, but it might work.

"Alright. One day. But tomorrow, we get back in the tank and try to paddle toward Chesapeake to find a real boat. Christ, even a stolen bathtub would be more seaworthy than this piece of shit."

The first step involved clearing out the workshop and figuring out if there was anything useful left behind by looters. Boxes and paper were strewn across the floor, piled up against the walls and old boat parts hung from the rafters above their heads. That's where Kelly noticed something which looked suspiciously useful.

"David," she said excitedly, pointing above them. "Look."

David studied the mess of metal cables and wires.

"That... looks like a mast."

This was too good to be true, to Kelly at least. David lowered his gaze to Kelly, then pointed to the sailboat carcass.

"But will it fit this thing?" he asked, skeptical. Though, even he had to admit this was quite a find.

"Let's find out. It might even be the mast for this actual boat. I mean, why else would it be stored up there?"

Kelly grabbed a ladder which lay on the floor, climbing up to retrieve the mystery mast.

"It looks like it has a sail attached to that bit that sticks out."

"The boom," said David, having sailed a few times as a kid. Kelly tugged at the mess of metal cables and slid it down onto the floor with the loud clang of metal on concrete.

"Jesus!" David said, reaching for his gun and hobbling to the edge of the workshop door. "Kel, please be careful."

Fortunately, aside from their own clanging and movement, there seemed to be no signs of human activity in the bushes surrounding them.

Connecting the mast aside, the largest immediate problem they faced was getting the boat upright and onto a trailer. For this, David came up with a plan. He limped over to a smashed-up RAM 1500, abandoned in the parking lot, and rummaged through it, returning triumphant with the truck's jack and handle.

"Kel, look what I found. I'm gonna try to lift the boat up, one block at a time. It'll take a while, but I reckon we can do it."

This news made Kelly smile, knowing that her initial plan was working and her hunch was correct. All she had to do was convince him to get involved and he'd put in whatever effort was needed to complete the operation. She'd tell him about her little con-job in the future, if they could get out of there, and if they weren't going to die of cancer in a week, caused by radiation exposure. David began turning the jack against a series of blocks and planks to right the hull, inch by inch. It was slow going, but progress was being made. Kelly, meanwhile, was untangling the wires attached to the mast, spreading them out on the workshop floor, determining where on the boat they attached. At the risk of raising her hopes, she allowed herself to enjoy the feeling that this might just work - aware that she'd made such mistakes before.

"Kel," said David. "I can't do it myself, having been shot and all, but can you bring over that boat trailer sitting across the lot?"

She rolled her eyes. It's already begun, she thought. Checking the coast was clear, Kelly pushed the trailer by its hitch across the lot and into the workshop, the trailers rear edge sitting against the bow of the boat. David was making good progress on righting the vessel, but how they were to get it aboard the trailer was another problem. The solution happened to be messy and not particularly environmentally friendly: paint. Opening one of the many cans of marine paint ignored by looters, David poured a messy line of paint in the middle of the floor, which would allow the boat's small, retracted keel to slide on the ground somewhat. With the vessel mostly upright, he attached the cable connected to the trailer's hand-operated winch to the bow, hoping to bring this discarded piece of flotsam back to life. The next idea, courtesy of Kelly, was to attach the front of the boat to the rafters above them via a pulley, helping to lift it into the trailer in an upright position, but also creating the risk of it pulling the roof down onto their heads.

Heaving, David turned the winch handle with the cable becoming tighter, resulting in the boat's hull making a couple of dry cracking sounds.

"That can't be good," David announced, the handle now refusing to move under the strain.

"Turn it!" Kelly said, pulling on the rope which ran between a ceiling beam and the boat's front anchor guide.

The roof frame above them creaked under the strain. David managed to turn the handle another half turn, the bow of the small sailboat finally beginning to climb onto the trailer. Kelly was now acutely aware as to why the looters gave up on this particular challenge. As the boat's patchy-colored hull met the trailer's side rollers and inched upward, Kelly began to loosen the pulley above her head, allowing the craft to put the majority of the strain on the trailer's rollers instead of the roof beams. It was only a few more turns of the winch to victory, and David, damp and frozen, began to smile. That was the first time Kelly had seen him smile since they found the plastic water tank and set sail to uncertainty. The winding of the winch came to a halt.

"Fucking well done!" Kelly said.

David nodded, wearing a broad grin. This was teamwork, though it was also the realization of more work to be done. Kelly climbed aboard the boat and sat at the tiller on the stern, suddenly aware of how small it was.

"This thing must only be about twenty-five feet long."

"Yeah, it's just a trailer sailer," answered David. "But it's like a hotel compared to the plastic bucket we rode in on."

David stepped back, putting weight on his leg, causing him to wince. He stared at the white hull with pink and red repair patches, sitting on the trailer before them.

"This thing really to sticks out like a sore thumb. We're gonna be shot dead before we even get it in the water."

"Hang on," Kelly said, an idea forming in her mind. "All that paint. That paint you poured on the ground. That was black. Let's paint the damn thing black!"

Actually, David thought. That was a brilliant idea. There was plenty of paint and it didn't have to pretty. He decided to go one step further.

"Let's do that, and while we're at it, let's paint our white hazmat suits black too. That make us impossible to see at night."

Kelly nodded. That wasn't a bad idea either, she thought.

By the time the day had begun to transform into evening, David and Kelly had managed to attach the mast, which they discovered was designed to be removed easily to transport it under bridges, and they'd painted the entire craft black, from top to bottom, including the sail, the four small windows, and themselves. Of course it was the absolute worst time to paint a boat, with the air hovering just above freezing, which meant the paint remained sticky and wet, getting everywhere, but they had to put the boat in the water that night.

The cramped interior of the boat had been stripped of anything of value. It still had its seat cushions, but its gas small cooker had been ripped out, leaving a rectangular stainless steel hole. There was a small gas-powered outboard motor in the corner of the workshop too, but there was no fuel anywhere to be seen and its basic circuitry was possibly fried from the EMP attack some months before. David hauled it aboard anyway, along with firewood and anything else he could find, and returned to the abandoned truck in the parking lot. He removed the large battery from its engine bay, also climbing underneath to put a hole in its gas tank. Twenty seconds later he'd climbed back out, hobbling to the boat sitting outside the workshop on its trailer, disheartened.

"Fuck's sake."

"What is it, Dave?"

"Someone's already punctured the tank. It's dry." Someone had beat him to the gas tank idea, with the truck sitting empty in the lot. Kelly paused for a moment and had another plan.

"What about taking its starter motor?"

"For what?" David asked.

"That."

Kelly pointed to the outboard motor sitting on the workshop floor. She was right. That was a smart idea, if it worked.

With the sun down and the sky nothing but a sheet of dark gray, they loaded their bags into the cabin of the sticky, black sailboat, and dragged the trailer across the lot, stopping at the edge of the boat ramp.

"Ready?" Kelly whispered, sitting in the cockpit, the black, sticky sail hanging off the boat's mast and her painted hazmat barely visible in the evening darkness.

"Ready," David answered.

He climbed up the trailer and aboard the small craft, his black suit leg adhering to the sticky, black cabin wall. David got himself into position at the tiller, not that he would have much control over the vessel. They certainly couldn't sail at night without seeing where they were going; at best, they could continue floating downstream until they reached the James River, some six miles away. If they somehow made it that far, then they'd take whatever came next, head-on.

Kelly climbed back down onto the tarmac and pushed hard against the back of the trailer, feeling it start to move. She aimed the trailer toward the boat ramp and pushed with all her might. As the metal trailer reached the top of the boat ramp, its speed began to increase quickly, and the trailer soon slipped out of her grasp. She reached for it, but it wasn't there anymore, causing her to lose balance and trip over on the ramp. Kelly fell to her knees, looking up as it continued on without her into the darkness. She inadvertently held her breath during those next three seconds, with the rattling sound of a dark boat jiggling on a trailer immediately being replaced by the sound of a splashing water.

"David?" she whispered loudly.

"Kelly!" he whispered back.

"What happened?" she asked.

"I think it floats!" came the reply.

Kelly walked down the ramp until her shoes made a sloshing sound and her feet immediately turned cold.

"Where are you?" she called, her hands outstretched.

"Over here," he whispered. "I'm still on the trailer but it's definitely floating."

Striking the metal structure in front of her, which could only be the trailer, Kelly touched the back of the boat. The water was up to her knees, but the trailer was stopping the sailboat from being free. She positioned her legs apart and pushed hard against the trailer. It begrudgingly moved a few feet, followed by the front of the trailer dipping down. Kelly grabbed the back of the boat and climbed up over the trailer as it submerged.

"The trailer's gone off the edge of the concrete ramp. We're free!" she whispered.

David stood slightly, reaching out to grab her, with both of them hitting their heads on the boom.

"Ow," Kelly said, sitting back down on the sticky cockpit seat.

"Yeah, better get used to that," David replied. They were moving once again - this time in an actual boat designed to move people on actual water. The taste of freedom was becoming palpable.

They'd drifted about twenty miles throughout the night, banging into the shore several times, taking turns in pushing themselves off the bank. This was a more difficult task than in the plastic tank, given the sheer weight of the sailboat, but the seat cushions and their foil blankets allowed them to take turns sleeping. This was a task made easier by being able to lie down; a luxury most people take for granted. By the time the blackness of the sky had begun to transform into a pale gray on the horizon, Kelly surmised that, if they hoisted the black sail and moved under the power of wind, they'd only have one more complete day of traveling before reaching the ocean. After that, who knows, but for now, they still had to fight to survive.

David opened the cockpit hatch and stuck his head out, looking up at Kelly.

"Hey," he said. "Where's your mask?"

"Hey yourself. I took it off. You sleep alright?"

"You know, actually I *did*. I'm still damp and I smell rancid, but I got a good couple of hours' sleep. Got any idea where we are?"

"I reckon we're about 60 or 70 miles from the sea. If we sailed, we could probably make that in a day or so, but, seeing as we can't sail at night, it would mean sailing during the day."

"Hm," David responded. "That would mean sailing in daylight right past Norfolk."

"Yes, but I have some good news."

"Finally," David replied. "What?"

"Look up at the top of the mast. See that wind needle? I've been checking it since it got light enough, and my compass says that it's mostly blowing a direct northerly. That's why I took off the mask. We're probably not being irradiated."

"That's a good sign. Though if we get spotted, someone would probably shoot out our hull and sink us just on the chance we had a chocolate bar onboard."

"Well, to be fair, we have two," Kelly replied. "We've almost eaten all the food and we only have one bottle of water."

"Oh, about that. My turn for good news. There's still water in the tank onboard. It's smells as stale as hell, but we've got some chlorine tablets. Oh, did you take your iodine tablet this morning?"

"Not yet. They're inside."
David lowered himself back inside the cabin and reached for the iodine tablets, popping one for himself and one for Kelly.

"Here you are, ma'am. One continental breakfast."
Kelly laughed, shaking her head.

"Yeah, 'bout that. I'd like speak to the manager."
The boat swirled in the early morning light, entirely out of control, but still moving. The river moved slowly, but it was much wider now.

"I reckon we should try sailing," David continued. "There's no houses here and the wind is light so it should be safe. I'll show you how it works."
David pulled on a rope, the black, sticky mainsail peeling off itself as it took its first leap skywards. He pulled again, the sail reaching another foot in height.

"Pull the tiller toward you, and when the sail starts to fill up with air, keep the boat aimed in that direction."
Some rope pulling later, the black sail was fully hoisted and secured and the boat began to move under its own power. Both of them had become used to traveling purely at the whim of the river current, so to be moving via actual propulsion was genuinely exhilarating.

"This is fucking brilliant!" beamed Kelly.

"It is, but you're going to have to have to turn soon, babe."
David stared as the opposite shore approached.
"Like, now would be good. Kelly... Kelly, turn the boat..."
Kelly pushed the tiller away from herself and the sailboat gradually began to change its slow course. The changing direction of the wind gently pushed the lapping sail in the other direction with the boom swinging around and thumping into Kelly's head.

"Ow!" she said.

"Yeah. You'd better get used to that."
Kelly soon got the hang of sailing, tacking to port and then to starboard, zig-zagging slowly down the James River, while David sat with his rifle on the bow of the small sailboat. Other than an occasional cliffside house above them, there was no sign of human activity, but sailing during the day was still incredibly risky.

"What are we gonna do when we get to Hampton and Norfolk?" Kelly asked. "There's gonna be crazy and desperate people there."

"I honestly don't know," David replied.

Kelly studied the slowly approaching curve in the river, mentally charting how close she could get to the bank before having to tack to port once again.

"You know, we're gonna have to sail right between them, a city on either side. Straight through the gauntlet."

"I know," David replied.

Raindrops started falling on the water around them, tapping against the surface of the dark, sticky cockpit. David got to his feet, exhaling in pain, and opened the hatch on the bow. Kelly watched as he reached down into the tiny front cabin and pulled out a bucket, placing it on the bow, between his legs to catch a few precious drops of water.

"What if we just sail as fast as we can, right past the city and straight out to sea?" Kelly asked.

"I want to, but someone would definitely see us. Anyone who sees a person on a sailboat, even a piece of shit like this, would probably assume we're stocked up with food and water."

"Well, we're certainly not," said Kelly.

"Yeah, but no one else knows that."

David gazed across to a grassy, bushy area on their starboard bow. It looked like a wildlife reserve. This immediately made him think of food. God, he was hungry. If they made it to sea they could catch a fish. They just had to wait another day, he thought.

"I've been thinking," he continued.

Kelly wanted to make a "Really, did it hurt?" joke, but this wasn't the time.

"What were you thinking?" she asked.

"What if we stopped the boat over there for the night and then, first thing in the morning, we make a break for it, sailing right through the city."
Kelly was just eager to get the hell out of there.

"I was also thinking," she continued. "There's not really any wind in the mornings, so what if we just kept going today and took our chances and tried to reach the sea tonight?"
David had wondered the same thing, but it was such a risky proposition.

"I thought about it too, but honestly, I really don't want to get shot again."
Kelly pondered if that was the second or third time he'd mentioned that he'd been shot.

"What if we just take the sail down, let it flop around in the water, hide inside and just drift out to sea?"

"I've thought of that too. Problem is, we're so close to the sea that this river's now tidal. I don't know when the high tide is, so we could be sitting ducks, floating around in the harbor, going nowhere."
The two sailed in silence for a couple of minutes, moving slowly at around one or two knots. David was the first to break the silence, the raindrops tapping on the water surface around them.

"I have an idea."

"I'm listening," Kelly replied.

"I could try and rig up that outboard to the car battery I got from the truck yesterday. I've got the truck's starter motor inside, and there's a chance I could mate the two together to turn the propeller."

"Do it!"

"Well, don't get too excited. That battery probably doesn't have much power in it, after sitting there for three months, but if I could somehow make it work, it could get us about a mile. Maybe. Plus, when we get sailing and the propeller is running in reverse, the whole thing could be used to generate power to recharge the battery."

"Babe. Try it anyway. We have nothing to lose." David nodded, lifting himself up onto his good leg and picking up the bucket, holding a thin sliver of water in the bottom.

"Here. Rainwater," he said, handing it to Kelly.

It had taken an hour of effort, but David had moderate success in removing the small outboard engine and replacing it with the truck's electric starter motor. With a hacksaw and basic tools he'd sourced from the workshop, he'd scraped slots into the starter motor's shaft and the propeller shaft of the outboard motor. Using rope and a lot of duct tape, he managed to convince the two shafts to lock together, at least temporarily. He connected the positive and negative leads of the motor to the battery. Inside the cabin, the propeller spun.

"Kel! It actually works," came the cry from inside the cabin, followed by David's head poking out, a look of mild triumph on his face.

"I mean, there's no guarantee the shafts will stay connected, and God only knows how much power is left in that battery, but it might help us in a crisis." Running a cable from the truck's battery in the foot-well of the cockpit, he placed the outboard contraption on the motor mount attached to the stern, ready to lower it into the water if necessary.

"Let's just hope we've got the tide on our side," David added.

255

Chapter thirteen

The ocean or bust

Nighttime approached, as did the dock area of Hampton, both getting closer by the minute. They needed some kind of plan.

"We need some kind of plan," said Kelly.

David nodded.

"I know," he responded, looking up at the black mainsail, growing dim in the evening light.

"We have a choice," David continued. "We can try to gun it, sailing right through the middle of the city, or we can drop the sail and try to drift, making any crazies think that it's an abandoned, worthless boat."

Kelly sat in silence for a few seconds.

"I reckon we should go for it, guns at the ready," she suggested. "I've had enough. I just want to finally get away from people."

"Oh," David replied, that not being the plan he had in mind. "I was thinking that we should try to drift through, hopefully ignored."

They looked at each other.

"Rock, paper, scissors?" asked Kelly.

"Seriously? Our lives are going to be decided by a game of rock, paper, scissors?"

"Well, there's a higher risk of being seen if we try to sail, sure. But look at the tide. It's not moving. If we drop the sail we'll just sit here like targets," said Kelly.

"Yes, but if we keep that giant sail up, anyone waiting up ahead with a gun will just blow us out of the water. It's suicide."

The docks were now becoming visible on the port bow in the evening light.

"Alright," David said, sighing. "Rock, paper, fucking scissors."

Kelly, sitting at the tiller, prepared her fist, raising it towards David, sitting with the rifle on the bow. He shook his head in frustration, raising his arm and closing his fist into a ball.

"Ready?" Kelly asked.

"No. But let's do it anyway. On three."

The rain pattered on the river surface as they rhythmically shook their fists up and down, counting, "One... Two... Three!"

The result, both of them having paper, caused a collective groan.

"Alright. Try again. Ready?" David asked. Kelly nodded.

"One... Two... Three."

It was a tie, with both of them choosing rock.

"For God's sake, exclaimed Kelly, wanting to laugh but not having the energy. "Alright, let's try again. Ready?"

David closed his eyes for a moment and exhaled, nodding his head.

"Ready."

Kelly took a breath, her fist raised to her chest.

"OK," she said. "One... Two... Three."

They looked at each other's hands, their potential fate chosen by a children's game.

"Well, congratulations," Kelly said.

David didn't reply, pulling himself to his feet with a gasp of pain. He hobbled to the rope holding up the mainsail and pulled it free from the cleat, the mainsail above them slackening, David pulling it down and draping it over the side of the boat, into the water.

"Let's get inside," he said.

The tide was high as the boat bobbed about in the evening rain, their vessel not moving. Like sitting ducks, they cowered in the dark interior, hiding from any eyes on the shore, their painted-over windows making it difficult for them to see each other's faces in the darkness. The looted waterfront buildings of Hampton city were now sitting just a hundred yards to their port side. David's outboard motor contraption sat partially submerged in the water, in case it was needed.

"I reckon the tide should begin going soon. I hope," said David. "Until then, we just wait."

God, thought Kelly. They were so damn close.

She looked at David's silhouette, the last of the late evening light appearing in the window above his head, illuminating through a part they'd missed while painting.

"You're gonna need a bigger boat," she said.

"What?" he asked.

"You're gonna need a bigger boat. From the movie Jaws."

"1975?"

"You got it," she said. "Your turn."

David paused, thinking through his mental archive of famous movie lines.

"Mama always said life was like a box of chocolates."

"No," Kelly said. "Give me a hard one."

"Alright," David replied, staring at the ceiling. "OK, how about 'Keep your friends close, but your enemies closer'."

"Godfather!"

"Yep, which one, though? And what year?"

David could make out Kelly's tongue poking out the corner of her mouth, a sign that she was deep in thought.

"It's got to be the second one; Godfather II."

"Good work, Sherlock. And the year?"

Kelly pondered in silence for a moment. A faint sound of a splash appeared outside in the twilight, interrupting their distraction.

"A fish?" Kelly whispered, hopeful.

Another distant splash sounded, followed by a faint clunk. David spun around and looked through a patch in the black, painted window.

"Something's out there," David said.

Kelly reached for her gun and tried to peer through the painting flaws in her own window. She thought she saw a person for a split second, maybe two. The darkness was playing tricks on her eyes.

"I think there's a guy in a dinghy, heading towards us!" she whispered, breathing quickly.

"Get the rifle," David ordered.

David stood up, approaching the cockpit door, but staying back against the wall in the darkness. As their sailboat drifted around, he saw it.

"There's a boat. A little rowboat. It's coming toward us. There's two people in it."

"What do we do?" Kelly asked, rifle in hand.

David's eyes darted around the cabin. If those guys had survived this far, they were certainly armed and no doubt happy to kill David and Kelly in order to get their hands on the boat.

"They probably think it's abandoned, so we have the element of surprise. I say we just shoot them now."

Kelly pictured the look on the face of the guy she'd killed
some months before. She didn't talk about it, but the
image of his frightened, confused face still haunted her.

"Should we give them a warning? What if they're
unarmed?" she asked.

"Kelly, I promise you, they will kill us if they see
us. They must be armed."
The rowboat approached, about forty yards away now.
They were so close to freedom, she thought.

"Fuck them," Kelly whispered angrily.
If she was going to die, she'd die fighting for her
freedom.

"You connect the motor to the battery and I'll
shoot the bastards."
Sitting on the cushion inside the dark cabin, Kelly raised
the Springfield M1A semi-automatic rifle slightly, ready
to stand up and empty the magazine's contents at the two
closing in on them, while David placed Kelly's Glock 19
and his own Desert Eagle on the floor at his feet. He
picked up the positive wire and held it above the battery
terminal. It wasn't going to move them fast, maybe one
mile per hour, but it was movement.

"Ready?" David asked.
Kelly looked over at her husband, the following second
of silence feeling like a full minute.

"I love you," she said.

"I love you," he replied.
With a nod, David wrapped the wire to the positive
terminal of the battery, causing a spark. A whirring noise
began from outside the boat. At the same time, Kelly
leaped to her feet, placing the butt of the rifle against her
shoulder. It took a second to spin around and locate the
rowboat, some twenty yards to their side, positioned
between them and the worryingly close city shoreline.
She froze, as did the two occupants of the boat, oars in

hand, a man and a woman, about their age. She didn't expect to see a woman.

"Shoot!" David yelled.

Yet, she froze, standing there, blocking the hatchway. David grabbed the pistols and crawled to the front hatch, throwing it open and rising up, arms outstretched, a gun in each hand. He turned and aimed them at the rowboat, to see both occupants; one with her hands raised, another with oars raised, frozen still. Maybe they were unarmed after all, he thought. There were no laws but they were still human beings. The boat's electric motor propelled them forward slowly.

"Please don't shoot us," pleaded the woman in the rowboat.

"Why not?" Kelly demanded.

"We thought the boat was abandoned," the woman continued. "We just wanted to escape the city. It's just nothing but death there."

The sailboat's humming electric motor began to put a few yards of distance between them, though they were all still too close for comfort.

"Stay there," Kelly added. "And we won't shoot you."

"But if you move a muscle, you're dead," David added, hoping that he could leave this scene without them both being cold-blooded murderers.

"Please take us with you," the woman begged.

Neither David nor Kelly responded, but each of them considered it. After all, they'd abandoned Steve, Maureen and the kids in the name of self preservation. They were already proven as selfish monsters. Kelly wondered if, perhaps by saving these two souls, they could redeem themselves in the eyes of God, or whatever. Kelly flicked a quick glance over at David, his head and arms sticking

out the bow access hatch, the dark ocean ahead of him.
She suspected David was thinking the same. He was.

It wasn't clear at first where the bullet came from, but the
man in the boat flew backwards onto the woman, who
screamed. It looked as though Kelly had chosen to end
the misery of these two tragic souls. Another shot rang
out, a bullet hitting the rowboat, right on the waterline,
evident by the thud and splash of water. David looked at
Kelly, only to see her spinning around, searching for the
source of the bullets. It wasn't her, after all.
Another shot rang out, with the unmistakable thud of a
bullet hitting flesh. The problems of the future were
solved for the couple in the rowboat, both now dead and
slumped over, their little boat taking on water, but Kelly
and David's problems had just begun.
        "There! There's a muzzle flash!"
Kelly opened fire, her gun aimed at the source of the
gunshot on the promenade. David turned back around,
facing the shore. The vague silhouette of the man, made
darker by the lack of light, ducked behind a smashed-up
car.
        "Get the sail up!" Kelly yelled.
David panicked for a moment, as it meant having to get
into full view.
        "I'll cover you!" she added.
David climbed out of the hatch and over the top of the
cockpit, pulling on the halyard to hoist the sail. It was
incredibly heavy, hanging over the railing and draping in
the water, the drag slowing the efforts of the electric
motor.
Kelly steadied her aim in the gently moving sailboat and
fired two shots at the center of the vehicle she believed
the gunman was hiding behind. David, meanwhile, had
lifted the sail out of the water and was pulling hard on the

rope, raising it skyward, its blackness almost matching the darkness of the sky.

A flash of orange light was visible from the shore, followed by the sound of a bullet whizzing by Kelly's head, arriving at the same time as the crack of a gunshot from the shore. The bullet was close, but the muzzle flash gave away the location of the gunman, still behind the car. Kelly pulled the high-powered rifle's trigger, firing six shots into the side of the vehicle, knowing they'd travel all the way through it and hopefully wipe out the guy on the other side.

David pulled frantically at the rope, the sail now reaching the top of the mast, before pulling the rope through a cleat in the cockpit and grabbing the tiller.

The rowboat was now about fifty yards behind them, slipping below the cold surface of the water, its occupants floating lifelessly. The outgoing tide was now aiding them in their escape, but only just.

"Get down!" Kelly yelled.

David dropped to his hands and knees in the cockpit, just as another flash occurred from the shore, the bullet tearing a perfect hole in the sail above his head.

David and Kelly both fired at the source of the flash, awakening the entire city to their whereabouts with deafening sounds and muzzle flashes. The combination of the electric motor, the full mainsail, and the outgoing tide meant that they were now moving at about four miles per hour. A muzzle flash from somewhere else on the shore resulted in a loud cracking sound from the hull, but it was now getting too dark to see what was happening or if they were taking on water. It was clear they now had two gunmen on the shore, firing at their craft. Kelly raised her rifle in the dark and squinted, looking for the source. Another muzzle flash from somewhere around the first gunman then resulted in a spray of water a few yards behind them.

"There's more than one now!" Kelly said, panicking.

David, crouched next to her, watched the silhouette of her gun as it moved left and right, hunting for the target in the enveloping darkness. Another muzzle flash on the shore was replaced by the sound of a bullet zipping past. Kelly looked down the sight of the rifle.

"Don't shoot back!" David ordered.

"What?! Why?!" demanded Kelly. "There's more than one out there!"

"They're losing us. They're shooting blindly. They can't see the black sail. You shoot; they'll see us!" With another gunshot from the shore, David and Kelly leaped inside the boat cabin and lay down on the floor, waiting expectantly for a bullet to hit them. The dry crack of gunshots rang out across the harbor, bullets peppering their general location, but missing them as their black sailboat blended into the dark sky, edging toward the ocean.

The gunshots had stopped, gradually being replaced by the sound of lapping waves slapping against the side of the sailboat. The craft was moving about much more now, the tension being felt on the tiller. The battery for their makeshift outboard motor had gone flat but now they were operating on sail power alone and didn't need it. Perhaps they were going in the right direction, perhaps not. Perhaps they'd cleared the harbor, or perhaps they were heading straight for a rock.

"So much death," Kelly said, holding the tiller tightly as the wind pushed against the sail.

"It's all over now," David replied, sitting down next to her.

Kelly rested her head on David's shoulder, the two of them safe, at least for now.

"Things are always better in the morning."

To Kill a Mockingbird

The dawn light revealed a spectacular scene. The expanse of the Atlantic Ocean spread forth on the boat's port side, while the eastern seaboard of the United States occupied the starboard. The cold salt air was heavy in the lungs, as Kelly raised her head from the seat cushion, rubbing the sleep from her eyes. She looked through to the cockpit, seeing her husband, looking across the ocean, his unshaven face and greasy hair flapping in the breeze.

"Hey," she said.

David looked down to meet her eyes.

"Hey yourself," he said, a smile appearing on his face.

He patted the seat next to him.

"Come up here, babe."

Kelly climbed out of the cabin and sat alongside David, putting his arm around her waist, the small sailboat rocking across the tops of the waves.

"So, what's for breakfast?" asked Kelly.

"Anything you want, as long as it's fish."

Kelly laughed. God, she thought. It felt good to laugh. It felt good to just *talk* without the fear of being overheard. Kelly lifted her head back and looked up at the sky. She took a deep breath and let out a long scream, surprising David. After all, for three and a half months they'd lived in silence. Kelly looked at her husband, smiling. David saw the joy on her face and let out a scream himself. It was instantly therapeutic, releasing months of frustration, anger and misery.

Kelly and David Shepherd from Lynchburg sat on the back of their stolen sailboat, the cold salt spray dusting their faces. It had taken months, but they'd done it. Digging into her pocket, Kelly pulled out her small compass and steadied it in her hand.

Looking from compass to shore, she turned to David.

"So, captain. Where are we going?"

David stared into the distance for a moment, adding a dramatic pause. He turned to his wife, sitting by his side, her greasy hair wet with salt spray, but still the most beautiful woman in the world.

"Somewhere warm."